Father,
Dear
Father

Other titles in this series

VOLUME II   I Love You, I Love You, I Love You

VOLUME III   How to Travel Incognito

Also by Ludwig Bemelmans

The Eye of God

The Best of Times

Dirty Eddie

Hotel Bemelmans

The Blue Danube

Now I Lay Me Down to Sleep

Hotel Splendide

The Donkey Inside

Small Beer

Life Class

My War with the United States

VOLUME I IN A NEW

H James H. Heineman   New York   1992

Father,
Dear
Father

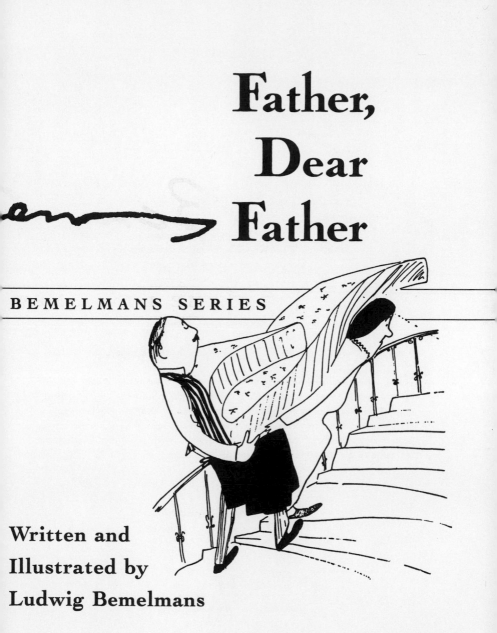

BEMELMANS SERIES

Written and
Illustrated by
Ludwig Bemelmans

Printed in the United States of America

First published in this edition
in the United States of America
in 1992

H

James H. Heineman, Inc.,
475 Park Avenue,
New York, NY 10022

Contents

Father,
Dear
Father

1.

Little Bit and
The *America*

"LOOK, WHAT a lovely day we have for sailing," I said, pointing my pen toward the lit-up greenery outside the open window. The birds sang in the trees, and the sun shone on a deck of brightly colored luggage tags which I was filling out. Under "S.S. *America*" I had carefully lettered my name, and I answered the gay question of "Destination?" with "Cherbourg."

I was about to fill out a new tag when I noticed Barbara's silence. She was standing at the window, staring at me. I saw clearly the symptoms of wanting something, symptoms long

3

known to me and always the same. I remembered that the day before she had said something about a dog, but I had been called away before I could talk about it at length.

For the most part, Barbara is a sweet and normal child; when she wants something, she changes. The child is then under great stress. A trembling of the lower lip precedes the filling of the beautiful eyes with tears. I am allowed to see these hopeless eyes for a moment, and then, as a spotlight moves from one place to another, she averts her gaze and slowly turns, folds her arms, and looks into the distance, or if there is not distance, at the wall. The crisis is approaching. She swallows, but her throat is constricted; finally, with the urgency of a stammerer, and with her small hands clenched, she manages to convey a few dry words. The small voice is like a cold trumpet. The last word is a choking sound. There is a long, cold silence.

On the morning of sailing I recognized the first stage of this painful condition that overcomes her from time to time. I could tell it by her eyes, her mouth, the position she stood in, the peculiar angles of her arms and legs. She was twisted in an unhappy pose of indecision. Not that she didn't know precisely what she wanted: she was undecided about how to broach the subject.

After the tears, the gaze into the distance, the silence, Barbara blurted out, "You promised I could have a dog."

I steeled myself and answered, "Yes, when we get back from Europe you can have a dog."

An answer like that is worse than an outright no. The mood of "I wish I was dead" descended on Barbara. She stared coldly out of the window, and then she turned and limply dragged herself down the corridor to her room, where she goes at times

4

of crisis. She closed the door not by slamming it, but with a terrible, slow finality. One can see from the corridor how she lets go of the handle inside—in unspeakably dolorous fashion; slowly the handle rises, and there is the barely audible click of the mechanism. There is then the cutting off of human relations, a falling off of appetite, and nothing in the world of joy or disaster matters.

Ordinarily the comatose state lasts for weeks. In this case, however, Barbara was confronted with a deadline, for the ship was sailing at five that afternoon and it was now eleven in the morning. I usually break down after three or four weeks of resistance. The time limit for this operation was five hours.

She decided at first to continue with standard practice, the manual of which I know as well as I do the alphabet.

From the door at the end of the corridor came the sound of heartbreaking sobs. Normally these sobs last for a good while, and then, the crisis ebbing off, there follows an hour or two of real or simulated sleep, in which she gathers strength for renewed efforts. This time, however, the sobs were discontinued ahead of schedule and were followed by a period of total silence, which I knew was taken up with plotting at the speed of calculating machinery. This took about ten minutes. As the door had closed, so it opened again, and fatefully and slowly, as the condemned walk to their place of execution, the poor child, handkerchief in hand, dragged along the corridor past my room into the kitchen. I never knew until that morning that the pouring of milk into a glass could be a bitter and hopeless thing to watch.

I am as hardened against the heartbreak routine as a coroner is to postmortems. I can be blind to tears and deaf to the most urgent pleading. I said, "Please be reasonable. I promise you that the moment we get back you can have a dog."

I was not prepared for what followed—the new slant, the surprise attack.

She leaned against the kitchen doorjamb and drank the last of the milk. Her mouth was ringed with white. She said in measured and accusing tones, "You read in the papers this morning what they did in Albany."

"I beg your pardon?"

"They passed a law that all institutions like the A.S.P.C.A. are to be forced to turn dogs over to hospitals, for vivisection— and you know what will happen. They'll get her and then they'll cut her open and sew her up again over and over until she's dead."

"What has that got to do with me?"

"It has to do with the dog you promised me."

"What dog?"

"The dog that Frances wants to give me."

Frances is a red-headed girl who goes to school with Barbara.

"I didn't know Frances had a dog."

Barbara raised her eyebrows. "You never listen," she said, and as if talking to an idiot and with weary gestures she recited, "Poppy, I told you all about it a dozen times. Doctor Lincoln, that's Frances's father, is going to Saudi Arabia to work for an oil company, and he had to sign a paper agreeing not to take a dog, because it seems the Arabs don't like dogs. So the dog has to be got rid of. So Doctor Lincoln said to Frances, 'If you don't get rid of her, I will.' Now you know how doctors are—they have no feelings whatever for animals. He'll give her to some hospital for experiments."

I resumed filling out baggage tags. When I hear the word "dog" I see in my mind a reasonably large animal of no particular breed, uncertain in outline, like a Thurber dog, and with a rough, dark coat. This image was hovering about when I asked, "What kind of a dog is it?"

"Her name is Little Bit."

"What?"

"Little *BIT*—that's her name. She's the dearest, sweetest, snow-white, itsy-bitsy tiny little toy poodle you have ever seen. Can I have her, please?"

I almost let out a shrill bark.

"Wait till you see her and all the things she's got—a special little wicker bed with a mattress, and a dish with her picture on it, and around it is written 'Always faithful' in French. You see, Poppy, they got Little Bit in Paris last year, and she's the uniquest, sharpest little dog you've ever seen, and naturally she's housebroken, and Frances says she's not going to give her to anybody but me."

I was playing for time. I would have settled for a Corgi, a Yorkshire, a Weimaraner, even a German boxer or a Mexican hairless, but Little Bit was too much. I knew that Doctor Lincoln lived some thirty miles out of the city, and that it would be impossible to get the dog to New York before the ship sailed.

"Where is the dog now?" I asked with faked interest.

"She'll be here any minute, Poppy. Frances is on the way now—and oh, wait till you see, she has the cutest little boots for rainy weather, and a cashmere sweater, sea green, and several sets of leashes and collars—you won't have to buy a thing."

"All right," I said, "you can have the dog. We'll put it in a good kennel until we return."

The symptoms, well known and always the same, returned again. The lower lip trembled. "Kennel," she said—and there is no actress on stage or screen who could have weighted this word with more reproach and misery.

"Yes, kennel," I said and filled out the baggage tag for my portable typewriter.

"Poppy—" she started, but I got up and said, "Now look, Barbara, the ship leaves in a few hours, and to take a dog aboard you have to get a certificate from a veterinary, and reserve a place for him, and buy a ticket."

To my astonishment, Barbara smiled indulgently. "Well, if that's all that's bothering you—first of all, we're going to France; the French, unlike the English, have no quarantine for dogs, and they don't even ask for a health certificate. Second, you can make all the arrangements for the dog's passage on board ship, after it sails. Third, there is plenty of room in the kennels. I know all this because Frances and I went down to the U.S. Lines and got the information day before yesterday."

I stared into distance. At such times I feel a great deal for the man who's going to marry Barbara. With all hope failing I said, "But we'll have to get a traveling bag or something to put the dog in."

"She has a lovely little traveling bag with her name lettered on it, 'Little Bit.'"

The name stung like a whip. "All right then." I wrote an extra baggage tag to be attached to the dog's bag.

Barbara wore the smug smile of success. "Wait till you see her," she said and ran out of the room. In a moment she returned with Frances, who, I am sure, had been sitting there waiting all the while. The timing was perfect.

Little Bit had shoebutton eyes and a patent-leather nose and a strawberry-colored collar; she was fluffy from the top of her head to her shoulders and then shorn like a miniature Persian lamb. At the end of a stub of a tail was a puff of fluff, and other puffs on the four legs. She wore a pale blue ribbon, and a bell on the collar. I thought that if she were cut open most probably sawdust would come out.

A real dog moves about a room and sniffs its way into corners. It inspects furniture and people, and makes notes of things. Little Bit stood with cocksparrow stiffness on four legs as static as her stare. She was picked up and brought over to me. I think she knew exactly what I thought of her, for she lifted her tiny lip on the left side of her face over her mouse teeth and sneered. She was put down, and she danced on stilts, with the motion of a mechanical toy, back to Frances.

I was shown the traveling bag, which was like one of the pocketbooks that WAC colonels carry.

"We don't need that tag," said Barbara. "I'll carry her in this. Look." The pocketbook, which had a circular opening with a wire screen on each end for breathing purposes, was opened; Little Bit jumped into it, and it was closed. "You see, she won't be any bother whatever."

The bag was opened again. With a standing jump Little Bit hurdled the handles of the bag and stalked toward me. Tilting her head a little, she stood looking up, and then she again lifted her lip over her small fangs.

"Oh, look, Barbara!" said Frances. "Little Bit likes your father—she's smiling at him."

I had an impulse to sneer back, but I took the baggage tags and began to attach them to the luggage. Then I left the room, for Frances showed signs of crisis; her eyes were filling, and the heartbreak was too much for me. Little Bit was less emotional. She ate a hearty meal from her *Toujours fidèle* dish and inspected the house, tinkling about with the small bell that hung from her collar.

It was time to go to the boat. The luggage was taken to a taxi, and Little Bit hopped into her bag. On the way I thought about the things I had forgotten to take care of, and also about Little Bit. It is said that there are three kinds of books that are always a success: a book about a doctor, a book about Lincoln, and a book about a dog. Well, here was Doctor Lincoln's dog, but it didn't seem to hold the elements of anything except chagrin. I wondered if Lincoln had ever had a dog, or a doctor, or if Lincoln's doctor had had a dog. I wondered if that side of Lincoln, perhaps the last remaining side, had been investigated as yet or was still open.

We arrived with Doctor Lincoln's dog at the customs barrier, and our passports were checked. The baggage was brought aboard. In our cabin we found some friends waiting. Frances and Barbara, with Little Bit looking out of her bag, inspected the ship. The gong sounded, and the deck steward sang out, "All ashore that's going ashore!" The passengers lined up to wave their farewells. The last of those that were going ashore slid down the gangplank. Good-by, good-by—and then the engine bells sounded below, and the tugs moaned and hissed, and the ship backed out into the river.

There are few sights in the world as beautiful as a trip down the Hudson and out to sea, especially at dusk. I was on deck until we passed the Ambrose Lightship, and then I went down to the cabin.

Little Bit was lying on a blotter, on the writing desk, and watching Barbara's hand. Barbara was already writing a letter to Frances, describing the beauty of travel and Little Bit's reactions. "Isn't she the best traveling dog we've ever had, Poppy?"

The cabins aboard the *America* are the only ones I have ever been in that don't seem to be aboard ship. They are large—more like rooms in a country home—a little chintzy in decoration, and over the portholes are curtains. In back of these one suspects screened doors that lead out to a porch and a Connecticut lawn rather than the ocean.

I put my things in place and changed to a comfortable jacket. I said, "I guess I better go up and get this dog business settled."

"It's all attended to, Poppy. I took care of it," said Barbara and continued writing.

"Well, then you'd better take her upstairs to the kennels. It's almost dinnertime."

"She doesn't have to go to the kennels."

"Now, look, Barbara—"

"See for yourself, Poppy. Just ring for the steward, or let me ring for him."

"Yes, sir," said the steward, smiling.

"Is it all right for the dog to stay in the cabin?" I asked. The steward had one of the most honest and kind faces I have ever seen. He didn't fit on a ship either. He was more like a person that works around horses, or a gardener. He had bright eyes and squint lines, a leathery skin, and a good smile.

He closed his eyes and announced, "Dog? I don't see no dog in here, sir." He winked like a burlesque comedian and touched one finger to his head in salute. "My name is Jeff," he said. "If you want anything—" And then he was gone.

11

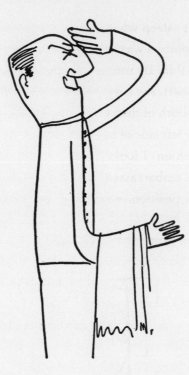

"You see?" said Barbara. "And besides, you save fifty dollars, and coming back another fifty, makes a hundred."

I am sure that Little Bit understood every word of the conversation. She stood up on the blotter and tilted her head, listening to Barbara, who said to her, "You know, Little Bit, you're not supposed to be on this ship at all. You mustn't let anybody see you. Now you hide, while we go down to eat."

There was a knock at the door. Silently Little Bit jumped to the floor and was out of sight.

It was the steward. He brought a little raw meat mixed with string beans on a plate covered with another plate. "Yes, sir," was all he said.

Barbara was asleep when the first rapport between me and Little Bit took place. I was sitting on a couch, reading, when she came into my cabin. By some magic trick, like an elevator going up a building shaft, she rose and seated herself next to me. She kept a hand's width of distance, tilted her head, and then lifted her lip over the left side of her face. I think I smiled back at her in the same fashion. I looked at her with interest for the first time—she was embarrassed. She looked away and then suddenly changed position, stretching her front legs ahead and

sitting down flat on her hindlegs. She made several jerky movements but never uttered a sound.

Barbara's sleepy voice came from the other room. "Aren't you glad we have Little Bit with us?"

"Yes," I said, "I am." I thought about the miracles of nature, how this tough little lion in sheep's pelt functioned as she did; with a brain that could be no larger than an olive, she had memory, understanding, tact, courage, and no doubt loyalty, and she was completely self-sufficient. She smiled once more, and I smiled back: the relationship was established. Life went on as steadily as the ship.

On the afternoon of the third day out, as I lay in my deck chair reading, Barbara came running. "Little Bit is gone," she stammered with trembling lower lip.

We went down to the cabin. The steward was on all fours, looking under the beds and furniture. "Somebody musta left the door open," he said, "or it wasn't closed properly and swung open, and I suppose she got lonesome here all by herself and went looking for you. You should have taken her up to the movies with you, Miss."

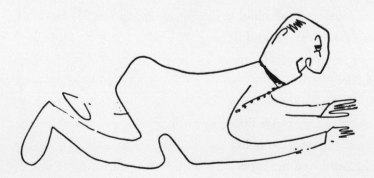

"She's a smart dog," said Barbara. "Let's go to every spot on board where she might look for us."

So we went to the dining room, to the smoking room, the theater, the swimming pool, up the stairs, down the stairs, up on all the decks and around them, and to a secret little deck we had discovered between second and third class at the back of the ship, where Little Bit was taken for her exercise mornings and evenings and could run about freely while I stood guard.

A liner is as big as a city. She was nowhere.

When we got back the steward said, "I know where she is. You see, anybody finds a dog naturally takes it up to the kennels, and that's where she is. And there she stays for the rest of the trip. Remember, I never saw the dog, I don't know anything about her. The butcher—that's the man in charge of the kennels—he's liable to report me if he finds out I helped hide her. He's mean, especially about money. He figures that each passenger gives him ten bucks for taking care of a dog, and he doesn't want any of us to snatch. There was a Yorkshire stowing away trip before last; he caught him at the gangplank as the dog was leaving the ship—the passenger had put him on a leash. Well, the butcher stopped him from getting off. He held up everything for hours, the man had to pay passage for the dog, and the steward who had helped hide him was fired. Herman Haegeli is his name, and he's as mean as they come. You'll find him on the top deck, near the aft chimney, where it says 'Kennels.'"

At such moments I enjoy the full confidence and affection of my child. Her nervous little hand is in mine, she willingly takes direction, her whole being is devotion, and no trouble is too much. She loved me especially then, because she knows that I am larcenous at heart and willing to go to the greatest lengths to beat a game and especially a meany.

"Now remember," I said, "if you want that dog back we have to be very careful. Let's first go and case the joint."

We climbed up into the scene of white and red ventilators, the sounds of humming wires, and the swish of the water. In yellow and crimson fire, the ball of the sun had half sunk into the sea, precisely at the end of the avenue of foam that the ship had plowed through the ocean. We were alone. We walked up and down, like people taking exercise before dinner, and the sea changed to violet and to indigo and then to that glossy gunmetal hue that it wears on moonless nights. The ship swished along to the even pulse of her machinery.

There was the sign. A yellow light shone from a porthole. I lifted Barbara, and inside, in one of the upper cages, was Little Bit, behind bars. There was no lock on her cage.

No one was inside. The door was fastened by a padlock. We walked back and forth for a while, and then a man came up the stairs, carrying a pail. He wore a gray cap, a towel around his neck, and a white coat such as butchers work in.

"That's our man," I said to Barbara.

Inside the kennels he brought forth a large dish that was like the body of a kettledrum. The dogs were barking.

"Now listen carefully, Barbara. I will go in and start a conversation with Mr. Haegeli. I will try to arrange it so that he turns his back on Little Bit's cage. At that moment, carefully open the door of the cage, grab Little Bit, put her under your coat, and then don't run—stand still, and after a while say, 'Oh, please let's get out of here.' I will then say good evening, and we

16

both will leave very slowly. Remember to act calmly, watch the butcher, but don't expect a signal from me. Decide yourself when it is time to act. It might be when he is in the middle of work, or while he is talking."

"Oh, please, Poppy, let's get out of here," Barbara rehearsed.

I opened the door to the kennel and smiled like a tourist in appreciation of a new discovery. "Oh, that's where the dogs are kept," I said. "Good evening."

Mr. Haegeli looked up and answered with a grunt. He was mixing dog food.

"My, what nice food you're preparing for them. How much do they charge to take a dog across?"

"Fifty dollars," said Mr. Haegeli in a Swiss accent. There are all kinds of Swiss, some with French, some with Italian, and some with German accents. They all talk in a singing fashion. The faces are as varied as the accents. The butcher didn't look like a butcher—a good butcher is fat and rosy. Mr. Haegeli was thin-lipped, thin-nosed, his chin was pointed. In the light he didn't look as mean as I expected; he looked rather fanatic, and frustrated.

"How often do you feed them?"

"They eat twice a day and as good as anybody on board," said Mr. Haegeli. "All except Rolfi there—he belongs to an actor, Mr. Kruger, who crosses twice a year and brings the dog's food along." He pointed to the cage where a large police dog was housed. "Rolfi, he is fed once a day, out of cans." He seemed to resent Rolfi and his master.

"You exercise them?"

"Yes, of course—all except Rolfi. Mr. Kruger comes up in the morning and takes him around with him on the top deck and sits with him there on a bench. He doesn't leave him alone. There is such a thing as making too much fuss over a dog."

I said that I agreed with him.

"He tried to keep him in his cabin—he said he'd pay full fare for Rolfi, like a passenger. He'll come up any minute now to say good night to Rolfi. Some people are crazy about dogs." Mr. Haegeli was putting chopped meat, vegetables, and cereal into the large dish. "There are other people that try to get away with something—they try and smuggle dogs across, like that one there." He pointed at Little Bit. "But we catch them," he said in his Swiss accent. "Oh yes, we catch them. They think they're smart, but they don't get away with it—not with me on board they don't. I have ways of finding out. I track them down." The fires of the fanatic burned in his eyes. "I catch them every time." He sounded as if he turned them over to the guillotine after he caught them. "Ah, here comes Mr. Kruger," he said and opened the door.

Kurt Kruger, the actor, said good evening and introduced himself. He spoke to Mr. Haegeli in German—and Mr. Haegeli turned his back on Little Bit's cage to open Rolfi's. The entire place was immediately deafened with barking from a dozen cages. The breathless moment had arrived. Barbara was approaching the door, but the dog-lover Kruger spotted Little Bit and said, "There's a new one." He spoke to Little Bit, and Little Bit, who had behaved as if she had been carefully rehearsed for her liberation, turned away with tears in her eyes.

Mr. Kruger and his dog disappeared.

Mr. Haegeli wiped his hand on his apron and went back to

mixing the dog food. The chances for rescuing Little Bit were getting slim.

"Where do you come from, Mr. Haegeli?"

"Schaffhausen. You know Schaffhausen?"

"Yes, yes," I said in German. *"Wunderbar."*

"Ja, ja, beautiful city."

"And the waterfall!"

"You know the Haegeli Wurstfabrik there?"

"No, I'm sorry."

"Well, it's one of the biggest sausage factories in Switzerland—liverwurst, salami, cervelat, frankfurters, boned hams—a big concern, belongs to a branch of my family. I'm sort of a wanderer. I like to travel—restless, you know—I can't see myself in Schaffhausen." He looked up. He was mixing food with both hands, his arms rotating.

"I understand."

"Besides, we don't get along, my relatives and I. All they think about is money, small money—I think in large sums. I like a wide horizon. Schaffhausen is not for me."

"How long have you been traveling?"

"Oh, I've been two years on this ship. You see, I'm not really a butcher but an inventor."

"How interesting! What are you working on?"

At last Mr. Haegeli turned his back on the cage in which Little Bit waited. "Well, it's something tremendous. It's, so to say, revolutionary."

"Oh?"

"There's a friend of mine, a Swiss, who is a baker, but you know, like I'm not a real butcher, he is not exactly a baker—I

19

mean, he knows his trade but he has ambition to make something of himself—and together we have created something that we call a frankroll." He waited for the effect.

"What is a frankroll?"

"It's a frankfurter baked inside a roll. We've got everything here to experiment with, the material and the ovens. I make the franks and he makes the rolls. We've tried it out on the passengers. Mr. Kruger, for example, says it's a marvelous idea. I might add that the experimental stage is over. Our product is perfect. Now it is a question of selling the patent, or licensing somebody—you know the way that is done. You make much more that way."

"Have you tried?"

Mr. Haegeli came close, the inventor's excitement in his eyes now. "That is where the hitch comes in. On the last trip I saw

the biggest frankfurter people in America—they're in New York. Well, the things you find out! They were very nice. The president received us and looked at the product and tasted it. He liked it, because he called for his son and a man who works close to him. 'I think you've got something there,' said the old man. I think with him we would have had clear sailing, but he had one of these wisenheimers for a son."

As Haegeli talked he forgot completely about the dogs. He gesticulated with hands that were sticky with hash, using them as a boxer does when he talks with his gloves on. Standing close to me, he held them away lest dog food soil my clothes. He stood exactly right, with his back turned to the spot where Barbara was slowly reaching to the door of Little Bit's cage. It was all foiled again by the return of Mr. Kruger and Rolfi. Mr. Kruger kissed his dog good night and stood waiting while Rolfi slowly walked into his cage. He said to Rolfi that it was only for two more nights that he had to be here, he wished us a good night also, and after a final good night to his dog he went.

"Where was I?" said the butcher.

"With the frankroll, the old man, and the wise-guy son."

"Right. Well, the son was looking at our product with a mixture of doubt, so he took a bite out of it, and in the middle of it he stopped chewing. 'Mmmm,' he said. 'Not bad, not bad at all. But—' He paused a long time, and then he said, 'What about the mustard, gentlemen?'

"I said, 'All right, what about the mustard?'

"So the wise guy says, 'I'm a customer. I'm buying. I'm at a hotdog stand. I watch the man in the white jacket. He picks up the frankfurter roll that's been sliced and placed face down on

21

the hot plate—he picks it up in a sanitary fashion—and he takes the skinless frank with his prong and puts it in the roll and hands it to me. Now, I dip into the mustard pot, or maybe I decide on a little kraut, or maybe I want some condiments or relish. Anyway, I put that on the frank—' He held out his hand.

"So I said, 'What's all that got to do with our frankroll?'

"So Junior says, 'A lot. Let me explain. It's got no appeal. Practical maybe, but to put the mustard on the hot dog the customer would have to slice the frankfurter bun first, and that leads us straight back to the old-fashioned frankfurter and the old-fashioned roll. The frankroll may be practical, but it's got no sizzle to it. No eye appeal, no nose appeal—it's no good.'

"Well, the old man was confused, and he got up and said that he'd like to think about it, and then he said he'd like to show us the factory. Well, you'd never think how important a thing a frankfurter is. There are two schools of thought about frankfurters, the skin frank and the skinless. These people specialize in skinless ones—because the American housewife prefers them without the skin—but did you know that the skinless come with skins and have to be peeled? This factory is spotless. There is a vast hall, and at long tables sit hundreds of women, and music plays, and they all have in their left hand a frankfurter, and in the right a paring knife, and all day long they remove the skins from the frankfurters—an eight-hour day. And at the end of the room is a first-aid station, because at the speed at which they work there is a great deal of laceration. The man in charge—"

"Oh, please, Poppy, let's get out of here!" Barbara broke in.

"The man in charge explained that in spite of elaborate safety precautions there was a great deal of absenteeism on account of carelessness. They had people who were working on a machine to skin the frankfurters. 'Now if you could invent a frankfurter-skinning device,' said the old man to me, 'you'd be a millionaire overnight.' Well, we're not licked yet. The beauty of working on a ship is that you have everything on board. One of the engineers is working with us on a skinning machine, and I have another outfit lined up for the frankroll."

The light in Mr. Haegeli's eyes faded. He wiped his hand again on his apron, and I shook it, and slowly we walked out on deck and down the first flight of stairs to A deck. I said to Barbara, "Run for your life, for by now he has discovered that Little Bit is gone."

We got to the cabin. Little Bit smiled on both sides of her face, and she bounced from floor to chair to dresser. There was a knock on the door—the thrill of the game of cops and robbers had begun. Little Bit vanished.

Barbara asked innocently, "Who is it?"

"It was the steward. "Did you find her?"

Barbara smiled.

"You got her back?"

Barbara nodded.

"Well, for heaven's sake, keep her out of sight. That crazy butcher is capable of anything—and I got a wife and family."

"From now on the dog must not be left," I said to Barbara. "She must go with us wherever we go, to the dining room, on deck, to the lounge, and to the movies. And you can't carry her in that bag—you have to cover her with a scarf or have her inside your coat."

Barbara started going about as if she carried her arm in a sling. The steward averted his eyes whenever he met us, and he didn't bring any more dog food.

Mr. Kruger said, "The kennel man suspects you of having removed the dog from the kennel."

"We did."

"Good," said the actor. "Anything I can do, I will."

"Well, act as if you didn't know anything about it. How is Rolfi?"

"Oh, Rolfi is fine. You know, he's never bitten anybody in his life except that kennel man."

Mr. Kruger offered to get Little Bit off the boat. He had a wicker basket in which he carried some of Rolfi's things, and he

24

would empty that, except for Rolfi's coat, and in that he would carry Little Bit off the *America*, for the butcher would follow us and watch us closely, and if he didn't find the dog before he'd catch us at the customs.

"Isn't he a nice man — Mr. Kruger? People always say such mean things about movie actors," said Barbara.

Camouflaged in a scarf, Little Bit rested on Barbara's lap during meals. On the deck chair she lay motionless between my feet, covered by a steamer rug. She traveled about under Barbara's coat, and she took her exercise on the secret after-deck, while I watched from above.

After the morning walk, the next day, the steward knocked. He looked worried. "The butcher was here," he said, "and went

all over the room. He found the dish with those French words and the dog's picture on it, on the bathroom floor."

"How could we be so careless?" I said, my professional pride hurt.

"And of course he saw the bag with *Little Bit* printed on it. I said I didn't know nothing about any dog."

We doubled our precautions. Little Bit's mouth was down at the edges with worry. I contemplated what to do. After all, there were only two more days, and if the worst happened we could sit upstairs with Little Bit, the way Mr. Kruger sat with Rolfi. I said to Barbara, "Perhaps it would be best to pay the passage and have it over with."

The symptoms were back. "No, you can't do that. Think of the poor steward and his family!"

"Well, we could settle that, I think, with the butcher. I don't like to cheat the line—"

"Well, Poppy, you can send them a check afterward, if that worries you, or drink a few extra bottles of champagne, or buy something in the shop."

Knock on the door.

"Who is it?"

"The purser, sir."

"Please come in."

The door opened. Behind the purser stood Mr. Haegeli.

"Just wanted to look and see if everything is all right. Are you comfortable, sir?"

"Everything is fine."

"By the way, sir, we're looking for a small white dog that's been lost. We wondered if by any chance it's in here."

"Come in and look for yourself."

"That's quite all right, sir. Excuse the intrusion. Good evening." The purser closed the door.

"What a nice man!" said Barbara.

The butcher was excluded from pursuing us in the public rooms of the ship; he couldn't follow us to the movies or the dining room. But he seemed to have spies. "What a lovely scarf you have there, Miss," said the elevator boy, and after that we used the stairs. The butcher came on deck in a fatigue uniform and followed us on the evening promenade around deck, during which Little Bit sat inside my overcoat, held in place by my right hand in a Napoleonic pose. We made four turns around deck. I leaned against the railing once, holding Little Bit in place, so that I could stretch my arms; Barbara was skipping rope, and the maneuver fooled him. He ran downstairs, and we caught him as he emerged from near our cabin—he had made another search. We saw his shadow on the wall near the stairs several times. He seemed to be nearing a nervous breakdown. Mr. Kruger told us that he had sworn we had the dog and meant to find it at any cost. There was one more night to go, and the next day the ship would dock.

At ten Barbara would deliver Little Bit to Mr. Kruger, and we would fill the bag in which she traveled with paper tissue, tobacco, soap, extra toothbrushes, razorblades, dental floss, and other things, which can all be bought in Europe but which for some droll reason one always takes along.

Little Bit was fed from luncheon trays which we ordered for ourselves in the cabin instead of going down to lunch.

The steward was shaking. "I don't know," he said, "when that guy butchers, or when he takes care of the other dogs. He's hanging around here all the time. I hope you get off all right."

On the last afternoon on board I became careless. Some passengers and a bearded ship's officer were watching the last game of the deck-tennis tournament, and others were lying this way and that in their deck chairs, forming a protective barricade. Barbara had checked on the butcher—he was busy aft, airing some of his charges.

I thought it safe to take Little Bit out of my coat and place her on deck, so that we all could relax a bit. She had been there but a moment when I heard a cry. "Ha," it went. It was the "Ha" of accusation and discovery, chagrin and triumph, and it had been issued by Mr. Haegeli, who stood with both arms raised. Fortunately he was not a kangaroo and was therefore unable to jump over the occupied deck chairs. I gathered up Little Bit, and we were safe for a few seconds. By now I knew the ship's plan as well as the man who designed her. We went down two decks on outside stairs, entered through a serving pantry, climbed one inside service stair, and then nonchalantly walked to the bar. I sat down and rang for the steward. I ordered something to drink. In a little while Barbara, with her lemonade in hand, said, "He's watching us through the third window!"

I swept my eyes over the left side of the room, and his face was pressed against the glass, pale and haunting. He kept watch from the outside, and ran back and forth as we moved around inside.

We went down to dinner. When we came back I got a cigar. He was outside the bar. As I went to the saloon to have coffee he was outside that window.

"Don't give Little Bit any sugar," Barbara said. "He's watching us."

The floor was cleared for dancing, and we got up to walk back to the library. There is a passage between the main saloon and the library off which are various pantries and side rooms, and it has no window. In a corner of it is the shop, and on this last evening people stood there in numbers buying cartons of cigarettes, film, small sailor hats, miniature lifebelts and ship models with "S.S. *America*" written on them. Here I suddenly realized the miraculous solution of our problem. It was in front of me, on a shelf. Among stuffed Mickey Mice, Donald Ducks,

and teddy bears of various sizes stood the exact replica of Little Bit—the same button eyes and patent-leather nose, the fluff, the legs like sticks, the pompom at the end of the tail, and the blue ribbon in its hair.

"How much is that dog?" I asked the young lady.

"Two ninety-five."

"I'll take it."

"Shall I wrap it up, sir?"

"No, thanks, I'll take it as is."

"What are we going to do now, Poppy?"

"Now you keep Little Bit hidden, and I'll take the stuffed dog, and we'll go into the library."

There we sat down. I placed the stuffed dog at my side and spoke to it. The butcher was on the far side of the ship, but he almost went through the window. He disappeared and ran around to the other side. I had arranged the toy dog so that it seemed to be asleep at my side, partly covered by Barbara's scarf. I told her to take Little Bit down to the cabin and then come back, and we'd have some fun with the butcher.

When she came back Barbara took the toy dog and fixed its hair and combed the fluff. Then I said, "Please give me the dog." We walked the length of the ship on the inside. The butcher was sprinting outside, his face flashing momentarily in the series of windows.

At the front of the ship we went out on deck. I held the dog so that the pompom stuck out in back, and I wiggled it a little, to give it the illusion of life. It took the butcher a while to catch up. He walked fast—we walked faster. He almost ran—we ran. He shouted, "Mister!" I continued running. As we came toward

31

the stern I asked Barbara, "Can you let out a terrible scream?"

"Yes, of course," said Barbara.

"One—two—three—*now*."

She screamed, and I threw the dog in a wide curve out into the sea. The butcher, a few feet away, gripped the railing and looked below, where the small white form was bobbing up and down in the turbulent water. Rapidly it was washed away in the wake of the *America*.

We turned to go back into the saloon.

We left the butcher paralyzed at the stern. He wasn't at the gangplank the next day.

Little Bit landed in France without further incident.

2.

My French Mattress

IN PARIS Barbara and I stayed at the Hôtel St. Julien le
Pauvre, an ancient favorite of students, writers, and traveling
American and English ladies, where I enjoyed the favor of the
team of chambermaid and valet. (In French hotels the valet and
the chambermaid work together, cleaning the room, turning the
mattress, and sweeping the carpet.) Once on a previous visit I
had given them a tip.

Upon our arrival the valet greeted us with his most elegant
phrases, and the maid wrung her hands with joy. The hotel at
this time had one good mattress, and this, they said, they would

get for me. They begged me not to lie down until then. They uncovered the bed, removed the mattress, and dragged it out of the door. A while later they returned with another one, which they installed. They waited for me to try it before bowing themselves out of the room.

The Hôtel St. Julien le Pauvre is built around a courtyard, and from the window of each room one can observe what goes on elsewhere. Barbara, who was taking advantage of this, suddenly turned and pointed an accusing finger to the window

of a room across the court and one floor up. Into this room the old mattress was being carried, and it had barely had time to settle before the occupant of that room, a very thin and aged lady, came in. She looked out her window and, after smiling at Barbara, produced a small American flag, which she waved.

"I hope you sleep well on that mattress, Poppy," said Barbara in her most dramatic fashion, saluting the flag across the way.

In the courtyard below lived an ancient turtle, and on the stairs and in the corridors six large striped cats. One of these took a swipe at Little Bit, who thereafter declared *mort aux chats* and with fierce courage chased them whenever she saw them.

The second day Barbara made friends with the old lady who slept on my mattress. She was from South Bend and was visiting a grandson who was a Marine corporal guarding the American Embassy in Paris. Barbara, Little Bit, and the old lady immediately formed an anti-French society. The old lady's grandson took Barbara along to the PX, and she came back with two cans of American spaghetti, which the old lady cooked on a Sterno heater. Barbara said it was the best meal she had in France. Also, she informed me, "The French don't curb their dogs, and as for their little boys and girls—it's disgusting—right on the Place Vendôme, and in front of Notre Dame."

I asked, "Did you look at Notre Dame?"

"Yes," she said.

"Isn't it beautiful?"

"It's all right. We're going to have meatballs and spaghetti tonight, and John—that's the Marine—is getting a case of Coca-Cola from the PX."

Little Bit was as disdainful of French food as Barbara and went along with the *cuisine américaine* on the floor above.

From Paris we were to go on to Vienna, where I had an assignment to write about the Russians. In order to see things one had to have accreditation and a card of identification with a photograph and fingerprints. I had such a card, but it was pointed out to me that it had expired.

I obtained a new one and pasted a passport picture on it. There remained only the problem of having my fingerprints taken. The American Embassy had no facilities for this, nor could they suggest any place.

One day, as we walked over a bridge to the Ile de la Cité, I saw two policemen standing at the elaborate gates of the Palais de Justice, and it occurred to me that here might be the answer. I approached one of them and explained the situation. Could the police be of help?

He saluted and called his colleague over. Together they studied my identification card. "Ah, monsieur," said the colleague, "but we are not equipped for that." They both saluted.

I asked them if it wasn't customary to fingerprint crooks.

"Yes, certainly. But monsieur is a man *comme il faut*, not a thief."

"Why not fingerprint me anyway, if I want to?"

They looked at each other, then stared at me. At last they made a tremendous decision. "All right," they cried.

"But where we are going is no place for mademoiselle," said the first one.

At the right of the stairs that lead up to the criminal courts is a restaurant, and there we left Barbara and Little Bit.

Walking up, my two escorts picked up a third, and they said to him, "Now then, Jacques, monsieur insists on going to the

Bureau de l'Identification Judiciaire to have his fingerprints taken. That, Jacques, is true democracy. This American is obviously a man of importance. Can you imagine any one of ours doing this?"

"Ah, *non*," said Jacques, "in France that would never happen."

We passed into the interior of the palace. At every door we were stopped and the story was repeated to a new set of guards. The scene took on a grim quality. There were iron doors, and the smell of iron and hinges, of prison, of dungeons. The light grew dimmer. We ascended a creaky stairway and stopped before a heavy door with iron bands and a peephole. One of the policemen pushed a button, and a bell rang as loud as a fire alarm. A piece of wood was pushed from the peephole, an eye looked out, and my escorts told the story again. There was an electric buzz and a click, and the door whined as it opened.

Inside was a narrow corridor with six doors on the right and six on the left, and then another mechanical door, and when this was past there were six men in worn black smocks. A functionary came and listened to my escorts and then disappeared to tell the chief of the bureau. There was a prison bench without a backrest and a narrow, worn plank for a seat. On this I sat with a policeman on each side and the third pacing up and down in front. While we waited several crooks were ushered through, and I received curious glances. They must have thought me particularly interesting, being so heavily guarded.

A messenger came, and we followed him to a small room in which stood a table. On this was an empty cigarbox without a lid. To the box a string was attached, and after my identification card had been dropped into it the box was pulled upward and

disappeared through a hole in the ceiling into the room above. When the box came down again a note was attached to it, and at last we went into the office of the chief.

The chief excused himself for not knowing a word of "Inglitch." He studied the note and the identification card. In back of him hung a photograph of De Gaulle. He took his pince-nez off his nose. He looked distraught. Addressing all in the room with a half swing of his arm, he said, "This is all well and good, but how do we know" — he held up my old identification card — "that these are the fingerprints of this person?"

"After all," I said, "my hands are attached to my body."

"Yes, yes, logic. That's easy enough to check. What I mean is, how do we know these are the prints of the man who is entitled to carry this pass?" He looked at me suspiciously and said to the others, "With so many things going on—secrets stolen, *agents provocateurs*, and so on around—one must be careful. This card tells me nothing."

"Obviously," I countered, "a man such as you suspect would not walk into the criminal courts building to have his finger-prints taken by the police."

"That is precisely what such a man might do," said the chief, putting his glasses back at the halfway mark, where his nose was pinched.

I suddenly had the feeling that I might be here a long time.

With false friendliness the chief said, "Sit down, monsieur, and tell us a little about yourself—where you obtained this card, where you live, who you are. Have you anything besides this paper on your person? Is there anyone who can identify you? And how is it that you who say you are an American speak a French which is not that of Americans?"

At such moments one can never find anything. While I told him that I was staying at the Hôtel St. Julien le Pauvre and knew a lady who had a grandson who was a guard at the American Embassy, I went through all my pockets and finally found a paper that impressed him.

After a call to the hotel, where I had left my passport with the concierge, he said, "Well, we shall see if it is you." He studied my photograph on the old card and compared it with my face. Out of his desk he took a stamp pad, and tore a sheet from a block of paper economically made from the backs of directives no longer valid. Holding my right thumb firmly, he moved it to the inked pad and then to the paper. Through a magnifying glass he compared the prints. *"Oui, c'est lui,"* he said.

They all smiled, bitterly disappointed. The chief motioned to
a door, the automatic buzz sounded again, and we walked into
the real fingerprinting room. *"Après vous,"* said the chief. He
waved away several crooks who already had their fingers
inked. They moved to the back of the room and remained there
like a chorus, their blackened hands held up, the palms flat
forward.

It was an elaborate performance, like Mass in an underground chapel. "You," said the chief to one of the black smocks,
"run and get water, soap, and a towel, so monsieur can wash his
hands."

The chief smiled while an assistant passed the roller with the
black stuff over a pane of glass. "Now, if you will give me your
little finger," said the chief delicately, and he took it and rolled it
carefully, like a Chinese eggroll in flour. He carried it across to
the new identification card, and there rolled it again. "Ah," he
said when it was done. *"Voici, c'est fait comme il faut."*

After I had washed my hands I offered American cigarettes
to the officials and the crooks. They were accepted with polite
words of thanks. We went into the outer hall, and there, after
the door had shut behind us electrically, the chief said, "I ask
your pardon. You understand, monsieur, that I was a little
doubtful in the beginning, but such an event does not occur
every day. In fact, it has never before happened that anyone not
of our regular clientele has appeared to have his fingerprints
taken. My suspicions, *alors*, were on behalf of the same cause
you have the honor to serve."

We shook hands. We bowed.

There were again buzzer sounds, and the smell of iron, the

stairs down, the larger corridor, and then the courtyard and the sunlight and Barbara and Little Bit waiting where I had left them.

That day the old lady had taken an excursion to Malmaison and was not expected back until late. Barbara agreed to forgo the American spaghetti and eat out.

In the restaurant on the Rue Royale the glasses were clean, the linen spotless, and the headwaiter himself smiled at the dog. The French make much of dogs, and Little Bit received so much attention that Barbara softened.

In French restaurants dogs are spoken of as "your son," and the headwaiter asked, "What does he desire to eat, your son?"

"Oh, a little meat, and a vegetable," Barbara said.

"Very good," said the headwaiter. "And perhaps all this sprinkled with a little consommé, mademoiselle?"

"Yes, that would be very nice."

"*Alors,*" he said and gave the order for our and Little Bit's dinner to the waiter.

A small cloth was spread on the carpet, and a silver dish was brought out, and a napkin was tied around Little Bit. Our own meal was served with equal care.

"I'm glad we came here, Poppy," said Barbara.

The bill came. I hate to add up restaurant bills, but this one was really high. I called the waiter. "I think you have given me the wrong bill. Look—we had melon and chicken curry and salad and cheese and a bottle of wine. What's this steak for four hundred francs, and the string beans and the consommé?"

"Ah, *pardon,*" said the waiter, "that was the dinner for your son." He pointed to Little Bit.

I paid, and on the way out I stopped to speak to the headwaiter.

Outside, Barbara said, "What did you say to him, Poppy?"

"I gave him hell."

"Yes, I know," said Barbara, "with a five-dollar bill."

Among the mistakes I have made was the one of reading to Barbara a paragraph from a medical paper that said that at the age of thirteen the human being is at the height of his or her mental faculties and powers of observation.

3.

Visit to Versailles

ONE AFTERNOON while we were waiting for the visa to
Vienna to come through, we drove out to Versailles, to the Villa
Trianon on the Boulevard St. Antoine. This property, small,
compact, and what is referred to as "out of this world," belonged to Lady Mendl. I rang the bell, and a gentle old
Frenchman—who has the best name any gardener can possibly
have, Monsieur Fleurtry—opened the gate. I showed Barbara
the gardens and the elephant—a creature not zoologic but
botanic, being a tree whose branches were carefully trained to
form the outlines of an elephant.

In a corner of the property is a dog cemetery. On small marble stones are recorded the names and brief life spans of half a dozen such creatures as Little Bit. The miniature poodles of the Villa Trianon were gray and blue, and the last of them was named Blue Blue. Little Bit stood looking at the memorials of her distant relatives and then went off to chase a cat, of which there were dozens. Barbara went off after her, and I sat down near the elephant and thought of the past.

IN THE months since Elsie Mendl died, I have been reading now and then in the forty-two notebooks I kept during the time I knew her. In them she appears mostly verbatim: I hear her talk when I read; I hear the shrill cry of a sea bird when she laughed; and I feel her elbow poking me in the side when something had to be underlined. There is a lot of dull and meaningless stuff in notes, but these come to life and hum with originality and the impact of her being.

Here is a disciplined, no-nonsense woman, whose observations about dress, decoration, and "foiniture," as she called it, are for the textbooks. But there is ample humor, gallantry, generosity. It is above all amusing and gratifying that, as she suddenly stands before me on her little-girl legs, there is in this less than a hundred pounds of woman the equal of the combined forces of Price, Waterhouse & Co. and Catherine de' Medici.

In the deepest black mourning for her, I feel the world colder by her absence; vulgarity gains; and with her leaving there goes also a cabinet of curiosities, a parade of people who have been invaluable to me, for I shall never be able to afford to entertain them. I speak of the old skulls with hair pasted on them that came occasionally out of the château country, and with ancient perfumes enacted scenes of the past; of the American marquise with the bracelet-heavy arms; of the meticulous Duc de Castiglione, who wears dove-gray spats and who is so short that his legs leave the floor when he sits down. His nervous face is as distinguished as his name; he tilts it to a pretty girl, a Hollywood starlet, eighteen years old, wrapped in tulle, who points a marzipan-like finger at his spats and innocently squeaks, "And were you wearing those when the Germans put you in a concentration camp?"

The duke smiles and says, "No, dear, not these, but a pair like them."

The baby star ponders over the next question she will ask. The soft bosom rises. The rosebud lips open again. "Well, and didn't they take them away from you?"

"They didn't dare!" answers the duke, brandishing an invisible sword.

There in a corner is Prince Pierre de Monaco, whose dialogue is like Proust's. There are so many princes here that in order not to stand out I sign myself in the guestbook at Villa Trianon as "Prince de Bavière." There is Count Armand de la Rochefoucauld, a man fiercely determined to be an individual, a great connoisseur of wines and of life in Paris after dark.

Dali arrives with an entourage of his patrons, his wife, and a gazelle-like woman. A heavy-chested American Army sergeant in bleached khaki follows with his eyes a newly arrived Czech countess and then turns to Sir Charles Mendl and says behind a large hand, "I bet she's good in bed—look at the way she walks." The sage host puts him at ease. "Dear boy," he says, "that's only because she's wearing high heels; she's not used to them. She just escaped from behind—" There is a pause as Gilbert Miller passes between the two men, then Sir Charles adds, "—the Iron Curtain."

The variety of guests in an establishment whose doors were as wide open as those of Villa Trianon is astonishing. On the already broad stream of the *persona grata* swam the rafts of various minority groups, young men who rotated on their pelvic bones as they greeted each other and their elderly friends, who in France are known as *tapettes*. I once asked Elsie what she thought of them, and she answered, "All I can say, Stevie, is that without them my life would have been a good deal drabber than it was." There were all the good friends from Hollywood who arrived in Paris like relatives from the country; there were the climbers and elbowers; and here and there alone in the stream swam a rare specimen—an oilman, a hotel man of bombastic allure, a suspected grand-style confidence man with hair like a yellow chrysanthemum hanging on his forehead (that one stood most of the time in conversation with the second Paris chief of police, an extremely *beau garçon*).

At the beginning and at the end one could pick up snatches of enlightening conversation. For example: "Can the ugliest man in the world—with charm—get any woman?" "My God, don't take hope from three-quarters of humanity."

"She's *jolie, jolie.*" "Well, my dear, she isn't *jolie, jolie* at all; she's just a nice-looking girl."

"*Aber wie kann man denn auf einmal so ekelhaft sein?*" "*Ja, aber* everybody knew, he was a *mauvais garçon*, after what he did to that poor little what's-her-name girl."

During the party the hum of conversation carpeted the room; the stream flowed around such pillars of the international bridge as the Duke and Duchess of Windsor, Schiaparelli, Hilda West, Paul Louis Weiller, who on account of his love for the splendor of châteaux is called "Paul Louis Quatorze Weiller," Noel Coward, Cole Porter, Kitty and Gilbert Miller, Rosita and Norman Winston, the Duff Coopers, and several other stout hearts. As the parties thinned out you could pick up talk again.

"If I ever tried to be faithful!"

"I'm not happy, you're not happy, let somebody be happy!"

"Je suis une femme sans histoire, sans complications—"

"I'm going to marry either a Swiss banker or a famous American dentist."

Toward the end there remained always those who had mastered the art of feeding themselves from cocktail buffets; they came first and left last, and promised to come soon again.

It all vibrated; it was never dull.

Charles was indispensable to Elsie: he separated the wheat from the chaff; he slapped down the houseflies, the hangers-on; he controlled the percentage of fags and *piques-assiettes;* and while he had humorous understanding, he protected Elsie against her boundless generosity and hospitality. Thoroughly informed, socially and politically, he knew the background of everyone and his motives and value. The seating at table, which Charles determined, was as carefully weighed as at the most protocol-conscious embassy.

Charles and Elsie were a devoted couple. Lifting her lips over her teeth, all of which were still her own, and smiling in her de Wolfe fashion, Elsie would say, "I am so fortunate to have a husband who always thinks of me before he does of himself. But then I am a good wife to him." And hitting the table with her fist, she would ask, "Now is there any greater sign of love than for a wife to send a car and a baggage truck to the boat—mind you, a car with a bed in it—and a letter from the *chef de la préfecture*, so that Charles gets smoothly through all the formalities *comme une lettre par la poste?*"

IF EVER I am run over by a truck or otherwise mangled, the one I hope to find sitting by my bed as I open my eyes is Hilda West. She is in her own person the therapy for the ills of this life.

It is rare that a human who stands in the middle of the turmoil—against whom all manner of beings are thrown—can, over a period of years, retain integrity and hold on to a personality. Hilda is the illustration for Kipling's "If," with an extra stanza added: "If you can answer the telephone all day long—"

Westy was saved by a quick wit and a spontaneous retort. Once a woman telephoned to find out who the other guests were going to be at a large Sunday luncheon. She asked, "And who will be there? I mean what celebrities?" Hilda answered, "Well, there will be you, and Lady Mendl, of course." Hilda put up roadblocks against the too ardent—said "no" nicely to petitioners. She was Elsie's best friend, and in the last trying years the only sigh I heard from her was—"Oh, if I didn't have my kittycats and pussycats, I don't know what I would do." She had between eleven and sixteen of them.

I first met Elsie in Hollywood. She immediately changed my name. There was a war going on with Germany, and "Ludwig" was grating to her ears; so she changed it to "Stevie." I called her "Mother." In the last years I offered her a backrest for the spine that had become weak as boiled spaghetti, and so, sitting back to back and looking at each other via the mirrors in the room, we held conversations and laughed. She, equipped with endless stores of anecdotes and observations, never spoke ill of anyone.

Invited for a weekend, I stayed at "After All" for the length of time I was in Hollywood; the Villa Trianon in Versailles was my home in France. I had a notion that Elsie was fabulously rich. It never occurred to me until I read her will that she, poor darling, was relatively destitute. She left a million, which is a bag of money to be sure, but it's peanuts, considering her fashion of living, her travels, the employment she gave to a brigade of artisans and servants, the money she handed out, and the hospitality she dispensed.

I'm not an easy guest in the house; my hours are irregular, I bore easily, and I lack respect. I am also a professor of *gaffes* and have an unmatched talent for saying the wrong thing, always perfectly timed so that it falls in a silence and everyone at the table can hear it. Sir Charles, who is the embodiment of the Foreign Office and a walking textbook on protocol, always changed the subject with a light hand and never reproached me.

Once, at a dinner, the lady seated next to me asked whether I ever got a thrill out of bullfighting, and I said that I did on rare occasions, namely, when the bull tossed the toreador into the air. There was at the time no silence, so my table companion asked for attention and asked me to repeat my answer to her question, and it turned out that her husband, the guest of honor of that evening, was the only Englishman who was an amateur bullfighter.

I shall always miss the table at Elsie's houses and the cooking of Monsieur Fraise. What pleasure it was to go into his kitchen and talk to an honest chef, one of the few who did not tell you that he was a pupil of Escoffier! How neat his dishes were! How superb his simplest effort! I have never seen a chicken so well cooked and so cleanly sliced and put together again; you did not know it was carved when it came to the table. The rarest thing is a French chef who does not kill you with sauces and seasoning. The master of his trade, such as Monsieur Fraise is, knows how to season so that the suggestion is there, as the bouquet in wine.

Elsie liked dogs and people slim, and, while there was superb cooking and always enough at parties, when we were dining *en famille* there sometimes wasn't.

We sat at dinner in Versailles—Elsie, Charles, Hilda, Gayelord Hauser, and I—and there were "bitkis" on the menu. This dish is a super chicken hamburger, the chicken being scraped and shredded before cooking, and served with a sauce in which sour cream plays a part. There were a great many of these bitkis, but they were the circumference of a quarter each. Soon we had eaten all but one, and eventually the one left in a small splotch of its fine sauce was passed again. The butler wandered around the table with it. I wanted it very badly; Hilda wanted it; Elsie was the only one with character enough to wave it away; Charles wanted it most of all. There was a great restraining all around, and finally, with anguish in his voice, Charles said, "Give it to the growing boy; he needs it most." With that he sadly pointed to the biggest man at the table—to Gayelord Hauser. For a moment there was hope, because Joseph held in his other hand a large silver dish filled with the most beautiful green spinach, cooked exactly to the doctor's liking and according to his recipe. We all were certain that the prophet of vegetable juice and roughage would ladle himself some of his own medicine. The good doctor was a disappointment: unashamed, he grabbed the last bitki, waving the look-younger-and-live-longer stuff away.

During one of the last weeks of her life Lady Mendl had the Duke and Duchess of Windsor as house guests. On the occasion of the fireworks in Versailles, Elsie got the upper hand again for a while and came down from her room. She wore a magnificent piece of lace wound around her head like a turban. Her hands, badly twisted by arthritis, were as usual in white gloves; she considered it her duty to hide them. We sat near the fountain in her garden. *House and Garden* was brought down, and there was a picture of Elsie, a full-page reproduction of a painting.

"My God, look at that!" she said, sitting up like a West Point cadet. "I never gave permission for this awful thing to be printed. Why, I look as if I were dying! It's cadaverous, a leper picture of an old woman. Take it away! Send a telegram immediately and tell them that I'm very angry about it!"

The picture was a very good likeness, elegant, serious, and intelligent, not at all what she said. It was painted by Vertès, but it wasn't the picture of herself that Elsie carried in mind.

On account of Elsie's being cold, the house was overheated, and the Duke sat at dinner wiping his forehead. After dinner he wheeled her down to the fountain and then brought her back, and she went up to bed early that night.

Sir Charles got some cigars, much too good to smoke outdoors, but it was the only place anyone was allowed to smoke cigars. We sat down at the pool. At nearby Versailles fireworks started to light the sky, and the hunting horns sounded across the park. The Duke walked to the pool to turn off the fountain to hear better. He smiled sadly and walked to the side of the garden and tilted his head back to listen. "The sound of those horns is the most beautiful music to me," he said. We lit the cigars, and everybody sat listening.

The Duke had sat down next to his wife on a wicker chaise longue. I saw that he was without socks. The Duchess noticed it too, and she asked him why he wasn't wearing any.

"I was golfing all afternoon," he said. "And I came here from the course and the socks were woolen and so hot I had to take them off."

"But surely there were others. I packed them myself," said the Duchess.

"Yes, but they were in a room that is next to Elsie's, and I was afraid if I went in there I might disturb what little sleep she gets."

ONE DAY when she was ninety-two years old Elsie was sufficiently energetic to decide to go to Paris. She soon exhausted herself on the Place Vendôme, talking and waving to people. She bought four pictures and ordered some lamps. On the way home, near Ville d'Avray, a child ran out into the street, and the chauffeur had to stop abruptly. Elsie was thrown forward. She required four stitches from a cut suffered in that accident. "You know," she said, "we might all have been killed." A moment after she herself laughed at the remark.

The last time I saw her, I sat with her in the shaded spot near the fountain that was her favorite place. She said, "Stevie, you know one can order death, the way one can order breakfast in a good hotel, and Mother has ordered it."

I didn't believe myself what I said in answer—it was some nickel-dime philosophy. I said, "I don't want to get sloppy, Mother, but perhaps there is a beyond; perhaps God, whoever He is, will allow us another life. In this world in which all things have logic, one of the things that make no sense at all is that one should live only to die. Perhaps for people of courage and spirit a small table is reserved in the ballroom above."

She gave me the proper answer. "Don't talk nonsense, Stevie. I have talked to God. Between one and two in the morning is a good time to talk to Him. It's all here, and when it's over, it's over. All the good is right here—and it's getting more expensive every day."

I said that anyway there was a gambler's chance for those who have done good on earth. I told her the story of a man who went to the portals of heaven, and on the way up he tried desperately to think of whatever good things he had done on earth, but there wasn't anything he could remember. He searched his mind again and again, and then he remembered that he had once bought a newspaper from an old woman; it had been raining, he had been in a hurry to catch a bus, and he had given the woman a nickel—the paper was three cents—and the woman had had no change. Shouting, "Keep the nickel," he had jumped aboard the bus. He remembered this good deed just as he arrived at the gates of heaven. The gates opened, and St. Peter came out with an angel. The new arrival was asked what he had done to merit admission. He related the incident, and St.

Peter said to the angel, "Give him back his two cents and tell him to go to hell."

Mother gave me a poke in the ribs—her last—which had the usual fervor. She said, "If anywhere, Stevie, that's where we'll meet again."

THE SOUND of crunching gravel roused me from the past. I looked up. The elephant cast a long shadow, and along the walk came Armand de la Rochefoucauld, holding a small boy by the hand. Barbara and Little Bit appeared from somewhere.

There is an immense distance between little boys and thirteen-year-old girls, and also between small female poodles and little boys. Six-year-old Armand bowed his head in introduction. Barbara nodded coldly. I suggested, since cemeteries seem to hold great fascination for children, that she show him Lady Mendl's dog memorials. Whereupon little Armand started to cry bitterly, but after a while he asked to see them, and they went off.

"I am worried," said his father, "and perhaps you can help me out. I was determined never to tell my son a lie—I must say, I find it difficult to lie anyway—and it has made my life miserable.

"Last Christmas little Armand came to me and asked, 'Papa, is there a Santa Claus?'

"I said, 'I'm sorry, but there isn't. It is an invention.'

"He was very unhappy. Several days later he came running to me. His face was bright. 'Papa, you are wrong,' he said. 'There is a Santa Claus. I saw him on the street when

Mademoiselle and I were walking near the Galeries Lafayette, and Mademoiselle said that of course there is a Santa Claus, and then we went over to ask a policeman, and he too said there is a Santa Claus.'

"What was I to do? I said, 'Well, Armand, if the policeman said so it must be true. I've just never been fortunate enough to meet him.' Tell me, was that right?"

"Of course it was right," I said, "and the only thing to do. But why worry about it?"

"Well, since then I have had to lie to him about all kinds of things. And the reason he cried just now was because we had a dog—an immense old Briard, with soft motherly eyes, that let him ride on its back. He had had it ever since he was born, in the country and the city, everywhere. And this old dog died, and we buried it in the garden and had a stone made for it. Armand was disconsolate. He asked me, 'Do dogs go to heaven?' I said, 'Yes, of course.' I wonder if that was right."

"Poppy," said Barbara later, on the way back to Paris, "I wonder if there is a beyond. I don't mind dying, but not existing any more, forever, that's terrible."

We got back to the Hôtel St. Julien le Pauvre in time for the evening ceremony. When the American meal across the courtyard was ready, the kind old lady tinkled a little bell and waved the small flag. Little Bit, conditioned like the dogs in the Pavlov experiments, gulped and raced for the corridor.

My visa had arrived with sixteen stamps on it, and the next day we took the Arlberg Express, which runs via Switzerland to Austria.

4.

Of Cows' Milk and
Laval's Dog

BARBARA, WITH Little Bit beside her, sat looking out of the
train window at the passing landscape between Zurich and
Sargans. Children seem to take an instant liking to Switzerland.
"Isn't it clean!" exclaimed Barbara.

A truck rolled along the highway, gaining on the train. It was driven by a youth in white uniform and cap. I thought at first it was an ambulance. As it caught up with the train, it turned out to be a truck. On its side was painted a huge milk bottle, and around this, in sky-blue letters, was written, "Swiss Dairy Pasteurized Milk." To the left and right of the bottle were two cows, painted with such realism that one almost could hear them moo.

The train slowed for a curve, the truck gained and passed, and at the back of the truck was another immaculate, rosy-cheeked youth in snow-white uniform and cap. He stood against a rack of snow-white bottles with metal caps.

"Poppy, are there cows in Tyrol?"

"Of course we have cows in Tyrol."

"And is the milk white, or blue like it is in France?"

"I never noticed any blue milk in France."

"Of course not, you don't drink milk. I had to drink tea all the time, because the milk is blue, and it's served with a dipper out of a pail by a woman in an old sweater with dirty hands, and there are flies all over. Ugh! Is it like that in Tyrol?"

The word "ugh" is pronounced like a sound of strangulation, with both hands at the throat. It is also like the sound of seasickness starting.

"The milk in Tyrol," I said, "is white."

"And pasteurized?"

"Well, it's fresh and warm, as it comes from the cow."

"Where are the cows?"

"All day they are out in the fields, and toward evening they are taken indoors. In wintertime they stay in the inn."

"The cows live in the hotel?"

"Yes, the part that is toward the mountain is the stable, and Florian—he's the stableman—milks the cows and brings the milk into the kitchen in a pail."

"Ugh!"

At Buchs the train passed out of the control of the Swiss. Its shiny Brown Boveri locomotive was exchanged for a rusty Austrian one, and the meticulous Swiss dining car was dragged past us for the run back to Zurich and Basle. All this was observed with suspicion by both Barbara and Little Bit.

I have come to the conclusion that to children travel means little and landscape means nothing. Barbara barely glanced at the mountains and lakes. She was much more interested in the details of living, in animals, children, food, and people, in that order. She also had appointed herself a lighthouse far from American shores, which sent out constant flashes. The beam was mostly turned on me.

We left the train at Langen. In front of us rose the Arlberg, the mountain on top of which stands the inn where my mother lives in a room over the cows. There was fresh snow on the ground. Beside the station waited the sleighs with well-fed, strong horses that take the skiers up the mountain. It's a long, slow ascent to the tune of jingle bells.

"Poppy, does that one horse have to pull our sleigh all the way up to the inn?" Barbara asked as we got into one.

I had never heard anyone complain about this before.

A little while later she said, "Poppy, oh, that poor horse! He's been pulling half an hour, and he hasn't had a rest. You'd never see that back home! And look at the man's whip—"

"Barbara, in America there are mines, and in these mines, deep underground, there are mules that never see the light of day. They work and work. They live and die down there. And as for the whip—it is only cracked on narrow passages to signal oncoming sleighs to wait until we pass."

"Poppy, the mines in America are all electrified."

"Well, maybe now, but they weren't until recently. In fact, only the other day—and that might not make you like him, but it shows the force of his personality—I read that when John L. Lewis was a miner there was once a mule that refused to go, and he took a shovel and bashed in its brains."

"I don't believe it," said the lighthouse.

The jingle bells stopped for a moment, the horse looked around, then happily trotted on again. Little Bit sat on Barbara's lap. Arguments like this are always followed by silence. If there is ever going to be any more conversation, I have to start it.

I said, "The horse's name is Gretel, she's four years old, and she has another ten minutes to go. On top of the Arlberg is the Hotel Flexen, owned by an aunt of mine, and there she will get a rest and water. After that the road is easy, descending for fifteen minutes to Lech, and there is our inn, where she will get fed and rest."

"Does the horse live in the inn too?"

"Of course."

The sleigh approached the Hotel Flexen. The people there were all happy to see us, especially my aunt, Frau Anna Skardarassy, who immediately endeared herself to Barbara by feeding sugar to the horse and covering it with its blanket.

On the faded and frayed canvas deck chairs that stood on the terrace lay sixteen guests. All were the color of Brazilian tobacco, and their mouths, like those of clowns, were smeared with white grease—a cream for preventing the glacier burn that often raises fever blisters. They were further disguised by the darkest of sunglasses. Two of them had legs in plaster casts—the usual proportion of casualties in establishments of this size during the skiing season.

Water from melting snow descended, like a curtain of glass beads in perpetual motion, from the roof to the edge of the terrace. The sun lit up each drop as if it were a crystal fragment on a chandelier. The time was the rest period after the *Jause,* an in-between meal served at four.

We went indoors to the welcome of a hall and to a dining room almost as meticulous as the Swiss dining car. At a table near the vast window that looks out at the nursery slopes we were given tea, and white milk in little bright silver jugs; and on clean plates, on a clean tablecloth, pastry was served by a girl in a snow-white apron. She put the pastry on the plate with silver tongs, not with her hand.

All this was carefully observed by Barbara, and approved. The mood was almost right when something happened that made the lighthouse beam appear.

Below the hotel a little animal seemed to labor upward in the snow. It was brownish, and when it came close it turned out to be a small melancholy drinking companion and restaurant sitter of the neighborhood, a harmless, friendly incompetent, a type whom the French call a *Lustic.* He was coming up toward the hotel. He moved his arms with rowing motions. He was exhausted; he grasped the banister that led to the terrace, took off a derby textured like the wet nose of a dog, and wiped his bald head with a blue handkerchief. On the terrace he removed his coat and turned its mangy fur lining to the sun as he draped it over one of the deck chairs. Then he came into the dining room. His greeting was a blend of Viennese and the local speech.

He had a curious manner of entering a place. He had the quality of an apparition, the Tyrolean equivalent of Mr. O'Malley. He floated into the dark corners, the warm places of inns. Gradually he took on weight. His hat in hand, and bent over, he talked earnestly in a low voice and smiled instantly when anyone looked at him. His face was round, his manner soft and apologetic. The most prominent thing about his face, despite a bushy mustache, was his large, brown, glassy eyes, the kind a taxidermist would set into the head of a Saint Bernard.

Wendelin was a fixture in every inn. He was given a jug of wine and a plate of food. He ate and drank with devout expression, and was deaf during his meals. He paid for them by singing the complete repertoire of Viennese sad songs, accompanying himself on a battered guitar.

After an hour of digestion he smoked awhile on his picturesque Tyrolean pipe, a piece of carving as elaborate as a cuckoo clock. He emptied a series of stout small glasses, called *Stamperln*, of schnapps, and then he unpacked his instrument and began softly to create that harmony and atmosphere typical of Tyrolean and other low-ceilinged inns. The highpoint came around midnight, when, with closed eyes and holding his head like a crowing rooster, he sang his ballads to the rafters and afterward, during waves of applause, passed his hat.

Since he never paid for food, drink, or lodging, and had gone about in the same costume as long as people could remember, it was suspected that somewhere, perhaps across the border in Switzerland, he owned apartment houses and had vast sums hidden away in various banks.

Wendelin is unattached, and one of the few really happy people I've known. He is also the only man of my acquaintance who wears a celluloid collar.

"Who is that poor old man sitting there all alone?" asked Barbara.

"That is Wendelin," I said, looking in his direction. He caught my eye and waved. He came to the table and mumbled, "Are we celebrating tonight?"

By "Are we celebrating tonight?" Wendelin meant, "Below in the inn the wine is on ice and the goose in the oven, and may I come along to make music for the homecoming?" I nodded.

He was standing outside waiting as we left. The horse blanket was removed, and he sat next to the driver. He managed to project his role of hapless, at-your-mercy creature from the back as well as from the front. Occasionally he turned and smiled a little sadly.

"Can't you give him a job?" said Barbara, looking at the back of the little man and his faded hat.

Things like that have happened to me before. I am a Defender of Furbearers, a contributor to the American Fondouk in Morocco, to the Horse-Watering Fund of the A.S.P.C.A., to the Christmas party given by the Humane Society, to the Emergency Shelter on the Bowery, and to the Washington Square Home for Friendless Girls—all under the aegis of Barbara and her mother.

Once the sleigh was under way, with the jingle-jangle tune that the dancing bells play when the horse trots, Wendelin turned around and inquired about Little Bit. All the dog questions were answered, about name, age, race, sex, and then he patted Little Bit's head and said, "Yoh, yoh, Waldi is going to be happy."

I said I hoped so. There is always the problem, when visiting a house, of whether the resident dogs will like the visiting dogs.

"Poppy, who is Waldi?"

"Waldi is a dog with a very sad history. On a windy night, some years ago, there was a knock on the door of the inn, and when my mother opened it, there were two men outside with hats pulled down over their faces and the collars of their coats turned up, and one of them asked, 'Do you like dogs?' My mother said she did. The man handed her a dachshund and a bundle of money and said, 'Please take care of him.' Then both of them, before anything could be said, disappeared. They were arrested at the Swiss border the next day. The man who had handed the dachshund over was Pierre Laval. The French in occupation of Tyrol took him to Paris, where he was later executed. The dog was unhappy for a while. The first day he ran after his master, following the tracks for two hours. He was brought back and mourned for weeks. He improved when some French skiers came and talked to him in their language. Eventually he began to feel at home and was as happy a dog as a dachshund can be. Once mature, they are inclined to introspection; they sigh occasionally and have an air of detachment.

"Waldi has a set routine of sleeping on a sofa, looking out of the window, and in the winter, when the snow reaches that high, of walking out of the window for small promenades over the white expanse that covers everything, rocks, fences, bushes—a blanket of snow twelve feet deep."

"Are there any other dogs?"

"Only one, the butcher's dog, a great Dane. There was no friendship, only a distant, barking acquaintance, between them the last time I was here."

"But Laval, he can't have been altogether bad if he cared so much about the dog."

"I don't know. I know only this, that if one writes propaganda against someone, one must not leave a good hair on them. Since this episode of the dog, whenever I think about Laval I can't feel that he was as awful as they say he was."

The mountains of the Lechtal appeared ahead between the snow-laden pine trees. Wendelin was conversing with the driver, and I translated for Barbara.

"What do I need money for?" he was saying. "I have my health, and a few possessions, and above all my guitar. I am free as a bird."

The sun went behind the mountain that stands at the entrance of the valley of Lech, and instantly the temperature changed. The water of the river roared in an abyss to the right. Wendelin pulled his coat tightly around him, and Barbara covered up Little Bit. She had retired into silence and remained so until the reception at the inn.

The next day, on a Sunday, the natives went past the window on their way to church, and inside the *Stüberl* sat Wendelin between my mother and Barbara. He was buttering bread and dunking it in his coffee.

"Poppy, there are also pigs and chickens living in the inn, and Waldi loves Little Bit. They are out playing together, and this poor man, Mr. Wendelin, has had to sleep on straw with the horses and cows all night."

I knew why Wendelin had slept on straw. He had celebrated my homecoming so thoroughly that he had been unable to make the stairs up to his room.

Wendelin wore his saddest face. In the coated voice of the disinherited he gave his poorhouse answers. Barbara had started a sociological study. The lighthouse was flashing.

"Did you know, Poppy, that Mr. Wendelin is a writer?"

I knew that Wendelin had sold flour and cigarettes on the black market and occasionally made deals, selling horses, cows, and arranging things between people as a kind of arbitrator. But I had not known about his literary talent.

"Yes, he has written for newspapers, and he has written a darling story for children, and all he needs is someone to illustrate it."

I was reaching for my hat to go out. There was a scream in the hall and the sound of porcelain and glass crashing. Waldi had chased Little Bit through the legs of a waitress, and two break-fast trays lay beside her on the floor. The dogs had run outside,

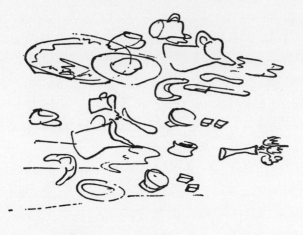

and the white fluff of Little Bit disappeared into the powdery snow, so that only the ribbon in her hair hopped along, and after her came Waldi. He seemed like a dark brown snake cut into pieces, the pieces jumping in the snow.

Barbara is a single-minded person. She ignored the disaster and held on to my sleeve. "It takes just a minute. Please listen to Mr. Wendelin's story."

"It's absolutely original, unpolitical, and safe," said Wendelin. "The story of my children's book goes like this: Hereabouts, in the high crags of the Alps, live a papa deer and a mamma deer. One day a dead-shot kind of hunter comes up from the valley below and spies the papa deer, who, unfortunately, is not young any more and is losing his eyesight and cannot see the hunter. Just as the hunter has his gun in position and is about to shoot, he gets his foot caught in the root of a big, benevolent pine tree which stands at the edge of an abyss. The hunter trips, and falls down the abyss, and is killed. The gentle tree, the friend of the deer family, had foresightedly, with one of its limbs, lifted the binoculars from the hunter's shoulder as he fell. They were attached to a shoulder strap, and now they swing on the branch of this tree, and all the papa deer has to do is walk there several times a day and look into the valley through the binoculars. He can see the approaching hunters long before they reach the mountain and go into hiding, and he and his family will live happily forever after."

Wendelin stopped talking. "Wonderful, no?" he said after a pause. "Of course, it needs a little polishing, and somebody to illustrate it."

"It's just perfect for you, Poppy," said Barbara.

I went out to look for the dogs.

Around noon Waldi chased Little Bit up the stairs, and one of the guests with a plaster cast almost came to grief as he descended for lunch.

"People seem to do nothing but eat up here," said Barbara.

The sad eyes of Wendelin were on his soup plate, and after the wienerschnitzel Barbara resumed her rehabilitation program. I listened as long as I could. Wendelin was telling her about his possessions, his life, and his ambitions.

"Most gracious Fräulein Barbara," he said, "I am a true Viennese, and I am homesick. I cannot stand it much longer. I want to go back to visit my little flat where I have my art treasures. I wonder if I shall find them. I left Vienna just before the Unknowns arrived. I must explain to you that by the Unknowns we mean the Russians. Unknown, because nobody really knows anything about them or what they are going to do next."

"Tell me about your art treasures, Mr. Wendelin."

"Yes, paintings, beautiful paintings. I have several Dürers,

also Michelangelo, Rubens, and Raphael—no modern junk. I used to cut them out of illustrated magazines and mount them on cardboard and then cover them with several layers of varnish and after that frame them myself in gold."

Barbara nodded.

"*Ja,*" said Wendelin, "and I have other magnificent possessions—all honestly come by. I have a small hand-carved wooden barrel, lined with glass, and with engraved glass cups hanging by handles on the outside. In this barrel you can make a punch and then serve it in the cups, with a ladle also of engraved glass and part of the set; it is wonderful. Also, Fräulein Barbara, I own a small locomotive made of bronze, and when you lift the lid of the smokestack you find an inkwell in it. That is, however, not all I possess. I have an antique hand-carved figure of a monk; when you take his head off, it turns out to be a liquor bottle. All that I have, and besides, furniture, silver, curtains and linen, and an oriental rug. These things, each more beautiful than the other, I have—if the Unknowns haven't taken them. That is why I want to go to Vienna."

Looking at me, Barbara said, "I think that's a wonderful idea."

A cold shiver ran down my spine.

5.

Gramercy Nocturne

WE HAD tickets to go to Vienna, but when the time came to leave I had a temperature and had to go to bed. The beds in Tyrol are made for sleeping rather than illness, but in this case it did not matter, for it turned out to be pneumonia, an illness of which I have become an habitué, even an *aficionado*. I have had it in Hollywood, in New York, and now I was catching it in Tyrol. The most beautiful indifference descends upon you when in this state. The patient floats away and comes back to the world, speculating whether to stay on a little longer or go for good. It detaches one from the ego. I recommend it as the best exit from life. On the edge of it, I have sensed a miraculous beyond. It gives the assurance of absolute repose in the arms of nature, which I find preferable to the promised paradises of all religions—with the exception of the Mohammedan heaven for men.

I manage to catch the disease by continuous celebrations, by riding in bad weather, by driving hatless and coatless in open cars after coming from warm interiors, and by extending myself beyond my capacity in my general enthusiasm for living.

The doctor arrived with his penicillin syringes. Barbara came and sat on my bed and after the obligatory inquiry said, "Now you can send Wendelin to Vienna."

"Why?"

"Because you can't go—so he can, to do the article for you."

"But darling, I have no idea if Wendelin can do it."

"I'm certain he can."

"And you know it's not so easy to send anyone into the Russian Zone. He needs papers. We must know about his politics."

"He has papers."

I fell back into my pillows, and, tiptoeing, Barbara left the bedroom. When I came to again, she was sitting in the living room, and I heard Wendelin's voice, answering her questions.

"Mr. Wendelin, have you ever been a member of the Nazi party?"

"Never," said Wendelin earnestly.

"Have you ever been a Communist?"

"*Nein, nein,* never!" Wendelin screamed.

"Well, then you better go in and explain it to my father."

Barbara brought Wendelin into the room, and he put his hand on his heart to testify. In New York, Barbara listens to a character on the radio called Just Plain Bill. In the semi-comatose state I was in, I thought, as Wendelin talked, that I was listening to that program.

"My father and his people were, since the fifteenth century, peasants. In the twentieth year of his life my father married the daughter of a neighbor, also five hundred years a peasant, two

hours from here, in that valley over there. That night, when the
ceremony was over and the guests had left the feast and my
parents were alone—that night the bride denied herself to her
husband. He was in low spirits. The next Sunday, after Mass,
he took his bride to the village priest and explained his disappointment. The priest drew the bride aside, made things clear to
her, and asked her if she did not want to please the Lord and
have children. Well, I am the result of that conversation. When
I was only ten days old I was carried down to church and
baptized a Catholic. Now, if you please, I can say with good
reason that I had nothing to do with becoming a member of the
Catholic faith. But when a grown man comes to me and says
that he is innocent of having joined the Nazi party at twenty-
one or thirty years of age, or at fifty, I tell him to his face that he
is talking nonsense, and there is no this and that and why and
maybe and because; there is only, Yes, I was a member, or, No, I
was not.

"I swear that I have never been a member of the Nazi party,
nor have I had any connection with communism. I have never
been a pink or a fellow traveler. If you wish to know, I'm a
Catholic and a royalist."

This simple affirmation of faith reassured me, and I floated
off again for a while. When I awoke, Wendelin was still there. I
thought I must have been out of hearing a long time, but it was
only half an hour.

"Poppy, you'll let Mr. Wendelin go?"

I nodded my assent and said that he should be given some
money in advance. Barbara handed me my wallet. Wendelin put
his hand on his heart again. His heavy eyelids sank down over

the glass eyes, and with earnest protestations he allowed me to press upon him a thousand schillings.

In a moment of clarity I asked him how much he thought the whole trip would come to. His hand went back to his heart. His eyes were as clouded as mine. Looking straight at me, he said, "I have made up my mind to remain an honest man until my end comes, absolutely honest—that is, honest within the limitations that the times impose upon us. You may trust me absolutely."

With that, he and Barbara disappeared.

My mother came and put her hand on my forehead. I was hot, and I asked for a jug of cold wine. The moments of thirst that occur during this condition are also glorious. I sank back into my bed. The phrase "until my end comes" still hung in the room, and outside the church bells tolled. The blue light of evening lay on the glaciers, and again I must praise the illness, for after the deep sleep it provides total recall. I remembered a quotation that fit the scene:

> My intention is to die in a tavern,
> May wine be close to my dying lips,
> That when they come, the choirs of angels say,
> God be merciful to this drinker.

After that I indulged myself, contemplating the tablet that would probably soon be attached to the outside of the tavern. It would be in German. In that language writers of no matter what caliber are bunched under the name of *Dichter,* which means poet. It would look like this:

The bells slowed down, the shadows deepened, and the evening star trembled in the sky. I folded my hands and closed my eyes and almost obliged myself by departing this life.

I returned to the here in the night and began thinking about the last such experience, which I had gone through some years ago when we lived in the old Stuyvesant Fish house on the south side of Gramercy Park. Barbara was then seven or eight.

As is only logical and good for the offspring of a writer, she even then knew the value of character and the importance of observation. Her studies of the people she met around Gramercy Park were thorough, untiring, and ranged from the delightful free entertainment that the patrons of restaurants who have trouble with knife and fork give—making faces while eating, food falling out of mouth, pieces of spaghetti stuck on chin, complaining of objects found in soup, etc.—to more complicated amusements like those provided by a friend, a fellow writer and naturalist, who, when he was with bottle, performed on the high iron fence enclosing Gramercy Park.

This show was best seen from the windows of our living room. My colleague would exchange frantic grips as he proceeded from stake to stake. He contorted like a limp acrobat past the gate that is in the center of the fence, sank, dipped, and came up by an ordinance ordering citizens to curb their dogs. At the end of the fence he embraced the four iron pickets that are welded into a column, swayed again awhile, looked around to get his bearings, checked on oncoming vehicles, and when he found the time had come he suddenly let go and, with his overcoat flying and flopping behind him, and fighting the downward pull of the sidewalk and the pavement, shuttled over toward Third Avenue. Reaching the pavement across the

street, he stumbled into a coffeepot, where he collapsed, one hand holding his hat down on his head, the other stretched across the counter.

Barbara was a regular customer of this establishment and spent a good deal of her allowance there on hot dogs and the specialty of the house, a fried cheeseburger enhanced by a rust-colored sauce maison.

Another esteemed client of the place was a Mrs. Peep. Around ten in the morning the proprietor of the coffeepot cleared the left end of his counter of dishes, wiped it clean with a moist rag, and, when he saw Mrs. Peep approach outside in the street, he hollered into the kitchen, "A sandwich, cut in six pieces." While his wife was busy making the sandwich he went to the icebox, took out a large piece of liver, cut a slice from it, and, after chopping it up, placed it in a saucer for Mrs. Peep's dog.

Mr. Woolly, the dog, a small poodle with dirty-white hair which was parted on top of his head, a small beard, and pale blue eyes, strained toward the coffeepot, piloting Mrs. Peep. She hoisted the poodle on the stool beside her own, patiently fed him, then wiped his face with a paper napkin. After that she munched her sandwich, drank two cups of coffee, and read the paper.

From a limp sack which she pulled up from the floor she took her purse, paid, and left a ten-cent tip. She replaced the purse, put the dog back on the tiled floor, and then walked out into the street, ready to cross Third Avenue — an undertaking as hazardous and fraught with the possibility of disaster for the little old woman as it was for my alcoholic friend.

In the years that Mrs. Peep had visited the coffeepot, her costume, her hat, and the sack that rode several inches above the ground as she walked along, all had achieved a sameness of faded hues such as is obtained by swishing a thick water-soaked brush over all the water colors in a paintbox. To this effect winter added a fur coat, cut like a bathrobe, of such age that on very cold, sunny days it blinked and sent out light signals. It was hard to tell at even a short distance whether it was made of tarpaper or chinchilla.

After a fresh snowfall Mrs. Peep would stop at each of the four corners of Gramercy Park. Her black sack, when put down, opened by itself. From its contents the old lady selected a whisk broom, with which she cleared a small plot of sidewalk. On this she poured bread crumbs from a paper bag, also carried in the sack.

The benevolences of Mrs. Peep continued undisturbed for

years until she appeared without Mr. Woolly. I heard the story
of what happened from Barbara, who got it in the coffeepot.

The people there informed her that Mr. Woolly was dead.
The proprietor of the coffeepot and his wife were upset, not so
much about the animal's passing but by the callous fashion in
which Mrs. Peep, who had become the neighborhood symbol of
kindness and protection to animals, had disposed of him.

A legless man, also an habitué of the coffeepot, was witness to this. He had been sitting on his box, sunning himself outside his house, when Mrs. Peep, who lived two doors down the street from him, came out of her home, carrying the dirty, dead little poodle — "just like that, by the scruff of his neck." She walked to the ashcan, took off the lid, and dropped Mr. Woolly in. She put the lid back on the can and returned to her house. "Now who would do a thing like that?" asked the legless man.

The first time Mrs. Peep approached the coffeepot after the tragedy the proprietor opened the icebox door and took out the liver. He was about to cut a slice off for the dog when he realized that Mrs. Peep was alone. He put the liver back, closed the icebox door again, and ordered a sandwich cut in six pieces. Barbara was there, and at the brief sight of the liver she began to cry.

Mrs. Peep sat down. She asked the child why she was crying. Barbara told her and then asked the old lady about Mr. Woolly and why she had gotten rid of him "like that."

"You don't have to cry," Mrs. Peep said to Barbara. "It's not sad at all. While I had him, I treated Mr. Woolly as if he were my baby. I got him when he was no bigger than a mouse — and I had a lot of trouble raising him. He didn't have a sad hour in his life. I never left him alone, he was never cold or hungry. Remember, little girl, remember this always: when you've been good to someone all his life, the way I was to Mr. Woolly, you don't have to be sad for a minute when he's gone."

This explanation was satisfactory to everyone in the coffeepot, especially since tears had started down the old lady's cheeks as she talked. The legless man cried too. It led to a great friendship, and from then on, whenever we went out, the old lady came to our house to sit with Barbara. She had an inexhaustible repertoire of stories about the neighborhood and particularly the old house in which we lived.

One fateful night when Mrs. Peep stayed with Barbara, we went to the theater. It seemed like a comfortable evening, and since I don't like to wear an overcoat or hat, I went without them. When the play let out, the theaters across the way were barely visible in the snowstorm. The street was jammed with people trying to get cabs. With blood thinned by six months of California, and run down with celebration, I went out into a sudden slush and snowy night scene. Holding the lapels of my jacket bunched close to my throat, I searched three wet city blocks for a cab, and with chattering teeth we rode down to Gramercy Park. My wife ran into the house and got off with influenza and a strep throat.

Paying the taxi in the windy street, I saw my friend, the naturalist, tossing on the park fence, blinded by the snowstorm. He gripped the icy stakes. His hat had blown away. He was only halfway down the fence.

"I don't need a cab," he shouted at me and the taxi driver through the wind. "I don't need anything, thank God. I went to school in New Hampshire. I can take care of myself. All I want from you is a small ax, a little bit of string, and some seed—and the key to the park. Don't worry about me, I'll get along."

The taxi driver asked him how he would get along.

"First," said my friend, "I'll cut those trees down and build myself a cabin. Then I'll chop me some firewood. And then I'll take some string and snare a cat and some birds."

"He's with the birds all right," said the taxi driver.

"I don't need any help whatever from you," said my friend, and, letting go of the fence, he fell on the ground.

We put him in the taxi, and I went home and was put to bed. Hours later I felt a cold cloth on my head and awoke. Through thick glasses I looked intently into eyes that looked intently at me. The glasses moved away and became part of a serious, extremely worried face—our doctor's face. He walked on tiptoe into the next room and said, "Have you a piece of meat in the icebox?"

"I'll have a look," said Mrs. Peep and walked into the kitchen. Without her hat and coat Mrs. Peep was another person. She had shed about fifty pounds and fifty years. She looked efficient and neat as she passed the bedroom door in the glare of the kitchen light. She opened the icebox and said, "No meat, but there seems to be a piece of liver."

"Good," said the doctor. "Take it out. I'll teach you how to give injections. I have to get some sleep. I can't get any nurses for any of my patients, and there isn't a bed free in any hospital. I haven't seen a bed myself for the last two nights. Now you'll have to give him these injections every two hours. Watch me closely. First we take a swab and some alcohol and we disinfect the spot where the injection is to be made. There's nothing to it. Next, watch me fill the needle. Now take a firm grip of the liver—don't be afraid of hurting him—squeeze it tight. Now jab the needle into it and push the plunger. That's fine. Now practice once more on the liver, and then I want to watch you try it on the patient."

Soon I was gently turned around in bed, the bottom part of my pajamas came off, and I felt the cold swab of alcohol and the sharp pain of an amateur injection.

"I was lucky to get the penicillin," said the doctor. "I got it from a friend. It's hard to get."

I was turned around again. There was so little enthusiasm in the doctor's face when he looked at me that for half an hour I thought about writing my obituary.

I must have sunk away into fever dreams, for Hendrik Willem Van Loon came into the room and sat down on my bed.

"Oh, it's you," I said to him. "Tell me, how does an author die properly?"

"No differently from anybody else. You're very lucky. For you, it's only a matter of leaning back a little farther," he said. "You'll be out of it in a second—it's no trouble at all."

"As for writing anything," I asked Hendrik, "have you any advice? I mean about a literary testament?"

"I had something very nice all prepared, but alas, I had no time. I hope you have," he said.

I asked him how he found things in the beyond.

He said, "It's heavenly. No publishers. Only thing I have to do is, once a week a group of librarians show up and I take them to lunch—the food is good, the wine superb—but, at the end, when I am about to sign my books, somebody comes and takes my fountain pen away from me." He sighed, picked up his hat, opened the window, and left.

"Please turn around," said Barbara and wiped my face with a wet cloth.

"Your father has virus pneumonia," said Mrs. Peep, filling the needle. I felt the alcohol swab again and the sting.

Barbara whispered, "I have two friends, two little girls—another Barbara and Elinor—who live downstairs. Could they come up and watch the next time?"

"I don't think your father would like that," said Mrs. Peep.

"They'll be very quiet," whispered Barbara, and after a while

she added, "And besides, Poppy won't know anything about it.
It's six o'clock now, and they could come at eight."

"Well, all right," said Mrs. Peep. "If they're very quiet. We
must leave your father alone now so that he can sleep."

When I awoke again Barbara, with a running commentary
and familiarity born of practice, was directing the operation.

"Now watch this," she said. "First we disinfect the part.
That's most important. Bob, you must come in too," she shouted
to our elevator man. "Now watch closely," said Barbara. "Now
comes the most important part—the injection."

It was Christmas Eve. The carillon of the neighborhood
church rang out "Silent Night," the tree in the living room was

lit, and below in Gramercy Park the snow fell and melted in the slushy path of tracks made by those hardy citizens who congregate there to sing carols.

At the foot of my bed, open-mouthed, stood the little girls and Bob, the elevator man, watching while the ancient angel of mercy injected me with the life-giving fluid. Mrs. Peep found the spot, as usual, by employing a method of her own, a combination of dead reckoning and the Braille system. The needle stung.

When it was over, I aroused myself sufficiently to turn around and with the newfound strength of the penicillin I whispered hoarsely, "Barbara, why don't you run over to the park and invite the people there? Tell them all that I'll give another show at ten, and also a special midnight performance."

My child ignored these feverish remarks. She addressed her audience. "Besides," she said, "it took a lot of trouble to get this penicillin—it's black-market penicillin—and if it hadn't been for Mrs. Peep here, poor Poppy would have died just like a dog."

But now, in Tyrol, as on that last bout, I came through. I lay, together with the broken legs and arms, the dislocated shoulder, and the sprained ankles of that season's skiers—so profitable to the doctor of Lech and to our inn—on the terrace, and got deeply sunburned.

Skiing is a passion—and the only sport in which the casualties refuse to leave but hobble about, looking with longing out on the slopes for another try.

Barbara received several cards from Wendelin in which he promised astounding results from his mission.

One day, as I was slowly recuperating, lying quietly and

covered with blankets in my chair on the terrace, Barbara said, "Poppy, if you had died, would you have wanted to be buried here?"

I said, "No, I don't want to be buried here. I want to be cremated and taken to America."

"And what would you want to have done with the ashes?"

"The ashes you can put in a shoebox and take back to New York with you, and then one very cold and freezing day you can take them and spread them over the ice on the sidewalk in front of Lane Bryant's or any other good maternity shop."

Children don't like levity in matters of life and death—she ran off to play with the dogs.

The rapport between Waldi and Little Bit during this time was such that I was seriously worried. Speculating on what the result of this relationship might turn out to be, I dozed off, but not for long. Barbara wakened me with the announcement that Wendelin was back from Vienna with his report on the city and the Russians.

6.

The Unknowns in Vienna

WENDELIN HAD covered Vienna thoroughly in matter and
time.

He removed his mangy coat and bowler and started right off.
"First of all," he said, waving his right index finger in front of
my face, "I must assure you that everything I tell you, every
word, is founded upon solid truth. I shall neither color nor
enlarge on facts, nor invent incident; neither beautify nor be-
smirch. I shall, as a good reporter, inform you only of what I
have seen and what I have heard and of those things told to me
by people whom I believe to be reliable. I am ready now."

Wendelin poured himself a *Stamperl* of schnapps. "As you know, I left on the Arlberg Express, with a ticket first-class for Vienna. Speaking as an experienced traveler, I must observe that it doesn't pay to go any other way, in spite of the fact that first class is filled with black marketeers and shady people. It is still the most comfortable—that is, it is comfortable in the French and American Zones. As you approach the Russian Zone the compartment gets crowded with people who flow over from second and third class.

"We sat packed together—eight people in a compartment for four. The baggage nets above sagged with the weight of bags, small trunks, valises, and rucksacks. At the last stop before the Russian Zone the door rolled back and there was one more applicant for room in our crowded compartment, a little man,

so pale, old, and pitiful that no one could refuse him. He begged to be let in, and when he saw that the occupants were of a mind to make room for him, he turned and shouted to a man outside, who lifted an enormous bag in through the window. The man inside was too small and frail to handle it, and for a while the whole compartment was upset. All the luggage in the nets above had to be rearranged and the big bag stowed away; and the seating also had to be changed—one man went to the other side, so that the little man could find space next to an old peasant woman, who, besides himself, was the only other thin occupant. He sat next to her, on the edge of the seat, and when he talked to her he had to look backward.

"The train went on toward the Enns Bridge, where the Unknowns are. It happens often that they go through every piece of luggage and take whatever they fancy, especially in the way of food. The people in the compartment started to yammer about this. The peasant woman said, 'Oh God, if the Russians take my stuff away, then all my trouble has been for nothing, and all my good money thrown away. I don't want to go home and look at the faces of my grandchildren if I reach home empty-handed. For two days I have gone from peasant to peasant to get a little food together.'

"The old man with the big bag turned his head and said, 'What have you got, good woman?'

"'Oh, I have two dozen eggs, a side of bacon, three chickens, and a kilo of butter.'

"'Let's hope for the best,' said somebody across the aisle, and a woman hopefully added, 'The Russians, after all, are human too.'

"Soon after, the train stopped and the Russians came into the cars to look at the people's papers, which must have twelve stamps. There is something typical about these stamps. On my card of identification the Austrian stamp says: 'This instrument is no proof of the Austrian citizenship of the bearer.' On this same card the Russian stamp says: 'This card is proof of Austrian citizenship.' These Russians just count the number of stamps. Then come the customs inspectors. One of these came in and asked, 'Anything to declare?' The people said no and shook their heads—all except the little man who sat beside the old woman. He leaned his head in her direction and said, 'She is trying to smuggle through two dozen eggs, a side of bacon, three chickens, and a kilo of butter.'

"'Is that true?' said the Russian to the woman. She was panicked and stared at him. The Russian said, 'Which is your stuff?'

"We all pleaded with him, saying what a tragedy it would be for the poor woman if he took her food away.

"He said, 'Show me what you have.'

"So finally she started to unpack. With trembling hands she undid the knots of a colored cloth and held up three skinny chickens. As she was about to open another sack the train whistled, and the Russian said, 'Keep it.' He left, and there was silence until the train started moving and was on the bridge.

"Then everyone began calling the little man bad names; some said he should be hung; a woman offered to scratch his eyes out. He sat looking out of the window as if none of it concerned him, until they had exhausted themselves. Then, as if it were the most natural thing, he calmly asked the man who had put his heavy bag into the net above to take it down again, because he was getting off at the next station. After the bag was taken down, he unlocked it and from one corner took some American chocolate bars and gave them all to the old peasant woman. He got out his wallet and handed her a hundred-schilling note, and as the train slowed down he said, 'Dear woman, you have done me a great favor. I regret that I had to do what I did, but it was necessary to divert suspicion from my own luggage, and I knew that no Russian would take anything from a poor little peasant mother like you. Forgive me. Good-by.'

"He was gone, and the opinion in the compartment was, 'Saccharine smuggler.' He had offered cigarettes all around also, and the woman who had said that she would scratch his eyes out now removed a bit of stale tobacco from her lip and lit one of the smuggler's cigarettes. 'These days,' she said, 'one should be very careful, and wait before passing final judgment on anyone.' The man who had helped with the bag told a current joke about smugglers, which goes like this:

"A smuggler approaches an Austrian customs guard, and the guard points at the first of two bags the man is carrying. 'What have you in there?' he asks, and the man says, 'A rabbit.' The guard says, 'Open it!' The man opens it, and inside the bag is a live rabbit. 'And what have you in the other bag?' asks the customs inspector. 'The food for the rabbit,' says the man. The guard asks him to open that bag too. 'But that is saccharine,' says the guard. 'Well, if he won't eat his saccharine, he won't get anything,' said the man.

"Everybody laughed at this joke, and the first observation I wish to make is that Austrian humor is not dead; also, that an

Austrian customs official would have confiscated the woman's property and seen to it that she was properly punished. That can be observed wherever they have authority. We got to Vienna without further incident."

"How about your art collection, the Raphaels and the Rubenses?" asked Barbara.

"All my treasures are gone," he said sadly. "The frames of the pictures—all of them gilded—are gone, and most of the paintings. The rest of them were torn and trampled. They left me one broken chair. All the light fixtures, and the buttons and switches and wires, and the telephone, were ripped out. They tore out all the telephones, switchboards, and wires of the exchange in my part of the city, and they shoveled the equipment on freight cars to take away to Russia.

"But in spite of all this the air of Vienna is good to breathe, even in winter. You see people smiling again in the streets— mostly the younger people. The old ones stand with blue faces, freezing, filled with sad thoughts, staring along the tracks on which streetcars come only after you wait and wait, and then are so crowded that you have to hang outside on the steps, where once it was forbidden to ride. How beautiful and bright our streetcars were! Now they are noisy, dirty crates that don't fit into the picture because the city is still beautiful.

"You will remember what I told you before I left, about how I feel about anybody who belonged to the party. I have in some respects changed my opinion about that—especially in the case of Professor Erdödi, who operated on me once. He was the head of a large clinic in Vienna. I knew him well, and he was, and is, a fine man, who has never done anything but good all his life. He held out as long as he could. Finally he was faced with the dilemma of joining the party or losing his clinic. He became a member in the last year. He never participated in political activities—the head of a clinic has no time for that.

"I visited him. His case is only now coming before the denazification board. He has many friends and colleagues who will testify for him, and he may be allowed to practice again and even to get back his position. But if someone who has been in a concentration camp is after his job—whether he is a good doctor or a mediocre one doesn't make any difference—then he won't get it. His future hangs on that and on the men who sit on the board, and they are Austrians.

"I asked the Professor what he would do if the board went against him. He said, 'I will have to become a helper in some trade, in order to get my food-ration card. I will not be allowed to work as a journeyman; I have to be a helper. What I would like to do is get a job in the library at the university, sorting and putting back on their proper shelves books that have been used. This would give me a chance to read and study, but I hear there are already several applicants for these jobs, all doctors and younger men than I.'

"I took him to a cheap restaurant. The Herr Professor ate a small goulash with great appetite and wiped the plate with the last piece of bread. The beer we were served was the first he had had since the end of the war. He told me, with the coffee, that he was always hungry. He said, 'You know, I dream often, very often, about my stamp collection. I owned a very good one. At the beginning of this dream I always carry my album to the large walnut desk that stood in my private office at the clinic, and I sit down and open it, and, stuck on the transparent paper of the album, which is like waxed paper, I find the most beautiful slices of sausage—instead of my rare stamps. There is salami, mortadella, liverwurst, and cervelat, and as I turn the pages I come to slices of smoked tongue, and then to hams— every kind of ham I have eaten on my travels, Westphalian, Prague, and prosciutto. The collection ends with an assortment of cold meats in which chicken predominates. The last time I had this dream I succeeded in carefully removing a large snow-white slice of breast of capon from the sandwich paper. I gently put this into my shoe, and carefully put the shoe on, so that no one would discover it. I wanted to take the slice of capon home to my wife. I got out of the clinic, but from there on frightful things happened, always with the shoe. I had to walk through a street newly tarred, still smoking and hot; I came to another that was strewn with broken glass. My foot began to ache terribly, and I took the shoe off to see if the slice of capon was still there. An ambulance came along and picked me up and took me back to the clinic. One of the doctors there, none of whom I knew, said, "Herr Professor, we shall have to amputate the leg." I protested, and that was when my wife woke me.'

"That much for the hunger of the Viennese," said Wendelin, who had gotten hungry himself. He called for the waitress and asked what there was to eat. He ordered soup, cold cuts with hot potatoes, and apple strudel and coffee. Here in Tyrol things were better than in Vienna.

He continued talking during the meal. "There used to be great feeling of neighborliness in all the quarters of Vienna, and there was friendship between high and low. The Professor lived in my neighborhood, and after my operation he would give me medical advice, gratis, on the street, whenever we met. We had a living newspaper, a woman old even before the war, Frau Brandl. She kept a small dairy shop. Now when she talks about the past you can see with how little people once were happy. These days she lives like a snail in a shell, in the basement of a bombed-out building. She said, 'Do you remember those wonderful times that never will come back again—when I had my little shop down the street here? I had to get up at four to get the milk and pour it into sixty-four small metal canisters. Then I would put hot rolls into sixty-four linen sacks and visit my sixty-four customers, climbing to their apartments all through the neighborhood. I would hang the sacks with the rolls on the doorhandles, so that when they opened the door there was milk and fresh warm bread outside. And on every one of the sixty-four I made, year in and year out, two cents a day profit. One could live nicely on that. Now they get their own bread—if they're lucky—and they have to stand in line for hours for their milk.'

"In that hole in which Frau Brandl lives with her husband they have two chickens, and in the morning she takes them down to the Danube and lets them run and scratch around, and in the afternoon her husband takes them under his arm and carries them to a place in the sun. It's the only work he ever does. The eggs are sold to a man who is an important official. Herr Brandl also had a boxer until last week, a big dog which he let run around loose. The papers are full of ads from butchers asking for dogs.

"I asked Frau Brandl if she knew how I could find out what

happened to my belongings, and she said the best way was to go to the hairdresser of the neighborhood, because he was very important and could do anything with the Russians. He had once persuaded a Russian officer to have a permanent wave, and afterward the officer was so satisfied he gave the hairdresser all the money he had with him. Since then the shop has been crowded with Russians getting their hair waved.

"The hairdresser listened to me and gave me his business card with an address and a name written on it. I spent a whole day finding the right office, gaining admittance, and waiting in the hall on what people call 'the anxiety bench.' This Russian colonel I went to see was a rug fancier. He had rugs all over the floor, under the windows, and hanging on the wall, and he had one rug cut down to fit the top of his desk. He sat with the fingers of both hands spread out, for the nails to dry, because he had just had a manicure. He held his two immense hands over the rug in front of him and admired his freshly lacquered nails while he listened to what the interpreter said about my property. He seemed very interested when he heard about the various items, but the time was wasted. He merely wrinkled the brows under the wavy hair and told the interpreter he would look into it. Nobody took my name or address. They did not even ask me to fill out forms.

"When I got back Frau Brandl said, '*Ich sehe* black.' The Viennese now mix a little English into their phrases, and everybody uses English words, such as pullover. There are also signs in the hotels announcing the 'Cocktailstunde.'"

Wendelin drank again and continued. "A curious thing that people tell you often is that the Russians enter a room as if water were running in: they come in silently on soft boots. 'They pour in,' people say; first one, and suddenly the room is filled with them. One came into the room of a neighborhood friend in this fashion, aimed his machine pistol at my friend's chest, and asked for cigarettes. My friend said he didn't have any. The Russian searched the place and found nothing. 'Wait here,' he said. My friend was frightened and did not know whether to wait or run away, but then he decided that he didn't care any more what happened and sat down. The Russian came back with a handful of cigarettes. 'Cigarettes for you,' he said and started to drink from a bottle of schnapps, which he then handed to my friend. They are unpredictable, the Unknowns.

"It seems that the average has courage only as long as he has a loaded gun in his hand, or is with others, or is very drunk. The following example will illustrate this. A man who lives in our block walked home late one night, and on a deserted street corner he met a Russian. The Russian pulled a gun on him and asked for his watch. This is the most usual request they make; they just say the German word *Uhr.* The man now says he does not know how he did it, but he lifted the cane he carried and hit the Russian so hard over the wrist that the Russian cried out in pain and dropped the gun and ran as fast as he could down the street. The other left his cane lying beside the gun and ran as fast as he could in the other direction.

"Before I left I visited Frau Brandl once more. She rounds out her income and supports herself and her no-good husband by collecting old woolen garments, such as mufflers, baby caps, and old socks. She unravels them, then sorts out the good strands of yarn and reweaves the bad, and after dying it a dark hue she knits pullovers. She also does laundry and cleaning, and she told me about a house to which she goes once a week to help their Excellencies keep their place in order.

"Her employer, a once rich aristocrat and former high official, not burdened with Nazi taint, now lives on a pension in three rooms of his former palace, in the American Zone. The establishment is poor but still has accents of elegance. The most evident is the presence of a butler, who eats at the same table with the count and countess and is in general sloppy as far as protocol is concerned, except on days when there is a party, when he becomes aloof. The butler has relatives in America and shares his CARE packages with his employers.

"One day the count put an ad in the paper—one finds curious ads in the papers these days—reading: 'Non-smoker wants a petroleum lamp.' 'Non-smoker' is the legal way of saying: 'I have cigarettes or tobacco, which I will trade for something I want.' And he found a lamp. The tobacco which was traded was, of course, provided by the butler.

"The family gave a party for the lamp. On such festive days the butler dons the splendid livery he wore in the old days. An old friend, a former cavalry officer still fiercely loyal to the old regime, a man whose face and body bear the marks of dueling and automobile accidents, contributed two bottles of wine. And because the true Austrian aristocrats are democrats in the truest sense of the word, their friend Frau Brandl was also invited.

"The butler polished the belly of the lamp all afternoon. The lamp was lit only after everybody was present, and it was done as if it were the Christmas tree. Frau Brandl said it stank, but it was the most beautiful stink in the world. The cavalry officer proposed a toast to the lamp and then played on his guitar. After a while the butler put protocol aside and sat down, and they ate food from a CARE package, and everyone sang and cried and was very happy.

"You know," said Wendelin, "Heine once said that the Viennese have no character, and maybe that's true, but they certainly have a great heart. Frau Brandl said they all stayed up until half-past eight that evening—usually they go to bed and lie and think as soon as it gets dark.

"That night the count said, 'Maybe now the Hungarians and the Czechs and the others in that club will remember with nostalgia how nice it was when Franz Josef was emperor.' 'Yes,' said the cavalry officer, 'if only the world had been ten per cent more intelligent,' and the impertinent butler, who had had a good bit to drink, added, 'Or if the Hapsburg had been five per cent more intelligent.'

"That is about all I have to report," said Wendelin and looked at me with the large glass eyes. "Of course," he said, "I have not been able to cover all of Vienna for you. There is more, another world. I have told you about the Russian Vienna, as you asked me to, but there is also the Vienna of the French, the English, and the Americans, of night clubs, racetrack, and nylon stockings. I have left that for another trip, but I shall have to have a little more money for expenses."

He put his guitar on the table and started to thumb softly the chords of Haydn's Imperial Hymn, which to most natives is still the best Austrian tune. Then he played a gay Viennese song. "I wanted to see if I could do it, stay in Vienna and make a living. I took my guitar and went to one of the *heurigen* restaurants on the outskirts of the city. I sat down and started to play, and it was just like old times. There was good wine, and everyone was in a good mood and sang and danced. I passed the hat, and there was enough. It was as if the old fiddles hung in the sky again.

"There's one thing that I can't get out of my mind. Nobody is bitter. Let the Unknowns go, and in no time it will be gay Vienna again. The old Ferris wheel is still standing in the Prater; it's rusty now, but it's there. They'll paint it again one day."

7.

Rome Express

WE WENT back to Paris when I was well enough, and now we were going to take the Rome Express.

I am never late for a train. The romantic scenery of a French railroad station attracts me even when I am not going anywhere. The pleasure of travel, for me, starts long before the train departs. I like to walk up and down the *quais*, as the platforms from which trains leave are called, and watch the thousand things that go on—the farewells, the reunions, the embraces and tears; the gymnastics of the porters and the many details of travel; the conductors, some alert, some tired;

the sleeping-car attendants, the cooks in the cramped quarters of the dining cars preparing meals. All this is set to the concert of the pumps of a dozen locomotives and the high yammering of the French train whistle; the sounds echo in the vast hall as in a mountain valley. The air is filled with carbon, and a soft blue light bathes the scene.

Barbara, with Little Bit on her arm, pulled my sleeve and said, "Look, Poppy, here comes one of your characters." Two porters passed, pulling and pushing a cart burdened with the most luxurious luggage—twelve assorted bags of crocodile hide with heavy fittings, each with a leather luggage tag. The owner's worried servant was running alongside, and in back followed the man who belonged to the load. The valet recognized me and gave me a quick smile; he had at one time worked for Lady Mendl.

"You see," said Barbara, "I was right."

The bags were taken by the porters into the sleeping car in which we had our compartments. The owner of the bags was a nervous man; his legs and arms moved as if he were a marionette. In contrast to his small, perpetually agitated limbs, his body was vast, like that of a bug. His head belonged neither to the limbs nor to the body, but looked like the head of a statue. His eyes were large and sad. He took off his hat and wiped the top of his head. I had seen him here and there for years.

He is at Cannes at the height of the season; he swims in an old-fashioned bathing suit at the Eden Rock. He walks in the snow at St. Moritz in plus fours and high shoes with the back straps sticking out, and wearing a pea-soup colored jacket which he himself must have designed; it has pockets like a rucksack and a collar of red fox fur. Whenever I've seen him he's looked as if he were listening to a requiem. His name is Ugolino Patrizzi.

Here at the Gare de Lyon he leaped up the steps, his legs making an intense effort but his body hanging back like a rabbit whose stomach is filled with lead. He squeezed through the narrow corridor, pushed the valet aside, and, as a crab disappears into sand, backed into his compartment. The Rome Express jerked three times and then moved out of the station.

In the dining car, as the result of an invitation tendered to me by his valet, Barbara and I found ourselves seated at Patrizzi's table. He brought along his own food and wine, which the steward served, assisted by the valet. We were the object of unpleasant stares from the people being served the ordinary table d'hôte.

On such occasions Barbara falls into a state of suspended animation. Her face is a mask; the sides of her mouth slope downward; her eyes are cold, and her brain becomes a recording machine. She eats like a bird while she feeds Little Bit, who sits in her lap. To questions she gives the briefest possible replies in a flat voice.

Since European children are taught not to talk at table her behavior was correct. She watched the darkening landscape, gave Signor Patrizzi the usual statistics on Little Bit, and left the table as soon as she could.

I sat with him, and we drank his special brand of Italian coffee, made at the table in a portable machine. He took an immense cigar etui, also of crocodile leather, from a special coat he had changed into, and proffered large Upmanns. I accepted one, and the valet brought forth the kitchen matches with which these cigars are properly lighted. Patrizzi's sad eyes

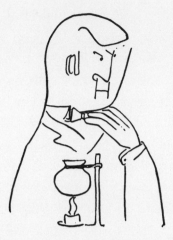

moved from the coffee cup to my face. He leaned back. With the cigar in his mouth, he employed both of his stubby arms to lift one of his short legs over the other. He sighed and, taking the cigar in his right hand and moving the glowing end back and forth under his huge nose, closed his eyes and said that he wished he were dead. Finally he opened his eyes to ask where I was going.

"To Capri," I said.

"Oh," he said sadly, "then we will be traveling together. Not that we will have any fun. As for me, I have to go there."

After a while he added, "I have been in Europe three years now—God, what I have been through! If I had known what it was like, wild horses could not have dragged me." He let out a long wheeze and wiped his forehead. "When I first arrived I could not sleep in Paris, not even after the fourth week. I was an unhappy man every hour. In my club the doorman looked like a figure out of the attic of a museum. First I thought it was merely dust on his cap, but it was dirt; and the gold braid hung like lace on his cuffs and tails. Inside the club the servants had grease stains on their vests, and no coat matched another. One had green sateen breeches, also spotted, and with them wore a faded blue coat. Another had holes cut into his pumps to accommodate his bunions, and the collars and shirts and faces of all were dirty. I wrote to my friends in Brazil. 'Don't come back,' I said, and underlined it. 'You wouldn't be able to live here any more. I'm coming back to Brazil.' But by that time they all were on the way, and it was too late to warn them. Imagine, the telephone in my room did not answer! The manager himself often stood outside in the street, shaking his head because he could not get me a cab; I was compelled to go to Maxim's on foot. All the people one used to know were in hiding—some for stupid political reasons, others because they were so poor they couldn't even use the Metro. They came and went on foot, and there were holes in the soles of their shoes. Their evening trousers were like those of the servants in the club; only the grease spots were lacking, because, alas, they had nothing to eat. I said over and over to myself, This is not Paris. God, let me out! I told myself I would divide my time between Rio and New York. I could not bear to see these unhappy people, and I could not help all of them. Besides, they have their pride and they would be hurt if I offered to buy them shoes or a new hat.

"But I steeled myself and stayed. I had a car shipped over and hired a chauffeur, and also this individual who is serving us. I got him in England. And isn't it remarkable that the land which produces the perfect gentleman also produces the perfect servant? He knows his place always. He's like the butlers you see in American films. My friends arrived and, as Goethe says, 'Shared sorrow is half sorrow.' I stayed, and things got slowly better, and now it's almost livable, as far as Cannes anyway. But now I have to go to Italy. I'm Italian—that is, I'm of Italian descent—and I have an income of a million lire a day in Italy, but I have to go there to spend it. Can you imagine anything so stupid?"

Suddenly he became agitated again and bowed his head. I glanced around and saw an Italian of great beauty, a Botticellian kind of Madonna, coming down the aisle. She wore a blue hat and was severely dressed; she was followed by a distinguished-looking man with a white spade beard. They sat down at one of the tables for four and studied the menu. Patrizzi watched her, his eyes sadder than ever.

After a while he said in a muted voice, "How small the world is! Would you believe that, over thirty years ago, that woman was my love, and that she still is the only one? I knew this trip would be awful.

"Ah, it's terrible to think of it. She is looking intently at the menu but she is not reading it. She is saying to herself, 'So that is Ugolino—I knew him when he had black hair and a small waist and was always gay.'" He continued regarding her in one of the many mirrors of the dining car. "Now she is looking up, and she is saying to herself, 'And here I sit with you, you stupid!' He is, incidentally, a prince. She is still beautiful, rich, and unhappy. I've met her here and there, and always after nodding she looks away, and I look away too, because I am responsible for her marriage to that penurious bastard who has ruined her life. They are going to Capri also; she has a villa there. Everybody has a villa in Capri. I know it's going to be awful. You can imagine now," he said, "with what feelings I approach Capri. I can't stay here any more—it hurts too much to look at her." With these words he rose and hurried from the car.

In the compartments of European sleeping cars there is hardly room to turn around when the beds are made. The door between mine and Barbara's was open. She was sitting up in bed, with Little Bit beside her, eating a can of American spaghetti, which she had heated on an alcohol stove. She was taking to Italy a supply not only of this specialty, but of American dog food for Little Bit.

"Oh, how I love a full-sized train, and a full-sized conductor, and a clean green compartment with its own little bathroom!" she said as she finished.

"Well, this one has cut-glass vases, and a place to hang your watch, and it's done in solid mahogany."

The train went "ta-dang, ta-dang, ta-dang, ta-dang," then changed over to "cluck-cluck, clickety-cluck," and then resumed its "ta-dang, ta-dang, ta-dang, ta-dang, ta-dang." The rhythm was very conducive to thinking, and easy to set words to. I swayed back and forth, standing at the window. I can stand there for hours very happily, especially in the night.

Before retiring, I called into the next compartment, "Barbara, are you still awake?"

"Yes. Has that character of yours finally gone to bed?"

"What do you mean by 'that character of yours'?"

"Oh, international society—counts, dukes, Mrs. Whoozit, General Leonidas Millefuegos—your snob friends."

"I beg your pardon?"

"Well, Poppy, the people you write about and sometimes draw and paint."

"What's wrong with them?"

"Well, you're very fond of them, and you make them out the only people worth while."

"Some of them are my friends. Some of them are very interesting. Some of them are complicated and rare people who entertain me—I don't mean with wine and food, but by their curious nomenclature and the details of their personalities—their dress, ideas, means of locomotion. I love to watch them."

"And some are awful—most are."

"Yes, some are awful, and I have portrayed them as best as I can. I have written some very bitter social satire."

"Well, I'm sorry, Poppy, but I never got that. You make them all charming and too, too utterly divine."

"I'm not a prosecutor. I don't condemn. I put the form, the shape, the being, on canvas and on paper, and I let the reader decide for himself."

"Well, maybe you start out that way, and then, no matter how awful, you fall in love with your characters, and they all turn mushy and nobody is really bad—they're just odd. In fact, sometimes the bad are much more lovable than the good. And now that I come to think of it, almost always. Anyway, it's not social satire."

"Well, maybe it's not social satire but comedy of manners—and in a world in which there are less and less manners, especially among the young, it's a very hard thing to write. As for hating people, I'm sorry, but I find it hard to hate anybody, and impossible to hate anybody for long."

"That's what Mother says. She says you love too many people."

"What else does Mother say?"

"She says that you're very fortunate."

"Why?"

"Because everything that makes you happy can be bought."

111

I listened to the "ta-dang, ta-dang, ta-dang" of the wheels and hoped Barbara would go to sleep.

"Poppy, are you still awake?"

"Yes. What else?"

"Oh, nothing. I was only thinking about what other kinds of people you write about, and I remembered. It's bums and crooks, and they always come out all right too. So you write about the bottom and the top, but never about the between."

"The people in between?"

"Yes. What's wrong with them—the normal people, the people—"

The lighthouse was flashing again.

We passed several minor stations while I busily searched my mind for plain people that might have appeared in any of my works.

The lighthouse said, "Come to think of it, even the animals are strange in your books, like that little dog that belonged to the magician in *Hotel Splendide*."

"Well, a magician wouldn't be satisfied with an ordinary dog."

"What are you thinking about, Poppy?"

"Ordinary people."

"Well, what's wrong with them?"

"Nothing's wrong with them. I love them, and I'm sure I've written about them with understanding—sometime, somewhere."

"Your common people, Poppy, are all headwaiters with Cadillacs, and valets and gardeners." A few seconds passed, and then she added, "Or French."

"I admire the French, because they refuse, the lowest and middlest of them, to be caught by life."

"What do you mean by 'caught'?"

"Oh, to lead lives of quiet desperation."

"Who leads lives of 'quiet desperation'?"

"Well, the phrase comes from a writer by the name of Thoreau."

"French?"

"No, he was American."

"And who was he talking about?"

"The mass of men."

"Did he travel in Europe?"

"No, darling, he was born in Concord, New Hampshire, and stayed around there all his life."

"What was he like?"

"Well, ask Mother when we get back. All I know is he lived in the woods all alone and he wrote a book called *Walden,* which is very popular in Europe, because I read it there when I was a boy."

"What was the name of the book?"

"*Walden.*"

She yawned—at last—and asked, "He wrote a book about Waldi?"

I said, "Yes," and thought, Thank God, she is falling asleep.

"Poppy—how can you justify a man like that Signor Patrizzi, who lives off the fat of the land and never does anything?"

"Look, darling, in the circle in which I have responsibility, in which I function, toward the people who are dependent on me, I am responsible and fair. I am kind to everybody and as generous as I can afford to be. I pay my taxes, I don't commit any crimes. Beyond that I have dragged your dog around the world, I have put up with all kinds of nonsense, I have joined all kinds of societies—and if everybody would behave the way I do, the world would be a paradise."

"That is not enough."

"Darling Barbara, if a man today, especially a married one and a father, goes through life without ending up in the electric chair, in a strait jacket, or a suicide, he has already done enough. In fact, he is a tremendous success, a hero, an accomplished and perfect specimen. And now shut up and go to sleep."

"Ta-dang, ta-dang, ta-dang," went the Rome Express.

8.

The Spaghetti Train

AT THE first stop the next morning I took Little Bit for a run alongside the train.

Barbara was dressed when I came back and rearranging the remaining five cans of American spaghetti in tomato sauce — and sighing over the one she had opened last night. She opened the first can of dog food and proceeded to feed Little Bit. This takes ten minutes, because Little Bit is very dainty and licks food off the extended forefinger of the right hand.

Then we went to the dining car, where Barbara gave Signor Patrizzi the frigid good morning of extreme politeness and shot several lighthouse flashes over the scene before sitting down on the edge of her chair.

The breakfast sitting was almost over, and most people had left the car. Patrizzi, spurning the menu proffered by the steward, looked with a pained expression for his valet.

He went, "Psst," and snapped his fingers. "Tell my man to bring us a can of shad roe. I'm hungry, and it will be about two before we can get a decent lunch." The valet came and set up a large table, and we were moved to that. Barbara watched the landscape for a while. The steward brought orange juice that looked like blood, but she made no remark.

"I'm still very hungry," said Patrizzi. The steward assured him that a chicken had been put on the fire.

"He doesn't know anything about women—the beard—at any rate, nothing about a ravishing creature like her," said Patrizzi.

The valet came and held the dish of chicken close to the face of his master, who grunted with satisfaction. The steward offered another dish and said, "The asparagus now?"

"No," said Patrizzi and shook his head. Looking my way, he announced sadly that he had had a terrible nightmare.

"You don't want the asparagus with the chicken?" asked the steward.

"No, he doesn't," said the valet.

"Would you like some string beans, signore, or tomatoes, or french-fried potatoes?" persisted the steward.

"Will you go away?" Ugolino screamed, and the valet said, "He wants his asparagus after."

Barbara punished Patrizzi with a long look.

"As you like," said the steward, injured, and walked away.

Patrizzi ate the chicken with his fingers and then licked them.

"May I be excused?" Barbara said icily.

"Steward," said Ugolino, "what time do we get to Milano?"

"We're a little late—at eleven-twenty, signore."

The railroad station at Milan is one of the monuments to the memory of Mussolini and is proudly pointed out as such by Italians. It is grandiose and almost of the dimensions of the Pennsylvania Station in New York. There was a delay between trains sufficient for a tour of the city.

I changed some money, not very much, but when I wanted to pocket the Italian notes I got for dollars, it was like trying to put the Sunday edition of the *Chicago Tribune* into my trouser pocket.

I told a taxi driver that we had a few hours and asked him to take us to the places of interest. He stopped briefly at the gas station on the steel beams above which the bodies of Mussolini, his mistress, and several others had been hung for display. He stopped briefly at the cathedral and then raced out of the city to the fairgrounds, where he offered to show us the most interesting sight in Milan. He parked his cab and led us to a scene both modern and of singular importance in this land. In a hangarlike exhibition hall the products of several competing firms were on view. In back of stout ropes protected by watchmen stood monstrously complicated machines, the size of small houses, making sounds such as come from the interior of establishments in amusement parks that are called "Fun Houses," places where people fall downstairs, get lost in mazes, and have air squirted at them.

In this hall the sounds of joy came from the outside of the fun machine; all other sounds, the hissing and the falling, came from the inside. We followed our driver as he pushed his way through the crowd, and I saw that the big machine made spaghetti. From many openings on the underside of the apparatus, a steady, endless rain of spaghetti came down onto a conveyor belt and was thus transported to another machine, operated by attendants in white suits and gloves. The spaghetti, the driver pointed out, was real, and that was very important, because close to the machine which was of Italian make stood one made by a Swiss firm, and nobody looked at this, although it appeared even more modern and elegant. It was running but made no noise, and the frugal Swiss had substituted artificial spaghetti made of nylon—in which no Italian had any interest. The driver also pointed out other machines and told us that those manufactured macaroni, ravioli, and so forth.

It was getting late, and I had to pull the driver away from the exhibition. When we got back the train for Rome was made up.

Patrizzi and his valet were in a rage because the accommodations they had engaged were not in order. Barbara and I had each been alone in a compartment from Paris to Milan. Now we found ourselves in another sleeping car. Barbara was still alone in her compartment, but I was sharing mine with another passenger. He came aboard with an Italian girl, and both of them inspected the compartment carefully. He walked out into the corridor with the girl, and, as the departure of the train was announced, he enacted a farewell scene with her that was ardent even for Italy.

"I think it's disgusting," said Barbara, "the way these Italian men behave!"

He then ran to the compartment, pushed up the window, and threw kisses at her as the train got under way. Finally he took a large handkerchief from his pocket and waved it. He wanted to run to the end of the car, and, trying to get past Barbara, he said in unmistakable New Yorkese, "Excuse me, Miss, I wanna get by."

He was dressed in a polyglot costume of yellow corduroy jacket, gray flannel slacks, neglected gray suede shoes, and a Borsalino hat. He carried a cane and had a raincoat over his arm, and the suitcase he put on the bed was old and worn. Like Patrizzi, he was heavy, a man weighing a little less than Alfred Hitchcock. He had taken possession of the lower berth as a matter of course. No one could expect of him the gymnastics necessary to gain the upper.

After dinner, some hours out of Milan, and after a great deal of attention to getting ready for bed, he turned out the light. He seemed nervous; he kept turning and moving; and the noise of his bed was added to the rattling of the train. Later he got up, raised the window shade, stared briefly out into the night, went back to bed, got up again. I let him know that I was awake, and he excused himself, saying, "In a moment she will come." I became a little worried and asked him who would come.

"My bridge," he said excitedly, adding, "In a little while the train will slow down."

I thought that perhaps he wanted to jump off the bridge. I remembered his passionate farewell at the station, and for the next few seconds I debated whether I should try to stop him, pull the emergency cord, or let him jump.

"Here she comes!" he said. He pushed up the window and leaned out. As the first girder of the bridge slowly took shape in

119

the dim light cast by the train window, he reached out, touched it tenderly, and said, "Hello, old girl." I felt better when at last he pulled his head back into the car. "You know," he said, "I built this bridge during the war."

He leaned out again and watched until the whole train had crossed the bridge. It took a while, as most Italian bridges are still under repair.

As the train resumed speed there was a commotion in the corridor. It involved an American girl and an Italian youth, the conductor and a middle-aged businessman from Chicago. The girl, it developed, had met the young man in Milan while they were staying at the same hotel. They had met again in the dining car and had a drink together. Later, as she was about to retire, she found the young man in the same sleeping compartment with her. She called the conductor, who listened with boredom while the young man explained that he had arranged the sleeping accommodations with the porter of the Milan hotel where he and the girl had stayed, and that it was customary to share train compartments with friends or even strangers of the opposite sex. The conductor seconded the young man and said that it was quite all right and that no one thought anything about it. The man from Chicago, who had also been drinking in the dining car, entered the argument. It was difficult for him to stand upright. Leaning heavily on the conductor, he offered his protection to the young girl.

She was bewildered until he explained that he was a father and a very important man, that he had a whole compartment to himself, and that he would put the young man with ideas into the vacant bed in his room. The young man quickly retired into his compartment.

Barbara opened her door and offered to share her compartment with her compatriot. This suggestion was accepted.

For a while it was quiet, and then the Chicago father reappeared and started to bang on all the doors. He wanted to rescue the girl, and he spoke a long piece on the moral concepts of Europe and especially Italy. Finally, at dawn, the pale conductor persuaded him to retire to his room. The conductor lay down on the folding seat at the end of the corridor and covered himself with his dirty blanket. The normal noises of the train took over.

The next morning Barbara said, "I'm having breakfast here." She was sacrificing a second can of her American spaghetti and sharing it with the older girl.

I came into the dining car late. Patrizzi was finished with his breakfast—that is, with the orange juice, toast, coffee, and egg part of it. The other passengers had left. The crew seated at the end of the car had faces like wax figures in the bright sunlight.

Patrizzi lifted his nose and sniffed. "Spaghetti," he said. "Real spaghetti?"

"Yes," said the steward, "we are eating now. Back there the cooks are from Napoli."

"I'd very much like some of your spaghetti," said Patrizzi. "Enough for me and my friend here."

The steward said the cooks would be delighted.

The spaghetti came, cooked with butter and garlic and with a handful of chopped parsley strewn over it.

"Some people condemn the Italian kitchen," said Patrizzi, "and also the French. They say they can't eat the food on account of the garlic. Now there is no good cooking except with garlic—but in the hands of a bad cook it is poisonous. It must be used with extreme care. The most reckless are the English; once they take to cooking with garlic they use it so freely it's impossible even for an Italian to eat it. For example, Somerset Maugham once served truffles wrapped in bacon, a very good dish. The truffles profit by the flavor of the bacon, the bacon is enhanced by the truffles, and I like it. But at that luncheon I bit into a truffle and inside was a whole clove of garlic. Both the truffle and bacon were ruined. And the garlic, which, incidentally, was also in the chicken we were served and on the toast that came with the cheese and in the salad—it was so predominant that the whole meal was ruined. Now take this spaghetti— simple, ultra-simple—but with a bouquet like the finest wine."

The train had stopped at a small station to wait for a clear track. Outside the window were the cars of a freight train. The boxcar doors were open, and inside were benches on which sat people most of whom had no shoes and all of whose eyes were fixed on the spaghetti and the bottle of wine on our table. I said that it seemed to me that in Italy there was a belief that God had made some people rich and others poor, and that the tragedy was that not only the rich, but the poor also, believed it, and consequently it would never change.

Patrizzi answered, "And don't you think this is as it should be and a very good arrangement? Have you ever seen an Italian peasant envious of those who have fine cars, or horses, or jewels? No, they admire those things, knowing they never can have them for themselves. They adopt a detachment, like people who go to the theater, or to an art gallery to admire priceless paintings. They are glad to know that these things exist, but they also know they never can own them. Just from looking at these things they derive a pleasure that possession never brings, because possession means worry." He snapped his finger. "More," he shouted back to the steward.

"You are going where?" Patrizzi asked with the coffee.

"To Capri," I said.

"Oh yes, you told me. I will see you on the train to Naples," he said and added that he would take a short nap and then look after his baggage himself. "I have asked the Italian ambassador in Paris if he could guarantee there would be no revolution for the next six months, and he promised there would be none. But then, Italians promise you anything. Incidentally, you have picked the worst season to come to Capri." With these final observations, and after handing the steward a royal tip, he left the car.

THERE WAS AN overnight stop in Rome. In the grill of the Hotel Excelsior, which is the equivalent of the Stork Club's Cub Room in New York, Patrizzi sat down with me.

"She is upstairs," he said, "the woman with the blue hat." He had a great capacity for wine, and I returned his hospitality with three quarts of Bollinger. Sunk in a Gargantuan leather couch, at four in the morning, with a few of the better street-walkers of Rome hanging around the bar, and dabbing at his eyes, Patrizzi told the story of the woman with the blue hat.

"How is it," he began, "that one never finds it a second time — the ideal love? I mean the kind of love in which the head, the heart, and the body are all in accord. I had the loveliest parents anyone could ask for. I was the only child, and they gave me everything. Maybe that's what's wrong with me. Until recently I had everything, and yet never was truly happy. But I was talking about my dear parents. They said good morning to each other with smiling faces, and they held each other by the hand for a long while several times a day. They loved each other so beautifully, and as only Italians can love. They sang together— that is, Mamma played the piano, and Papa sang opera in Italian and French, and songs by Schubert—and there was peace and happiness in their hearts and in our home. They never needed to go out. Each night before they went to sleep they sat in their bed and folded their hands and prayed aloud together like children. Once a year we left Brazil and came to Italy. On these trips we always went to Capri, and it was so beautiful then, because *she* was there—the woman in the blue hat.

"I long so for companionship like that, for the great love, but I can't find it because it comes to you only once, and if you are dumb and spoiled as I was, you let it go—you don't recognize it. Let me tell you how I threw away the only love I have ever had from a good girl. She was from one of the finest families; she was that combination of happy and serious girl that you find only in Italy—elegant, kind, beautiful, and proud. My parents found her altogether to their liking and blessed her as their own. I was eighteen, she was sixteen, and all was prepared for marriage. In nothing was there a flaw. We were both religious in the same degree, not too much, not too little; we liked the same things, and we did not have to speak, for we were happy just walking along hand in hand—oh, how lightly we walked! It was the perfect love.

"She came to me one day with six little leather books all carefully bound, and she said, 'Ugolino, since I will be your wife, you must know all about me, about every hour's happening. Here in these books is the story of my life so far, all I have thought and done. Take them and read them.' I took them. I must say I was frankly bored by what was in them — silly things, romantic nonsense, the life of a little girl; church, games, excursions, school, about a little new brother, about a new dress, stuff like that. I don't know why I bothered to read them in order — perhaps because I was so very much in love with her, and when she was not there in person she was there in the book. I had no thoughts but of her. So, in book Number Four, I came to a passage that said: 'Went to a concert with Alfredo.' He was a boy I could never stand. It went on: 'And we sat in the park on a stone bench and he was nice. He did not act at all fresh, he did not try to kiss me or put his arm around me, or even hold my hand. He sat there, and I felt that he was very glad I was with him, and I changed my mind about him and promised that from now on I would be nicer to him and treat him like a brother. On the way home I took his arm.' That was all there was in the book — or in any of them — about Alfredo. But the next page was empty — the only empty page in all the little books. Do you know, on account of that empty page I did not marry the girl. Crazy fool that I am, I was jealous of that empty page. I ruined my chance for happiness and hers. That's why I look away when I see her."

His hands, tightly clasped all during the story, relaxed. The streetwalkers sat along the bar like vultures, waiting.

"Nothing does me any good any more," he said, nodding in the direction of the women, "not even that. But the heart doesn't stop aching." He started worrying about his baggage again. "Tomorrow, early, I'll have to see to the packing," he said and got up.

The elevators in the Excelsior are like quick little taxis; they fly up with zest. "From now on," said Patrizzi, "it will be awful. Here you must take care of everything yourself—lock every bag, lock every door, keep your hands in your pockets."

He, speaking Italian, would be all right, he said. But of all foreigners—and especially Americans—beggars, porters, and other natives who come in contact with them have two opinions: first, that they are all millionaires; second, that all of them are idiots.

Patrizzi offered to take care of my baggage, but I had had our trunk checked through to Capri.

"I hope you find it there," he said mournfully.

I have one small bag which I always carry myself. The article that usually takes up most room in this bag is a book that has been at my elbow for years. It weighs three pounds and its pages have narrow margins; it is set in extremely small type and was printed in the years 1856 to 1877, by F. A. Brockhaus, in Leipzig. I recommend the volume to anyone who can read German. The title is *Wanderjahre in Italien,* and the name of the author is Ferdinand Gregorovius. I took the volume out of the bag the next day aboard the train. It was toward evening, midway between Rome and Naples. The landscape outside was on page 213 of the book. I translated it for Barbara:

> Who is able to paint it, this magnificent terrain, at the hour when all the hills glow in the purple play of evening and when the valleys below them sink into shadows? The night slides upward on the hills; its hand reaches up to the cities that stand on top of them, for one after the other, until all are taken in darkness.
>
> In the windows of the highest and most distant still

glitters the sinking sun in pale red rays—there in Seronne, in Rojate—and now only in Piglio—and now that last flicker is extinguished also.

I ride my horse here on this road—the impression of a great landscape is heightened for the thinking man when he knows how to rhyme it with history, for it is thereby animated.

This road, this strip of land beneath our feet, is the key to the kingdom of Naples, it is the strategic highway of the people of the Middle Ages; of the Goths, the Vandals, the Franks, the Longobards; of Delizar or the Ottones; even of Saracens, Frenchmen, and Spaniards; of uncounted people whose horses drank from the waters of the River Sacco.

The serene landscape now was in complete darkness, the electric train was rapid, and we had eaten aboard simply but well. Patrizzi, sitting opposite me at the dining-car table, had closed his eyes.

In my mind unknown places always have a very definite character, color, and shape, determined by hearsay, instinct, and reading. I imagined Capri a sugar-loaf-shaped mountain that rose out of lukewarm water. It was dark brown. On its rotund plateau was a city made up of luxurious hotels, bars, villas, and casinos. They were crowded at the proper season with the nomads from Palm Beach, Cannes, and St. Moritz. I expected to behold a shining tabernacle of ennui.

The steward tried to make conversation with Patrizzi, saying something about the state of the world. Patrizzi snapped, "I don't worry about the state of the world at all, you know. All I care about is to give pleasure to my friends. Bring us another bottle of wine."

Barbara kicked me under the table.

The steward hastened away, and Patrizzi said, "Did you see it? It's worse than in France. The steward is walking about in canvas sneakers, and one has a hole cut in it for the bunion. It was like that in my club when I first came back. It gives me pain to look at anything like that. There are in this life moments when one does not want to belong to the human race. Well, I am losing my appetite for living all over again."

I closed Gregorovius, which had been open to the chapter on Capri, the train slowed down, and the lights of the first houses of Naples moved across the windows.

A few minutes later we stood on the platform, and the valet handed the baggage out to several youths, one of whom, in charge of the band, was arguing with Patrizzi, who refused to pay what he demanded. In Rome, he said, there were uniformed porters and they had been honest, but here it was sinister. *"Banditti,"* he called them, and the money that he offered was refused. Either two thousand lire to deliver the luggage or nothing, the boy said. He finally got almost what he asked for.

The bargain was closed through the mediation of a friend of Patrizzi who had come to meet him. The *banditti* stacked the exquisite luggage on a small cart and, with several of them hauling it, disappeared into the night.

"I'll never see my luggage again," cried Patrizzi.

THE EXCELSIOR HOTEL in Naples is one of the cleanest I have ever seen. Its rooms are immense, the corridors slippery with polish, and on the tiled floor of the bar is a replica of the Bay of Naples. The alcoholic father from Chicago was sitting there gazing at the floor, glass in hand, studying the territory around Vesuvio and Portici. I took the elevator up to look at the view from the window of my room. The Bay of Naples lay in moonlight. Over on the crater of Vesuvio rested a crescent-shaped cloud; the lights of Sorrento and those of Ischia and Capri were flickering, and in the sea, like stars reflected from overhead, danced the lights of fishing boats. A tenor in an open-air restaurant below sang the worn-out melody of "Santa Lucia." It was like a souvenir postcard, but also, as most such places are, startling rather than beautiful until you become familiar with it. The eye takes inventory, the contours are traced on the mind, you drink it up. Slowly it becomes yours, and the postcard vanishes; the scene's magnificence puts you in bondage.

The next morning we took a hansom cab from the hotel to the pier.

Adjacent to a square as tumultuous as the floor of the New York Stock Exchange, and in which everyone is half naked, is a pier at which lie little boats that go to Ischia, Posilipo, and Amalfi. From here also leaves a small motorship named *Capri*. The fare is about fifty cents. The boat is something like a ferry. The seats are hard, and below deck is a bar.

It was a hot day. Patrizzi and his valet arrived late, and all the seats were taken. He had no baggage problem now.

"I knew it—I told you it was risky—they stole my baggage, all of it. I had to run out and buy shirts and shoes today. And it's no use complaining to the police. Oh, God, if only Mussolini were back! Those things did not happen then." He said that loudly, and the people around him nodded as he mopped his face.

"Listen to what happened here," said one. "A man had a new car, an American of course, and a boy came up to his car and spat in his face. The American stopped the car and got out to run after the boy, and another boy got in and drove off with the new car. He never saw it again. You know, my friend told me that the thieves are so well organized here that half an hour after the American Army landed in Naples, black-market American gasoline was for sale on the streets."

Patrizzi turned to the rest of the passengers and again told them about his luggage. They nodded in sympathy and agreed that something ought to be done.

"Ah," Patrizzi said to me, "the crooks that stole my luggage are perhaps here among us, nodding also, and smiling in sympathy, and looking to see what else they can pick off me."

The ship rolled as soon as it left the breakwater, and when it was abreast of Sorrento half the people were seasick. The roll changed to pitching as the ship came into the narrow channel between the mainland and Capri, although there was hardly any sea.

Jean-Paul Richter compared the shape of Capri to a Sphinx. Gregorovius said of it: "It's like an ancient sarcophagus whose sides are adorned with snaky-haired furies." It has been compared to a boot and to a crocodile. I did not find it to be similar to anything. It is as definite in shape as a table, a crocodile, or the Sphinx, but it has its own shape and compels your attention. You feel it to be as ancient as the sea; you look at it with the curiosity with which you would study the face of an interesting and perhaps disturbed person. It is altogether different from the picture that I had in mind.

The ship passed into calm water. At the entrance to the

harbor Patrizzi was telling a fellow South American in Portuguese about his baggage. Next to me sat a man and a woman, American tourists. The man had almost been seasick several times, and now, as the ship became steady, he talked to the woman next to him, resuming a conversation interrupted by his distress. After a few moments of his conversation I touched Barbara's arm and said, "Listen."

"Well, forty bucks a week was a lot of money and so I was a reporter for a while, and then that columnist wanted an assistant, and I went over there, and after a couple of years the columnist died. Oh, you know, he was a nice guy—nothing nasty—no keyhole stuff or scandal, just a kind of mellow column, faces along the avenue, stuff like that, and I was in—I was making three hundred bucks a week and the struggle was over. It's no use marrying unless you do it right and go the whole way. Well, we moved out to this community, and I said I didn't want to live there if they wouldn't accept us—I didn't want to have anything to do with them, in fact.

"Well, across the street from us was a house where they entertained a lot. Once they had the Earl of Derby or somebody like that—that kind of people, you know. Well, they asked us to the next party, forty people, that's twenty couples, and ever since then we've just been as welcome as that first time. All I can say, it's a lovely place and they're as nice folks as you can find. I'll tell you about a typical week-end. We get together, a gang, you know, about eight highly select couples, and we start out with a cocktail at the Ogdens', and then we go to a Saturday-night dinner dance at the country club—you know what that's like, it's pleasant living. It's really nice—a big buffet and nice people having a fine time. Well, that's where I'd like to be right now—

I'll go along that far. But Clarabelle—she's not satisfied with that. She's got to travel. She's got to follow them over here, and they own a villa—naturally, it's on Capri. And we've been invited to stay as long as we like. Well, I don't like it a bit. In fact, I don't care a damn about all this stuff. Now that man over there had all his luggage stolen yesterday, and Lord! the food."

The engines were signaled to stop, and the columnist got up to look for his wife. She lay on a bench, and the pleasant baby face that she must have worn at other times was old, and the utter misery of seasickness was in her eyes. With a weak smile she thanked a little unshaven padre for recovering a little ruined hat that had blown off her head. The columnist took the hat, and the padre held out a small box bearing a picture of St. Francis of Assisi. The columnist looked at his wife; he saw that she had closed her eyes again, and he put a folded bill in the poor box. Then he said, "Hey, Clarabelle, here's Capri."

The ship was now turning to back up against the pier, and on the pier sat the *banditti* of the night before, with all the luggage of Signor Patrizzi.

9.

The Isle of Capri

HERE IS A simple recipe for understanding the conformation
of the island of Capri: Place on the table in front of you, to the
left, a demitasse cup turned upside down; to its right, place a
full-sized coffee cup, also inverted, and preferably with a
chipped lip, toward you. Put a matchbox between the two cups,
move the three objects close together, and drape a pale green
handkerchief over the lot—and that is roughly Capri. You're
looking at it now as you approach it from the north—from
Naples. The small cup is Mount Tiberius (1096 feet), the large
cup is Mount Solaro (1920 feet), and in the valley between,

atop the matchbox, is the town of Capri. Rest a match end up on the table, leaning against the matchbox, and you have the funicular that takes you down to Marina Grande, the large port; at approximately the same spot on the other side of the island is Marina Piccola, the small port without benefit of funicular. On that side you can drape two limp strands of spaghetti, to simulate the roads that lead from Capri down to the water. Loop one piece generously for the serpentine turns — that's the one traveled by buses. Arrange the other in tight zigzags; it is the Via Krupp, a gift of the late munitions manufacturer. If you can expend two more pieces of spaghetti — a long one from Capri up to Anacapri, on the big cup, and another down to Marina Grande, you will have just about all the roads. A path leads to the top of the small cup, where the ruins of the Villa Jove are located. Like the houses of the great in Pompeii, it is restrained and simple. By comparison, for example, with Versailles, or with Mr. Hearst's San Simeon in California, it is merely a week-end bungalow. The fine pagan mood of this great ruin is marred by a badly sculptured modern Madonna planted in the middle of it, so that you cannot escape the clash of mediocre ecclesiastic art with the purity of the classic. Such clashes offend you again and again in Italy, and this is difficult to explain. For, with all the great models in front of them, and the blood of the best painters and sculptors in their veins, the Italians recently have produced very little in the way of good art.

There is the Grotta Azzura, the Blue Grotto, represented by the chipped place on the big cup; it also is decorated with an abominably executed Madonna that occupies a niche over the entrance. The roof of this tunnel is so low that you enter it sitting on the bottom of a small rowboat; even so, you have to duck while the boatman takes you in by pulling on a chain. At high tide you must lie flat in the bottom. The Blue Grotto is all that you have heard of it. The renditions of it that one finds on cheap souvenir paintings all over Capri come closest to the truth, and particularly accurate is the light effect on the top and the sidewalls. The local artists treat it as if they were showing a cavern with luminous, bluish worms crawling up the walls and across the vaulted ceiling.

On top of the smaller of the two coffee cups, on a rocky promontory that rises above Capri, is a villa with a sweeping view of the Mediterranean on both sides of the island. It is owned by Gaetano Parente, who has the long legs necessary to negotiate several times a day the two-hundred-odd stone steps by which the villa is reached. He is never without a small dog, a breed peculiar to the island and, like its population, of the most varied nomenclature.

"Without inflicting on you the tyranny of dates and too many names," said Gaetano Parente, "I will give you the briefest kind of history of Capri." We were walking down the Via Krupp. That is, he was walking—I ran.

"Almost everyone who has written a book here has taken something from a volume called *Ricerche Storiche sull' Isola di Capri,* by Rosario Mangoni. I recommend it to you, and also one called *The Book of Capri,* by Harold E. Trower, onetime British consul here. One cannot write about Italy without quoting from one book or another, or from inscriptions on ancient metals, stones, wood, canvases, or tapestries, that are in evidence everywhere.

"The story goes something like this: The Emperor Augustus

saw Capri's possibilities, and it was he, not Tiberius, who built it up. Tiberius came later and improved it, making of it for a while a rest place and camp for soldiers of the Roman Empire. His name is more in evidence here today than that of Augustus.

"After Tiberius, Capri for a few hundred years was left in solitude. I'll spare you history here, and we will move up to when it was rediscovered as a pleasure place, by Germans, who at the time headed a spiritual back-to-nature movement. They came here, shouted, '*Wunderbar*,' and walked about naked, carrying their children on both shoulders. They lived on fruits and vegetables, picked wildflowers, and named butterflies that until then had never been properly catalogued.

"After these blond nudists the English arrived—the Oxford boys, the Shelley and Keats group—and they were very impressed by the fine physiques of the native fishermen. Those romantic boys did a lot for Capri, constantly singing its praises. They never tired of adoring this happy, brown people, and, strangely enough, the propaganda brought on a great horde of British spinsters. There was no harbor then, and the ladies were carried ashore in the strong arms of the picturesque natives. Then came other English breeds, noblemen, industrialists, and archaeologists, who bought the best statuary and shipped it to the British Museum.

"Now Capri was really famous. The kings came, and the Russian grand dukes; the Kaiser visited on his yacht. All the world came—the old rich, the *nouveaux riches*, and tycoons like Krupp and Axel Wenner-Gren; also Lenin, and even Trotsky. Today an American woman, Mrs. Harrison Williams, is the Queen of the Isle. Of Italians, we have relatively few that are villa owners.

"Of all the things that have gone on here you find the remnants not only in the earth but also in the faces about you. Giovanni is a fisherman at Marina Grande—his face is out of the senate chambers of Rome in the time of Augustus. Put a toga on the fat chauffeur that drives the Anacapri bus, and you have Nero. Look at the man coming out of the Restaurant Hidigeigei every day after lunch; he wears his beard like Franz Josef of Hapsburg and looks like him. It's all preserved here as in an album, including some of the English, who still adore the native fishermen. The English spinsters are fewer now on account of travel restrictions, but instead we have the Americans, who outdo everyone else in letting their hair down and admiring everything, especially a few women hair-let-downers, who admire the fishermen even more violently than do the English boys."

With that much history we had arrived at a restaurant where, in a neat little kitchen, a simple and very reasonable meal was prepared. The curious regulations of the island forbid the sale of wine here, and in consequence it's the one place where one can't have spaghetti. To serve wine one must serve spaghetti, and this, constituting a proper Italian restaurant, demands a restaurant license. The woman who runs the little inn has never been able to afford the license, and so the place is called a tearoom. This small establishment, named the Pension Weber, is at Marina Piccola and overlooks a beach and rows of little bathhouses. The son of the proprietress waited on table, but he was not too gay, having been called up from the beach to help out.

A sunburned man with the small gold medal of the Madonna

hanging from his neck was telling a woman who sat at his table that he had come to Capri to look around for a villa.

Gaetano Parente said to me, "Here is the most important thing to know about Capri: Never say to anybody that you want to buy a villa. I will tell you all about villas. There are three main real-estate agents here. One is an old duke who is a Communist; another is an old Russian princess who was, some sixty-five years ago, very beautiful—one can see that even now—but one cannot understand a single word she says. Then there is a German baroness, also a beauty of long ago. This last one, being German, is of course methodical and knows what she wants, and she occasionally sells a villa. The others only go through the motions.

"Everybody else, from the priest of the biggest church in Capri to the last fisherman on the Punta Tragara and also the gatekeeper of the ruins of the Villa Jove, is a real-estate agent. Each is a poet, and mostly they sell places that exist only in their imaginations. Of course, most people who ask about villas don't want to buy them anyway, so it's just a Capri pastime.

"Let us assume you really decide to buy something—almost everything is for sale. You find the villa you like, knock on the door, and ask the owner what he wants for it. The owner says, 'I want ten million lire.' Not being an Italian, you say, 'Good,' and you go to the bank and come back with the money. Now he says, 'Ah, my wife—or my cousin, or my father—who owns half this house, will not sell for this price.' 'Good,' you say. 'How much then?' 'Twelve million,' he says. You bring the additional millions. Now he remembers that a grandchild of whom he is the guardian has an interest, and he cannot cheat the little one—he did not think about this before. 'Let's make it fifteen million and not talk any more,' he says.

"So you go and bring the rest of the money, and you think that finally the villa, at fifteen million lire, is yours.

"But there are other things. A relative who is a lawyer appears, and he speaks about a small commission due him. Then he tells you that the garden has to be bought and — another thing overlooked — in the attic lives the grandmother of the owner. She's so good and sweet, and she goes with the villa; you can of course make some other arrangements for her. Also, this lawyer draws you into a corner and whispers to you that you can't possibly want this peasant hut to live in. 'I will show you a real villa,' he mutters and describes a place like the Alhambra. By the time you have it, the usual villa comes to between ten and fifteen million lire, or to about twenty-three thousand dollars.

"Now I will tell you of the servants, but that part is pure joy. The servants are the best part of the villa. Born with shrewdness and skill, as are all Italians, they don't speak Italian at all, but a Neapolitan dialect. Yet they manage to understand English, French, German, Czech, or Swedish; other languages, like Hindustani or Arabic, they understand by merely looking intently at the speaker and reading his mind. They are very clean and they give you every comfort. They live only for you. They want to satisfy every one of your wishes. If one night you come home a little unsteady and gay and ask them for the moon, they will bring it to you, or else they will improvise something that is as good.

"The first party you give at your villa is very important to them. They watch everything closely. They want to see how you pour whisky, how fast the bottles of champagne are opened, what kind of flowers you order for your house, what tips you give to messengers, what orders you issue for food. From all this they determine exactly how much to steal. They do this so nicely that you don't mind it at all. The salaries they get are ridiculous, but of no great importance. What makes them happy is to cheat a little on the spaghetti, to move a bottle of wine from your side of the cellar to theirs.

"I forgot to tell you that among villas here you have the most extraordinary assortment to choose from. This isle has always attracted remarkable people, and so you may find yourself owning a place completely Chinese, including the opium pipes with which the last owner smoked himself to death. Or you may find a small castle with stone bulwarks and cannons. You may become the owner of a house whose builder was devoted to Mayan culture, tiger-hunting, deep-sea fishing, or the collection of ancient timepieces. If your house lacks decoration, take a shovel and dig in your garden. I came up with a jaw of a prehistoric animal and a bas-relief the first day. Now I have decorated one whole wall of my studio with the things I dug up. Some are so very interesting—I cannot show them to everyone."

I was most grateful to Gaetano Parente. Actually I didn't want to buy a villa, but I rented one. Its name was lettered on a piece of tile at the gate, together with a picture of the owner. It was something like La Balalaika. The house was nice, but the name didn't go with either the place or the island, so I changed it to Jovina.

I have a preference for irregularity in houses, and Jovina was just right. It stood hidden by olive trees extending halfway down to the sea and was bordered by little vineyards and an immense terrace that afforded a wonderful view. At the right of it rose the wall of Mount Solaro, beyond the top of which the sun passed at about four o'clock, leaving the terrace in pleasant shade for the rest of the day. The view included the Faraglioni— three rocks that jut out of the water off Punta Tragara—Marina Piccola, and the sea. Best of all, the place was completely lost, yet only a few minutes' shaded walk from the town of Capri. The rent was a hundred dollars a month, plus the food for four cats.

"How about the cats?" I said to the landlady on taking over.

"The cats go with the villa," she said, "and also Antonia."

Antonia was seventeen; she arrived at seven in the morning, left at nine in the evening, and got a salary of three dollars a month. Her first job was to pump water from the cistern below the villa up into a tank on the roof. This she did for three-quarters of an hour every morning, singing in Neapolitan.

Lithe and quick as the salamanders in the garden, she leaped to a boulder and up on the roof several times during the pumping to check the amount of water. Next she lit the charcoal oven and with a small fan got the fire going. She was beyond herself when her salary was trebled and her hours cut in half. My guests were her guests—whatever concerned us became her worry or joy.

"Poppy," said Barbara, "that poor girl has to get up on the roof several times a day to look at the water. Isn't there something we could do?"

So I climbed up on the roof with an empty bottle and a long piece of string. I tied one end of the string around the bottle, which I floated in the water tank. Then I lowered the other end

of the string, with a horseshoe tied to it, down the side of the
house. Next I marked a scale on the wall, so that Antonia could
read the water level in the tank without jumping up on the roof.
This invention raised her esteem to delirium, and all the water
girls of the neighborhood were called. They came running
barefoot and, shy as deer, appeared from the shadows of the
olive trees. "My signore did it," said Antonia, pointing with
pride at me and at the indicator of our water tank.

Whenever she saw us anywhere in Capri she would run to us
and walk by our side a while; or if she was in a hurry she'd wave.
She was always neat, and, in addition, she had humor. I was
invited to a party and I didn't want to leave Barbara alone in the
house. I said to Antonia, "Will you sleep here tonight?" and she
said, "Yes, signore, but I think I better ask my mama." So I said,

"Tell her that Barbara is afraid at night all alone, and I am going out tonight, and that's why I want you to stay with her."

She smiled and said sweetly, "Oh, for that I don't have to ask my mama."

A family renting a villa like Jovina, shopping in the markets and doing its own cooking, can live well in Capri on not much more than a hundred and fifty dollars a month. I know a couple of Swedes with healthy appetites who lived in comfort in Anacapri for seventy-five dollars a month. Reporting on the low prices of bargain paradises is a hazardous business. One should always append: It was so when I was there—I don't know what it is now.

When I took over the Villa Jovina the landlady presented me with a twenty-page inventory which carefully listed every broken cup and saucer, a broom that looked like an abused polo mallet, and even a dishrag. A lawyer came on her behalf. Everything was checked over when we moved in, and again when we departed. And in the meantime the landlady herself lived in a grotto under the house. She emerged early every morning and went down to the gate, where, with a wild yell and a rending sound such as is heard when a doctor rips adhesive tape from a wrenched shoulder, she tore off the sign "Villa Jovina." Right after breakfast—and without a word from me— Antonia always brought me a new piece of cardboard, India ink, and a brush, and, standing by, watched me paint the day's new sign. She held it in the sun to dry and then ran down the stairs, singing all the while, and attached it to the tile with new strips of adhesive tape. I painted the sign sixty times in all, staying there that many days. The four cats were fat when we left in spite of the eleven members of Antonia's family, who got half the meat and fish bought for the cats. There was also a little graft with the iceman. Otherwise Antonia was scrupulously honest.

Capri is very good for children — Barbara was in the water most of the day. It was also good for Little Bit, whose character underwent a great change. In back of the Villa Jovina was a second grotto, deep and resonant, and one day while Barbara explored the place with Antonia, the little dog went into this grotto and barked. The effect was tremendous: the bark was amplified to the roar of a great Dane. Little Bit lost no time adjusting her personality. She went for the biggest dogs on the island, and several times a day she went to the grotto to hear herself. She tried out growls and howls and became hoarse with barking.

The piazza, the center of the social life of Capri, is a stage on which movement, sound, and lighting seem to be manipulated by a director of untiring invention. The audience sits on the set, the set is on many levels. There is a complicated and interesting white church, reminiscent of the cathedral in Quito, Ecuador. It is the only church I have seen in the basement of which is a bar and café. There are vaulted exits and entrances to the piazza, and an open break at one side offers the cyclorama of the Bay of Naples. There, forming one side of that opening, stands a square clock tower with a set of bells that bongs every few minutes with such insistence that the glasses on the tables begin to dance and tinkle and people cover their ears. At the base of the tower is a police station the size of a telephone booth, and a newsstand where you can buy American magazines and comic books, the latter translated into Italian. Superman here is called *La Battaglia di Orson.*

The center of the piazza is crammed with the varicolored sidewalk tables of four competing restaurants and the tight-fitting, shapeless wicker chairs that belong to them. The greatest activity in the piazza is toward seven.

There are many people in Capri who, in less romantic and non-Italian regions, would find themselves in institutions, not permitted to walk about without men in white coats close by. There are among this group several outstanding and amusing ones. One little man, a retired civil servant from Naples, has a suit with electric bulbs for buttons, connected to a battery in his coat pocket. On high holidays he stands in the center of the piazza, where, from time to time and with great seriousness, he lights himself up. There is a poet who lives at Marina Piccola and writes an ode on the soles of his shoes every morning. Then, walking up to the piazza, he eradicates the daily inspiration in the sand of the road.

During one busy hour a native not given to bragging pointed out to me forty-six homosexuals sitting in the piazza. The crowd totaled perhaps a thousand people, and though this percentage seems high, I think it is equaled if not surpassed in other fashionable places over the world. The majority of them are respectable people, and unless you are especially allergic, they provide you with the stock comedy drama they perform everywhere. Their female counterparts are here in about the same number.

Toward nine various members of the sleeping-pill set and the narcotics squad march in. They are of mixed nationality and include several Americans. They are starry-eyed and dressed as for an elegant masquerade, the men in black or wine-colored

velvet slacks, golden sandals, rings the size of matchboxes, and lavalieres hanging on bronzed chests; the women exquisitely gowned.

I heard much talk of their orgies and attended several of them. Whatever happened there that was awful must have taken place inside their heads, for I never saw any of them behave badly. One of them had the face of a saint in perpetual ecstasy; many of them appeared to float past me and disappear. They remained alert all through the night and seemed to enjoy especially the early morning hours. Since they were all extremely young, there was as yet no evidence of punishment. Next day they were as radiant in the sea as on the ballroom floor.

The natives who labor pass through the piazza constantly. Mostly they are like a troupe of acrobats accompanying their equipment into a circus ring. Silently, on bare feet or straw-soled canvas shoes, they move along with dignity and grace. Two pull a small wagon while two walk behind with ropes with which to hold back the wagon on the sharp declines of the narrow streets. They are as alert as the addicts, and most of them are as gay. They slow down in the piazza, crying politely, "*Permesso*," asking people to let them pass, and as they pass they inspect the crowd with curiosity. Children and women in tattered clothes, carrying great loads on their heads, and men bearing produce and baggage, stones, sand, and timber in astonishing weights, cross through the piazza, for no automobile or horse and wagon can go beyond this spot. They sometimes stop to rest there, without removing their burdens. They stand and gaze at the crowds, astonished at first, like people looking at strange animals in the zoo. I have studied their faces, and in none of them have I observed envy or resentment; if anything, besides the expression of awe, there is a look of pity.

Add to these groups and individuals a dozen priests, a few fishermen, six Frenchmen at a table for two, a group from Hollywood, and some people from the ringside of El Morocco; include in the late hours a few rich American women with their hangers-on, a handful of international panderers, and here and there an honest-to-God tourist and his wife, and the picture of the piazza is complete. At the height of the season, when every hotel room is taken, old cars no longer in running order are dragged here, and weekend visitors from Naples, unable to afford the hotels, pay to sleep in them. Others sleep in caves or leaning against buildings.

During the war the piazza was deserted. "There," a man told me, pointing to the terrace beyond the bell tower that overlooks the bay, "the people of Capri lay. They lay flat, watching Vesuvio, whose glow guided the Allied fliers like a lighthouse beacon. Once a Capriote lit a pipe, and the German S.S. man on duty hissed, 'Put out that light! Stop that smoking!' 'You tell him over there to stop smoking,' said a voice in the dark, and,

looking over at Vesuvio, all of them laughed. Soon after that a lot of shooting was heard—the beach of Salerno is right over there, and there were American vessels in the bay.

"On a bluff near Marina Grande a battery of guns was mounted, commanded by a fiery captain of artillery. The sage Italian governor of the island heard that the captain wanted to open fire on the Americans, and he ran down as fast as he could and shouted as he arrived, 'Don't shoot! Don't shoot!' 'Why not?' asked the captain. 'Because they will shoot back!' replied the governor. The captain listened to reason.

"Most of the Germans departed. But Capri was a rest camp, and a few German heroes remained. So the people got them together and said to them, 'Why don't you go? You know the Americans will be here any day now. It's all over for you.' So the Germans, who were only twelve, said, 'All right, we go.' The people said that was fine. Then one of the Germans who was organizing the departure came and said they needed a little of this and that and some oil and so forth. The people gave it to them and they went away, so after that the people here said, 'We better get the Americans.'

"The fishermen collected all the clean bed sheets they could find and rowed over to the American ships—the water was filled with them—and waved the white sheets at them, saying, 'Come on, come and visit beautiful Capri. The Germans are all gone.' But the Americans said, 'Beat it, you bastards, we're busy. Get away, you wops, or we'll open fire on you.' So the Capriotes came back and said, 'We better bring the padre with us.' Next day they went out with the white sheets again, only this time they brought the priest, who stretched out his arms and said, 'Peace—all is peace—come to beautiful Capri. The Germans are gone. Come to Capri. Don't be afraid.' Well, soon after that they came, first with machine guns in hand, looking to the left and right and behind themselves, but then they saw that there was peace on our island and they took over—and how! Three loudspeakers in the little piazza, each one louder than the other, and jeeps running up the stairs."

BARBARA AND Antonia were always together, sitting mostly outside their bathhouse. I received long lectures on the lives, the joys, and the troubles of the mass of ordinary people, who, like the French, were poor but also refused to live in quiet desperation.

Under the platform on which stand the small green bathhouses at Marina Piccola are a few white-painted boats which are called *sandolinis*. This boat has the shape of a sardine as it is seen from above, and one balances on it as if one were riding a bicycle over a tight-rope with the hands off the bars. The *sandolini* is nine feet in length; midships is a square recess like a well, or cockpit, and in this sits the rider, propelling himself with a double-ended paddle. Once you know how to use the *sandolini* you can move along at a good speed.

I hired one of these every day and rowed to a rock from which I swam. In a week I became proficient enough to ride as the natives do—that is, sitting up on a small deck with the feet in the well. After two weeks of this, on a day the sea seemed calm, I started at Marina Piccola and, paddling past my rock and on westward beyond the Grotta Verde, I steered for the lighthouse at Punta Carena. In another two hours of steady and not tiring paddling I went by the Blue Grotto and came to the Baths of

Tiberius, where I swam and ate. I went on after an hour's rest and paddled to Marina Grande, and then set out to finish circumnavigating the island by skirting the massive cliff (the small coffee cup) on the top of which is the castle of Tiberius. A boat passed me, and the people waved. Going around the east end of the island, I came into the strait between Sorrento and Capri, and the color of the water changed from green to slate; and in the channel, suddenly, were whitecaps. I kept close to the rocks and paddled. The sea lifted me up about ten feet, and after every rise, in a sickening corkscrew motion, the *sandolini* sank down—or, rather, was sucked down and against the rocky bottom. It was too late to turn around, and in any case it would have been too difficult to paddle back, against the wind, to Marina Grande. I will always remember the stern of the boat from which the people had waved as it disappeared behind the mountain. I thought they were waving greetings, but found out later that they were trying to warn me and waving for me to turn back.

Along this coast are many grottoes, and from them come noises made by the action of the sea. Some sound as if a herd of thirsty beasts were drinking, while others roar; some, as a wave rises, make a hissing sound and shoot out a jet of compressed air mixed with water. There are grottoes that moan awfully—and sigh. I came to one that gave the illusion of the doors of a vast bank vault being shut. Every fearful noise of watery catastrophe was along this passage. I managed by rowing fast to keep the *sandolini* atop some waves like a surfboat. Looking up, I saw the rock from which Tiberius is said to have thrown people, and the height of the rock at this time only accentuated the depth of the water. It is easy to be brave when people are around. For a moment I had a flash of hope. Going around a rock and passing a clucking cave, I thought I'd come to some land, but I had miscalculated the distance. Next, rowing past the Grotta Bianca, I expected to see the Faraglioni and a small settlement of fishermen's houses. But there was not a ship or a house in sight, and there was no place I could get ashore without being dashed against the rocks.

At one spot there is a very small beach, but this was foaming in the tide, and the rocks periodically exposed had ridges like razorblades. I thought I'd never see my child again. I don't think I have invoked the help of God for myself since the days of childhood. It seemed to me on that stretch of dark travel, with no apparent exit from danger, that the bill was being presented to me and the time had come to pay. I once did the scenery for a play called *Noah* by André Obey. Pierre Fresnay played the title role, and toward the last curtain he raised his hands and, looking heavenward, said, "Thank you, dear Lord." I thought of that scene as I kept paddling methodically, and suddenly, with these same words and my paddle held up in both hands, I greeted the sight of Punta Tragara. By that time I was sitting in several inches of water.

The sea rose and fell as I approached the small landing. The fishermen had taken out all their boats, and now two of them came down and, after a great deal of waiting for the right wave to lift the craft close enough to them, they got me and the *sandolini* up on the rock. Before the next wave came they had hoisted me out of the boat. I was very thirsty, and presently I was on the way to the wonderful Restaurant da Luigi.

This place is characteristic of the isle, and here one can see why Capri has not suffered the fate of the Riviera. The Restaurant da Luigi is built on a platform supported by high, slim chestnut trees. Its roof is of straw mats; the chairs as well as the floor seem to be made of old orange crates. It all sways and creaks as you walk; it creaks as you sit down; and every time you move it moves with you. The food is fine and the diner is served with a special concern as if he were the guest of the family.

With all its fame, Capri never has been "developed." With the exception of Gracie Fields' Canzone del Mare, there is no casino in Capri. Nowhere has anybody done so much as build a pier for guests to go swimming, or even a stairway or a ladder down into the water. The tiny beaches are covered with egg-sized pebbles that hurt your feet, and all except the native fishermen stumble along the shore and into the water with both arms extended to balance themselves.

Besides, the submerged rocks are covered with sea urchins, a glasslike jet-black kind, wearing a bouquet of spines, long, black, and sharp, and arranged like those of an angered porcupine. When stepped on, these break off under the skin, and the exceeding painful removal of these splinters is an operation as frequent and casual as having cinders removed from eyes in New York drugstores. These urchins are most plentiful at the Baths of Tiberius and the Punta Tragara. The bathing cabins are little houses with a bench inside, made by the fishermen, and they are clean. Unless you swim from a boat, the best way to get into the water without pain is to buy tight-fitting rubber shoes—they are especially made for this kind of seashore, and are sold in several stores in Capri.

From time to time I hired a two-hundred-pound coachman

named Luigi Balsamo. The day we got off the boat in Capri, Luigi was there with the other coachmen, but he, unlike his colleagues, did not shout for patronage among the debarking passengers. It was raining, and Luigi let his horse eat in peace. In fact, he held an umbrella over it. I felt the tug on my sleeve again, and Barbara pointed out the benevolent coachman.

The horses here are reasonably well treated; the natives have learned that tourists don't like them to use the whip. Also, the horses have no bits, but, instead, a light, loose metal brace, sometimes cushioned with lamb's wool. The brace is placed over the horse's nose, the reins are attached to two bars that extend left and right. Wagon and gear are kept shined and polished, and the horses are washed and rubbed every day. Into the harnesses on top of their heads are stuck flags, feathers, or brightly colored artificial flowers.

The house of Luigi stands at the end of a narrow street in Anacapri. At the close of a day his horse is put into the clean and warm stable on the ground floor of the house and covered with a blanket and fed its hay. Upstairs the family sits down to spaghetti Milanese — eight pounds of it, every night. With it they drink a good local wine.

For a week I went up to Anacapri every day to paint, and came down toward evening. Sitting in front of the Villa Jovina, the terrace reflecting the heat of the sun upward into the cool evening, I watched the sunsets — the colors were of corals, rubies, and fire, and the sea turned to molten silver.

"Poppy," Barbara said one evening, "I met the nicest man today. We've seen him several times. I don't think you'd like him very much. I mean, he's sort of plain."

"What makes you think I wouldn't like him?"

"Oh, you know—he's an ordinary Italian. And besides, he's tattooed."

"I have many friends who are tattooed."

"Well, anyway, maybe you would like him. He has lots of money. He's been to America and has many friends there, and he says it's a great country. He invited Antonia and me to lunch

156

at his table down at Da Vincenzo's restaurant, and he showed me how to eat spaghetti the Italian way. It's not done at all the way we do it in America, where people take a spoon and turn the fork against it—that's for tourists. The real Italian way, you use only the fork and turn it, and pick up enough to eat. This man has a friend with him, also very nice, and he asked me where Mother was, and I told him she stayed in New York, because she's studying, so he asked where, and I told him at Columbia, and he knows all about New York. 'It's a great place,' he said, and also that he wanted to get back there. He's having trouble getting a visa or something. I said I would talk to you, because you know all about these things and have a lot of friends that might help him.

"They make the best spaghetti at Vincenzo's, with mussels and a little garlic, and then they put parsley on it. It's delicious—you must try it sometime. He said he'd be very glad to talk to you. He knows Italy well. He has a friend with a boat, and they would be very happy to take us along to Ischia. Please come and meet him."

I said that after I was finished with my Anacapri pictures I would be very happy to.

The next day Barbara reported that her newfound friend had ordered another wonderful dish for her, called *quadrettini*—which means "little pictures"—made of spinach with small squares of pasta and small pieces of prosciutto.

"He said it would be all right for Ischia next Monday, if you're finished with your pictures by then. He'd like to see the pictures too. He knows your name, he said. He's read some of your books."

It is always a great pleasure for me to hear that what Barbara calls "plain people," especially tattooed ones, read my books. "What's his name?" I asked.

"Charlie."

"That's odd for an Italian."

"Well, I told you, he's been to America. He has an American bathing suit, and an American wristwatch, and he says things like 'Whassamatta with you kids.' You must meet him."

When the pictures were done I took the girls to Vincenzo's so they could present me to their friend and invite him to lunch. But he had had to leave suddenly. He had gone to Naples.

"Oh, Charlie, he's a great guy," said Vincenzo, who had also spent some time in America, running a lunchroom in Passaic, New Jersey. "He would have shown you all around Ischia — for that matter, all around Sicily too. You'da seen things the ordinary tourist never gets to see."

With regret I asked about boats to Ischia.

10.

Cinderella Island

THE HEAD porter of the Quisisana, which is the Waldorf-Astoria of Capri, threw up both arms, and, closing his eyes, said, "If you want to see it, take a yacht and go there and float around it. But Ischia—I warn you—the natives there are indifferent, if not rude, to visitors, and there is not one good hotel on the island. Somewhere there are two sisters named Pirozzi or something, who cook in their home, but first of all you must know them, and next you must inform them ahead of time when you will come and how many you will be."

I still asked for the best way to get to Ischia, and he picked up a guidebook by Dottore Cesare Tropes. Its title was *Naples Environs,* and in it were listed:

Cumae	Capri
Herculaneum	Amalfi
Pompeii	Paestum
Sorrento	Capua

"You see, signore, as far as travel is concerned, Ischia does not exist. It is like Africa—if you insist on going there, you are on your own." With that he went to tie tags on the baggage of a group from Hollywood going back to the security of the Hotel Excelsior in Rome.

I sought out the agent of the American Express Company. "No," he said, "we have no itinerary for Ischia. It's not included in our program, but a boat goes there from Naples." The man from Cook's merely shook his head.

On our way home we stopped at a restaurant near the piazza, the Gatto Bianco. At a small table on our left sat a couple, formerly Italians, who lived in America and had come to Capri for a vacation. This was their first day here. They were speaking English, and each held a menu.

Husband: "You take the spaghetti?"

Wife: "You take the spaghetti. I—no. If I eat the spaghetti, soon I cannot get into that new bathing suit, and half my charm is gone."

She studied the menu for a while, then ordered the spaghetti anyway. The spaghetti eventually came, and she took off her sunglasses and said, "I just want to have a look at these beautiful spaghetti before I eat them." She put the sunglasses on again and ate the full oval platter of spaghetti—it must have been about two pounds.

I had a *langouste,* which is the European name for crayfish. It looked good but it had a very strong iodine taste, stronger than that of shrimp. The proprietor and the chef asked me how I liked it, and I answered that I preferred lobster to crayfish, that I thought Maine lobster was the best in the world, and that the *langouste* in Italy, on account of the warmth of the water, was not as good as the kind one gets in France. At the table to the right of us sat an Italian, a fat little Neapolitan, without neck, with hairy black hands and bags under eyes that seemed mascaraed. He looked down at the *langouste* he was eating and cleared his throat—he was obviously displeased with my remarks about the quality of Italian crustaceans.

A fisherman named Carmine came in, and I asked him how long it would take him to sail us to Ischia. About four hours, was the answer. The proprietor of the Gatto Bianco exclaimed, "Oh, you're not thinking of going to Ischia—not for any length of time."

I said that I would like to spend a week or two there.

At this the Neapolitan could contain himself no longer. He dropped his fork and the last claw of the *langouste.* "For heaven's sake," he said, "don't go! You would die there! Take my advice and stay away." He wiped his fingers and lips, put the napkin down, and turned his immense head toward me.

"Listen," he went on, "I have lived in America for years—I go there every winter. My sister has an apartment on Park Avenue—at an insane price. Imagine, last year she paid one hundred and twenty-five dollars just to have one chandelier hung!" He stopped to look at the ceiling and then at his audience. There were the proprietor and the chef; an elderly English gentleman with a young friend, seated near the kitchen; then a group of six—an Italian family; and the couple on my right. The Neapolitan addressed his words to all of them rather than to me.

"Oh, I know it so well, that great country, and there are many things that are wonderful about it. But Americans don't know how to live. Take restaurants. Americans always demand a certain degree of discomfort; a hole without air, badly lit, small, and hard to get into—that is the most important part of a successful place in New York. Not food, not wine—just make it hard to get into, so that to obtain a table at all is a mark of distinction. A kind of detective stands at the door, and when he nods his head you are in. The hole is then known as a 'swell place.'" He imitated the New York pronunciation of "swell place."

Everybody had stopped eating to listen to him, and he continued, "The Americans like to be served by an arrogant waiter—they think that too much service is undemocratic. The restaurant-keeper believes the same—he is never in his kitchen, but busy being democratic, shaking hands, calling people by their first names, kissing the women and slapping the backs of the men. The food we won't discuss." He turned to me. "What you said about American lobster is right, sure. But then—try to spoil lobster. It's like prunes. Who can spoil prunes?"

Barbara gave him her deadliest look.

He turned back to his audience and said with mock praise, "Here in Italy we have made every effort to please the traveling public. Great care has been given to establish 'swell places' all over the country, complete with bad waiters and with swing music blowing on the food. The American tourist will find himself at home from Milano to Taormina, but never in Ischia, for on that island is still comfort, the real old-fashioned comfort. It's a private place with modest charges and excellent hotels and restaurants; it's the Italy of Italians. There are a few English who live there and like it, but they are too few to spoil it"—I lifted my hand, but he kept on—"I don't say that all Americans are like that. But of those who come to Italy, only a handful has the courage to visit Ischia, and maybe one of them has a taste for that kind of place. Maybe you have—I wouldn't know."

The Italian-American on our left had by now turned purple. He was tall and blond, and he rose and delivered a long, impassioned address on America. He had a slight speech defect and could not pronounce *st*, so he ended by saying, "Bathads like you ought to go back where they came from."

"But I'm Italian," said the other.

"Go back to Napoli," screamed the tall one, who was from Tuscany.

The next morning Carmine got his small boat ready, and we sailed for Ischia.

THE ISLAND of Ischia has always played a Cinderella role. When the Emperor Augustus saw Capri, he traded Ischia to the Neapolitans for it, though Ischia is five times as large. Since then Capri has become famous, while Ischia still belongs to the natives. It has no tourist trade and, despite the words of the Neapolitan, there are no good hotels. It is, as the chief porter said, in parts as savage as Africa, and it is private. The people, if not unfriendly, appear indifferent to the visitor; there is no great comfort in sleeping or eating, unless you are invited to the houses of friends who live there. It is a place of great interest and is scenically as varied and interesting as Capri. If you suffer from arthritis you will probably find it the most wonderful place on earth—the hope against hope.

Ischia, the largest island in the Gulf of Naples, is volcanic, and on it are many natural hot springs. The Italian naturalist Tenore determined that these volcanic wells protected the plant life of the island during the glacial period when the rest of Europe's vegetation was destroyed. Today this vegetation is so varied that Ischia seems like a cramped encyclopedia of all the world's flora. Plants of the tropics thrive here, plants that are usually found only in the West Indies, Arabia, Central Africa, and India.

The island is dominated by the bulk of Monte Epomeo, which, along with other local mountains, is the result of ancient volcanic upheavals. The immense ash and lava deposits of Epomeo make plant growth as lush as it is on Vesuvio. In 1850 a forest of pines was planted on the largest of the tufaceous masses, the Lava dell' Arso, which ran down Monte Epomeo into the sea. The forest still stands today.

If the coloration of the rock along the coast of Capri is astonishing and bright, here it is of more subtle, softer shades; yet the landscape changes from the tame and idyllic to sudden savagery. While you are afraid to walk fast in Capri for fear of coming to the ends of it, here you can stretch your legs. While in Capri every road, every house and garden, every face becomes known to you in a few days, here is space and surprise, and the people lose themselves in foliage and on sandy beaches. The

existence of the people of Ischia is simple; here is still the patriarchal pattern of life. After a while one finds out that the natives are shy rather than indifferent.

The visitor may take part in the sorrows and joys of the people, but he will never disturb them by his presence or cause them to change their ways. For example, there are no feasts, no native dances or local celebrations, arranged for the benefit of the tourist, as in Capri. The men, with the exception of a few shopkeepers and government officials, are fishermen or peasants. The women repair nets or they are busy making straw baskets for wine bottles or for hanging cheese. The straw comes from Monte Epomeo. Almost all the girls of Lacco Ameno are called Restituta, that being the name of the saint of the whole north coast. This remarkable saint, according to legend, arrived from Africa on a floating millstone. The fishermen of Lacco Ameno waded out and took her ashore, and every year, starting on May fifteenth, the event is celebrated for three days with a regatta of fishermen's barks.

The women of the interior of the island, most of whom stay on Ischia all their lives, are nymphlike creatures of great beauty. They are devoted to flowers, a characteristic relatively rare in the South of Italy; they have lovely voices, which is even more unusual. They also have large eyes, even larger than those of their sisters on the mainland.

The young men have less to recommend them, and in the interior they are said to be hostile toward outsiders. A German historian I met on the island, Eckehardt von Schacht, said that their attitude is explained by their history; the islander's experiences with visitors have made him suspicious.

Since the fall of Rome, Ischia has been attacked, occupied, and pillaged almost without interruption. The Saracens began it in 813, followed by the Pisans in 1135, after which pirates took over; next came the Germans under Henry VI and Frederick II, followed by the Angevins. All these conquerors left their imprint on the native population, so that you see today a mixture of Nordic, Arabian, and Spanish strains. Under the Spanish occupation of Alfonso I, all the male population of the island was abruptly sent away, and men of Catalonia were brought in, and the women and maidens were forced to marry them. The frequent Spanish family name Pattalano is evidently derived from Catalano. In 1545 the Corsican pirate Barbarossa kidnaped four thousand additional Ischian men and sold them into slavery. Unlike the Spaniards, he did not replace them with

Corsicans. There was also much infiltration from Arabia and Morocco during that time.

In addition to invasions, the islanders suffered the terrors of earthquake and of the volcano which was in constant eruption, taking thousands of lives.

Under the pressure of these conditions many of the peasants took to the sea, and there developed in Ischia a type of tough fisherman who still sails small boats to the far fishing grounds of Sardinia, and carries cargoes of wine to France, Spain, and the North of Italy.

In 1580 an ancient medico, philosopher, and scientist named Iasolini published a book in which the mineral wells of Ischia were endorsed. The text of this prospectus is here translated word for word:

If your eyebrow falls off and you lose the hair on your eyelids as well, go and try the baths of Piaggia Romana.

Are you unhappy about your complexion? You will find the cure in the waters di Santa Maria del Popolo.

Are you deaf? Then go to the Bagno d'Ulmitello.

Blind? Then immediately go to the Bagno delle Caionche. Have you headaches, liver or kidney trouble? Take yourself to the Bagno di Fontana.

If you know anyone who is getting bald, anyone who suffers from elephantiasis, or another whose wife yearns for a child, take the three of them immediately to the Bagno di Vitara; they will bless you.

How much the followers of Iasolini benefited is not known. There are, however, in the National Museum of Naples, a number of votive tablets dating from the Greek period and bearing words of thanks for miraculous cures.

The most frequented baths are on the north side of the island and are fed by a spring named Gurgitello, from which source flow every day seven hundred thousand liters of hot water.

In the neighborhood of Casamicciola is the most famous spring on the island, the Terme Restituta. This well is of the highest radioactivity known, having been measured at 376 units Maché. The person who came to Ischia and discovered this fact, unknown until the twenties, was Madame Curie. The next most radioactive spring in the world is at Bad Gastein in Austria, and measures only 149 units Maché.

The baths on the north coast of Ischia are formal. Some of them have classical façades and remind one of European spas; on the south coast of the island there are just as many hot springs, but all are primitive. On walks along the beach from Sant'Angelo toward the east, one will occasionally hear an anguished moan coming from the interior of the earth. Farther on, the beach emits steam as if the skin of the earth were thin as paper. A hand extended over this surface is pulled back immediately; a kettle of fish can be cooked in this sand in a few minutes. But, close to the sea, it is cool enough for the natives to take steam baths in pools scooped in the beach.

Walking on, one comes to a narrow ravine which widens into a cave with perpendicular walls; it is called the Valley of the Violet Rays, or the Obscure Cave. As in the Blue Grotto on Capri all is blue and silver, so here every object is said to appear in violet light. Upon visiting it I noticed no such phenomenon — the light was plain daylight.

In a ravine rather than a cavern lies the oldest bathing establishment on the island. It is prehistoric in point of age, as well as in manner of operation. It is open to speculation with what instruments and by whom the bathing cabins were hewn into the rock. Your privacy is assured by a girl named Restituta, who hangs up a large cloth with the texture of a soggy dishtowel. Behind this you undress and put your clothes on a stone block; then you step into the bathtub, which, like the cave, is cut out of lava rock. In a loud voice you announce if you want any change in the temperature of the water. According to your directions, Restituta directs hot or cold water toward your grotto by the most primitive means — a system of channels hewn into stone.

Barbara and I bathed in two adjoining caves. As the benevolent ooze came flowing in, it produced in me the curious sensation of being very old — a thousand years. The charge was ten cents apiece, and a tip was proudly refused.

To the southwest, in back of Lacco Ameno, where the street leads over a pass across weathered lava, the landscape takes on a character equaled only in Africa; the illusion is supported by the architecture of the houses, which stand apart. The people are very friendly and hospitable. Near Forio, an engaging and prosperous town of six thousand, whose houses are also of African design, begins the zone in which Ischia wine grapes are grown; the vineyards reach south all the way to Panza, a distance of about two miles. The grapes ripen in glowing heat, the beaches are wide, covered with volcanic sand, and the land is watered with warm mineral springs. Here tomatoes ripen in April, to be exported to Naples and Rome. The specialty of the small village of Panza is a wine called *Sorriso di Panza,* which translates into "laugh of the stomach." It is sweet, and not everybody's drink.

Forio is the end station of the boat from Naples and is at the extreme western end of Ischia. In this remote community lives the widow of Mussolini with her two youngest children. I have read articles about both Countess Ciano and Donna Rachele Mussolini; one reported that in Capri, where she spends much time, Countess Ciano is ignored by local society and despised by the peasants. This is not true. It is difficult to treat anyone so marked in casual fashion, and I was impressed with the apparent polite unconcern shown by Italians of all classes as they passed the Countess and her children in Capri. There was neither staring nor open avoidance. Those who knew her greeted her; other children were friendly with hers. I heard an Italian explain it: "What do you want us to do? We hanged her father by his feet. Her husband was shot through the back and we took his property. What more do you want us to do?"

Rachele Mussolini is a strong-faced woman who has lived for her family. You might turn to look at her if you met her on Fifth Avenue in New York, but on Canal Street, or here, she doesn't stand out, because there are so many of her. She says, "In times past I didn't like this island. Benito was always amused about that and often said that eventually I would end my life here." You can still read Fascist slogans on the walls of gardens and houses around here, and some of them say: "Mussolini is always right." In this case he seems to have been right. Donna Rachele says that after three and a half years she has got used to Ischia and likes it.

She keeps house in a small oriental-looking building. She does all the housework, draws water at the fountain, buys the groceries, and does the laundry for the small family—herself, Romano, and Anna Maria.

Romano, who is twenty-two, crosses every morning to Na-

ples, where he soon hopes to pass the final exams at the Techni-
cal Institute. He is conscious of his appearance. "Benito," says
Donna Rachele, "wore only shirts which I sewed for him, but
Romano puts his hands up to his neck in agony and says that my
collars are old-fashioned and never sit well—and that it's very
important for him to look right." She has to reach into her purse
to buy the commercial shirts that he prefers.

Of all his five children, twenty-year-old Anna Maria looks
most like Mussolini. She has the same immense skull, the
energetic chin, and she speaks as her father did, in short,
staccato sentences. When Anna Maria brings home the latest
village gossip and recites it in the next room, Donna Rachele
says it sounds like Benito.

In the morning Anna Maria sits under a wide straw hat on the
terrace of the house or in her room, the walls of which are
papered with pin-up girls. She reads American novels and then
helps her mother with the housework. Afternoons she goes
with her friends to a sewing school, and in her free time she and
other girls climb the roofs of houses and engage in a peculiar
pastime: they throw live chickens into the air. It's an ancient
game on the island of Ischia, and they say the exercise is good
for the fowl and that they enjoy the sport.

In spite of this childish amusement Anna Maria already has
her *fodanzato*. He is the son of the greengrocer across the street.
"Honorable people," says Donna Rachele. "He has blue-black
curls and is two years older than the girl. Everybody is in
accord, but first," says her mother, "she must learn how to sew
and cook properly."

Donna Rachele is frequently visited by journalists, and just
as frequently she is surprised by what she reads after these

interviews. She has none of the plans of marriage, travel, or career ascribed to her. "I'll end my days in Ischia," she always says, "as Benito pronounced."

Barbara dutifully visited everything with me. She was mostly bored, and rather silent, except to say occasionally, "Oh, look — a dog! A cat! A donkey!" Once, she really came to life and pointed to a curious dwelling. A boulder shaped like a pebble, enlarged to vast dimensions and round as an orange, had been chiseled out, with infinite patience, to form a home. There was a door, a balcony, a window. I tried to take a picture of it, but the old woman on the balcony started screaming at the children standing by the gate to come in. The dog who lived there was also called in, the door was closed, and the curtain on the balcony drawn. They were afraid of the evil eye of the foreigner.

To come upon a new horizon unexpectedly and find a view which would be described as "breath-taking" in a guidebook is as great a discovery as finding a real Van Gogh in a junkshop. Of such astonishing surprise is the view that suddenly unfolds as you leave the magnificent, ancient, and dirty town of Panza.

Nearby, the land is like an immense amphitheater, with thousands of steps descending to the sea. The steps are in reality man-made terraces on which corn, figs, wheat, grapes, and olives grow. Deep stone cleavages framed in the red of poppies lead down to where the arena would be. In the exact center of the picture stands the Torre Sant'Angelo on a towering peninsula.

From this point starts the trip to Ischia Ponte, the principal town on the island.

The hottest and most crowded bus I have ever been in takes

the traveler on a road like a roller coaster. The saint whose job itis to protect autobuses on Ischia deserves the most beautiful niche and fresh flowers every day. Nowhere do people depend on saints as they do here; curves are taken blindfolded and at top speed, and if the curve is downhill, the pull of gravity is happily added to the motor's best efforts. The driver talks with his hands to a friend sitting beside him, waves at colleagues on other buses—and nothing happens. Along this route appear vineyards from which comes the wine that is sold as Capri wine. It is good wine, and its origin could be admitted without shame, but the power of labels is as strong here as anywhere else. After passing the vineyards we come to the pine forest on the Lava dell' Arso, and to Ischia Ponte, the seat of the Bishop of Ischia. The Bishop, a very round little man, crosses frequently to Naples. And as he walks the deck, blessing everyone who greets him, green and golden threads hang from his hat and wave in the breeze.

The landmark of Ischia, high on a narrow rock and visible for miles, is the Castello. It was built by Alfonso V of Aragon about 1450 and later occupied by the Syracusans, who subsequently fled the island during an earthquake. The poetess Vittoria Colonna, an admirer of Michelangelo, lived there. Now the fishermen of Ischia Ponte hang their nets there to dry. It's exactly like the castle you see when you close your eyes and imagine a castle on a rock.

In this already varied and interesting place, the harbor of Porto d'Ischia is an added curio, being the only harbor of its kind in the world. It was originally a landlocked crater lake, situated close to the shore. In the 1850s a passage was cut from the lake to the sea, an undertaking which took two years and resulted in the safest harbor in the Gulf of Naples. Here are found the classic coastwise sailing boats, still rigged with colored sails; their cargo is wine, fruit, and vegetables.

Near this unique harbor is a small park, and in the park is a bench which had a part in altering one of the traditions of the island. On the morning of July 17, 1943, a man sat on that bench gazing toward the sea, contemplating the beauty of his land, his new freedom, and the truth of the proverb that the mills of the gods grind slowly. Suddenly he was dead—and from that day on the people of Ischia have considered their unluckiest number to be, not thirteen, but seventeen.

The man's name was Lucetti. As a youthful anarchist he had had the courage to toss a bomb at Mussolini's car. The bomb struck the car's hood, bounded to the top, and rolled off without exploding. Lucetti was caught and sent to Ponza, where he was imprisoned for seventeen years until the Allied troops liberated him. He reached his home on the island of Ischia on July 17, walked to the bench, and sat down. And there he was killed by the last shell fired from Procida by the Germans.

During our stay on Ischia I made the acquaintance of Professor Giorgio Buchner, who lives in Porto d'Ischia, and who guided us to places of interest. But he did not guide us to the restaurant of the Sisters Pirozzi, at Ischia Ponte. We found that happy establishment on the tip halfheartedly given me by the head porter of the Quisisana in Capri. At the Sorelli Pirozzi I ate my ten-thousandth kilometer of spaghetti, and I can only say that it was as good as the best I have eaten in all of Italy. The cans of spaghetti which Barbara had brought along had been disposed of in Capri. She was now an Italian spaghetti devotée, and the enthusiasm had even taken hold of Little Bit. It was not necessary to obtain a formal introduction to the sisters, as the head porter had said, nor was I required to reserve a table in advance. All the dishes are cooked to order, and the prices are extremely reasonable.

So frugal is the life of the savant that when I mentioned this meal to Professor Buchner he said, "So-so—h'mmm—you had dinner last night at the Sorelli Pirozzi. Tell me, is it really as elegant as people say it is?"

"Have you never been there, Herr Professor?"

"No. Never."

"How long have you been on this island?"

"Oh, approximately forty years."

"And you never get tired of it?"

"Never. You know, it is incredible, but after forty years of taking walks I can still discover new ones."

We took him to the Sorelli Pirozzi that night, in Ischia exclusiveness.

As everywhere in Italy, uncounted saints are revered on Ischia, every one of which has his feast day. Every village has its own patron saint, and all of them are carried about in processions with singing, candles, flowers, and much rivalry.

During the big earthquake of 1883 the patron saint of Porto d'Ischia earned immense gratitude and praise. While there were thousands of dead on other parts of the island, and the neighboring town of Casamicciola suffered total destruction, not even a floor tile was loosened in Porto d'Ischia. The poor citizens do everything to make the feasts of this saint glorious, and spend a good deal of money on spectacular fireworks.

The favorite old song of the island is dedicated to St. Restituta. It goes:

> Oh, holy Restituta, thanks to thee
> The beans have grown,
> The quail are gone
> And so at last has the enemy.

There is also a limerick left behind by a visiting poet, scribbled on a washroom wall. At least it tells one how to pronounce Ischia.

> An Englishman living on Ischia
> Got gayer and fatter and friskier.
> Between dancing jigs
> And stuffing on figs
> He drank gallons and gallons of whiskia.

Having found on this island the strangest house I've ever seen, we now came upon the strangest animal act in the history of circus art. We were walking along the waterfront, waiting for the boat to Naples, when we heard a trumpet and noticed a crowd gathering. We went over. On a plank stretched between two sawhorses stood a row of empty Chianti bottles. A large man in a red-and-white-striped sweater was doing the tootling. When enough people had assembled he brought out a cardboard box with holes punched in the top and took from it a cat. As the animal stretched he brushed his hand over its fur. Then, from the same box, he extracted six white mice and placed them across the cat's back, three facing one way and three the other. He set the cat on the bottles and cracked a toy whip. The cat stepped along the mouths of the bottles, down the whole row. The crowd applauded as it turned and came back. At a crack of the whip the cat jumped down. The man picked the mice off, and they huddled close to the cat as if it were their mother. He rearranged the bottles in various designs, each more and more

complicated, on which the cat performed solo. Finally he took all but two off the board. The cat was loaded with the mice again, and at the crack of the whip leaped like a kangaroo and secured a foothold on the mouths of the two bottles, balancing itself on its hindlegs. The mice clawed desperately to hold on. The trainer cracked his whip once more. The act was over. He put a large smile on his face and commanded the cat to smile. *"Ridi, ridi,"* he hissed, until the cat smiled too. It was a painful parody.

In an awkward mouse gallop the six rodents went back into the cardboard box. The cat settled down and tried to put her fur in order, while the man went around collecting coins in his derby. I gave him a small bill.

"Why did you give him money?" Barbara demanded.

"So that the cat and mice get something to eat."

The boat whistle blew. We hurried aboard.

On the top deck we met a man bound for Procida, a small island between Ischia and Naples that was a regular stop. On Procida there is a sort of prison for the remaining Fascists of the upper echelons. About seven hundred of them were writing their memoirs. The man told us he was going there to visit a high-ranking "guest."

"The poor fellow," my informant began, "is locked up there — for love. His story starts in Rome, long ago. He and the girl are both of good family but poor. She loves him, but he is not only poor, he has no prospects. Her father says to forget him, that she must marry so and so, a rich boy the father has picked out. The girl promises her father she will marry the rich boy, and the poor boy is heartbroken. The poor boy's father dies that week, and he gets a small inheritance with which he runs away to England, where he knows a girl he met in Rome the winter before. She is rich and loves him; but the fool tells her of his lonesomeness for the one in Rome, who has jilted him to please her father.

"The English one is not flattered. She says to him, 'You know what men do here when something like that happens? They buy themselves tropical outfits and go off to hunt big game in Africa.' So she takes the boy to Fortnum and Mason's, where she helps him pick out things khaki and things canvas, and she sends him off.

"In Africa there is no one to engage his heart, and he devotes himself wholly to hunting. He soon knows Eritrea. He gets to know every waterhole, which, in Africa, is the most important thing to know. He hunts with Englishmen, Americans, Italians, and Africans, and his little capital is almost eaten up when Mussolini's war starts in Africa. It is a furious campaign with many losses—an officer in charge is killed, and the poor boy's hour of opportunity has arrived. Our hero is flown to Rome, and on account of his knowledge of Africa, and especially the waterholes, he is put in charge of the campaign. Overnight he becomes one of the youngest generals in the Italian Army. He is a success, he comes home in triumph, he is feted at banquets, he gets the biggest medals. Parades are held in his honor, and all the women are at his feet.

"One day there is a knock on the door—and who is it? The girl he was in love with and wanted to marry. She tells him that she has not followed her father's advice. She found she could not marry without love and she is still free. But the proud young general tells her it is too late. Her eyes fill with tears. She tells him her poor father, a noted anti-Fascist, languishes in jail. Will he help get him out? He promises. In fact, he actually gets the old man out. Time passes again. We see him once more as the poor boy, with shine on his general's pants. I have a gift for him in this package—from the girl. It is *she* who is trying to get *him* out now. She has married very well, she is still beautiful, and her position in Roman society is secure. Her father is still alive too."

He sighed and asked, "Why don't you make a movie out of this story, with shots of lions and tigers and shots of the war, and call it *The African* something or other? And, speaking of Africa, that reminds me of poor old Carlo Sforza, who tried to get back those waterholes in Africa. He asked the English to give them back; you know, the English do not mind giving away things that belong to others, but with what they have taken for themselves they are very careful."

The boat tooted. "Here we are," he said, and we walked up to the prison with him. Beyond the enclosure stood the man who had been one of the youngest generals in the Italian Army, with his arms stretched out to embrace his visitor.

"I was his adjutant for a while," said our informant.

I looked at Barbara. She was sad. I said, "Don't worry about the young general—he'll get out."

"I'm not worrying about him. I'm thinking of the poor cat and mice."

Traveling, one finds out that everything that can be imagined—form or smell or sound—exists somewhere.

We returned to the boat and reached Naples at dinnertime.

—

THE LOBBY of the Hotel Excelsior was filled with people. The dining room was also crowded. We waited for a table. Barbara waved at a man and said, "Oh, Poppy, there's Uncle Charlie!"

I got up and followed her. "This is Uncle Charlie," said Barbara, and I shook his hand.

Charlie looked well, relaxed and pleasant. He spoke softly, and he wore a warm smile when he wasn't talking. The man with him had a long name and title, and a strong handshake.

"See the tattoo?" Barbara whispered as Charlie lifted his arm and the headwaiter came running.

"We're all eating together," said Charlie. "You'll let me order?" he asked, looking at me. He debated the menu with the headwaiter and then took some time to choose the wine. "You smoke cigars?" he said to me. "I'll send up for some. I got the best Havanas in Italy."

I was very happy that Barbara had an instinct for real people.

A man in a gray suit approached and talked to our host. "Excuse me a minute," Charlie said and walked out. His friend also excused himself.

"Didn't I tell you?" said Barbara.

We were seated as soon as Charlie and his friend rejoined us. The dinner was excellent, and ended with a very good cigar. Later, I found a box of them in my room.

I said to Barbara, "What's Charlie's name? I have to write him a note of thanks."

"I don't know," she said. "Everybody just calls him Charlie."

The next day we were in the lobby when Charlie and his friend left in a large car. Near us stood the assistant manager of the hotel. He turned to me and said, "There goes one of our greatest tourist attractions, the man on the right."

"You mean Charlie?"

"Oh, you know him?"

I said, "I met him yesterday—my child always introduces people to me by their first names."

"That was Charles Lucky Luciano," said the assistant manager.

Barbara had a peculiar expression on her face. "Well, anyway, I like him just the same."

I said, "We'd better go upstairs and rest and then do a little work."

11.

Science and Man

I WAS DOING my Latin lesson, because I had developed a great hunger for learning. I was among the Latin poets with dictionary beside me. I looked up from my work—a sepia-colored cloud was at the foot of Vesuvio.

Barbara was doing her schoolwork. She sat on the balcony with Vesuvio in back of her. She was doing "Science and Man," a course she was taking by correspondence. I can never get over the fact that, in spite of an irregular existence and lack of prodding, Barbara is a conscientious student.

My experience with my child is that American children want

things solid. Parents are supposed to be of the type of members of the Parent-Teacher's Association, the parents of the insurance company ad. They should be serious. They can be plumbers, but they should not be foreigners, and certainly they need not be humorists.

The most desirable qualities are that they be believers in the rounded life as it is found in magazines and lived in suburban communities, subscribers to all the prejudices of that life, the patient disciples of the norm of things. Cynics are out altogether, and the least-wanted kind of parent is one who himself was a problem child.

I have, among other mistakes, made those of revealing to Barbara the details of my life as a scholar and that I was a problem child practically from the moment of arrival.

I sat through the first form of a provincial *lycée* for two years, and then was sent to a clandestine school for backward children to which the near idiots of the better families were relegated. I found great happiness there—good friends. I was quite at home, for they were amusing and had private minds. But there I failed also and was let go after a year, with low marks in all departments but religion and sports. Except for the labors of a French governess when I was small and a tutor when I returned from the "idiot" school and who gave up after six months, this was the sum of all my education. In the house of my mind there are vast, empty, unlit rooms.

All the above is not amusing to Barbara. At times she looks at me very worriedly. At others, when I ask a question concerning the higher things, she answers me with the anxious concern one extends to the blind at street corners.

"Barbara, Carlyle wrote a story of the Roman Empire, didn't he?"

"No, Poppy, he wrote a history of the French Revolution, and he wrote it in longhand, and then he had to write part of it all over again, because the maid had burned it."

Obviously then, in my position, one leaves the bright American lighthouse alone.

The only time I have been near one of Barbara's teachers was in her first year of school. We were in Hollywood at the time, and living in a bungalow on the shore of the Pacific in a place called Topanga. Before I drove Barbara to school on my way to the M-G-M Studio at Culver City, I would reach in the icebox to get her prepared lunch and put it into her lunchbox.

This went on without incident for a week. Barbara was very happy in the Topanga Town and Country School. It was a kind of outdoor school, with horses, cows, chickens, and a wonderful teacher, E. Phyllis Devey. Although she was married, the children, with that way they have of abbreviating titles, called her Mis' Devey. She had a large family whose health and activities were reported on daily. There was old Ping Pong, the Peke, eighteen at the time, and two adorable chihuahuas, who were inseparable. These lived in the house, while the two Dobermans and Rags stayed outside. Then she had an aquarium with two water newts, six canaries, two lovebirds, and a parrot. She had also owned a cockatoo, but she had given her to a friend who had a male, and now they had the loveliest babies. (How curious with what objectivity these prim ladies always arrange flirtations between their own pets and those of their friends.)

The cloud had moved; it was now like a school of whales halfway up Vesuvio.

The school in California had had a kind of belated sunrise service every morning which went:

> If I have faltered more or less
> In my great task of happiness;
> If I have moved among my race
> And shown no glorious morning face;
> If beams from happy human eyes
> Have moved me not; if morning skies,
> Books, and my food, and summer rain
> Knocked on my sullen heart in vain:
> Lord, thy most pointed pleasure take
> And stab my spirit broad awake.

This poem, called "The Celestial Surgeon," by Robert Louis Stevenson, was recited facing the sun and with hands on hearts.

After a week's attendance, a letter came from the principal, asking me to stop by. A stern young woman who, when I introduced myself, opened her mouth and closed it again, raising her eyebrows, showed me into a room furnished with lecture chairs so small that I had to sit sidesaddle in them with my knees up to my chin. She sat me there and with lips pressed tightly together left the room. In the corridor was a concert of slamming doors, little feet running, slamming doors again, and the incessant flushing of little toilets. The nostalgia for places where one has suffered overcame me, and I noticed that the smell of chlorine and small boys' pants that issued from the hall was the same as in the first schools I attended. The dreadful apparition of time when it takes on substance, when I become aware of the passing of it, paralyzes me. On the waves of the chlorine I floated into a black mood, from which the voice of the young woman awoke me. I followed her to the principal's office.

"What do you expect this school to do for your child, help turn her into an alcoholic?" said the lady principal, who looked like George Washington with his wig in a severe hairdo.

She stood up and advanced. She said that at first she suspected one of the teachers when it was reported to her that everyday after lunch a beer bottle turned up. Eventually it was discovered that it was Barbara who was quietly drinking the beer and then going for her rest period. It seems that in the morning when I packed her lunch I had absent-mindedly put a bottle of beer in her lunchbox instead of Coca-Cola.

I explained it as well as I could, and I said that at home she occasionally drank a glass of beer with lunch and wine with dinner.

The clear eyes of several assistants were upon me as well as those of the principal. She stopped my explanation by saying to the teachers, "That is Barbara's father."

I looked for the door, and made my exit, and, as hastily as the little boys did, got out into the open air and drove to the freedom of my little cell at the M-G-M lot, to devote myself to a picture called *Yolanda and the Thief.*

Since then I have stood aside, detached, and watched the progress of Barbara's education with fascination, from a safe distance. The most astonishing thing is the way she found the kind of school where even I might have learned something.

The choice of school was left to her. My wife (American)

said, "You can go to any school you like, to Miss Hewitt's classes, to Foxcroft, to any of those schools."

"No, thank you. All the girls I know who go there come out with a kind of speech impediment."

"Well, you can go to a public school, or to a convent school, or you can go to a school in France."

"Ugh!"

By herself she found, at last, a remarkable and enlightened institution. I have not visited the school as a parent, but I was once told to "just go and have a look at this wonderful place — you won't believe it otherwise." I went there impersonating someone who got off at the wrong floor.

The school is located in a downtown office building and as you enter it you think you are going to see your dentist or lawyer. The lobby has a newsstand displaying cigars, cigarettes, comic books, and candy, and a row of elevators and the operators thereof. I have always wondered, as I do about pigeons, what causes an elevator man or a pigeon to choose his particular neighborhood, the overfed Central Park pigeons compared with the windblown Brooklyn Heights and Bowery pigeons, the Park Avenue elevator man compared with the Broadway elevator man.

As I walked about the school I came to an empty classroom. On the blackboard was printed, in large, unhurried letters: "Let's kill Miss Stockes." The word "kill" was in red chalk and underlined, "Miss Stockes" in pale blue, and "let's" in canary yellow. The message was signed by several sponsors.

Some of the children come in cabs, and some have makeup on, and dyed hair. When Barbara first went there the boys from *Life with Father* lit up the corridors with their fiery coiffures.

190

Some of these kids support their families, some are ice skaters who get up at four in the morning to train. There are acrobats, pianists, comedians who practice on the teachers. This stable of circus *Wunderkinder* rushes out of the elevator into a corridor lined with the pictures of Maude Adams, John Barrymore, Maxine Elliot, Walter Hampden, Henry Irving—and you think you are at the Lambs Club.

Milton Berle is one of the alumni. There is a Gilbert Miller memorial room, although, happily, Gilbert is still with us. Helen Hayes presides at commencement exercises, and John Mason Brown comes to speak on Shaw, Paul Gallico to speak on cats.

To accommodate the actors among the children, who get to bed late, the school starts at ten and is over at two-fifteen. The teachers are as attuned to the spirit of this school as the pupils. Said one, "Please be good today, children. I don't want to keep you in, and my husband wants me home early."

One of the comedians in the class asked, "What's the matter, doesn't he trust you, dear?"

"My name is Miss Carson," said the teacher is an effort to reestablish order.

The kids cooperated, Barbara said, and school was out on time.

No parent-teacher's association could ask for closer rapport between teacher and pupil, or for more candor in their relationship. Pupils even feel free to correct the teacher on occasion—as is demonstrated by the following.

Mr. Trimble, the science teacher, said one day, "I'm very sorry but I couldn't correct your papers. You see, my wife has had to go to a family funeral in Oregon, and I have to take care

191

of our three little boys. Anyway, last night after school I went home, cooked dinner, washed the baby's clothes, and put them all to bed. Then I tried to sit down to read the paper, but the baby wouldn't go to sleep. I had to keep giving him his bottle. About eleven I went into the bathroom and found the middle one sitting on the floor. His name is Matt, so that was quite appropriate" — appreciative laughter for the bathmat joke. "Unfortunately, the floor was wet because I had given them all baths, and I had to change his pajamas.

"About twelve o'clock I finally got into bed. The baby had wet it, but I was too tired to do anything about it. I just slept to one side. A little later the oldest one crept into my bed, complaining of a pain in his stomach. Soon the middle one moved in too. The oldest one said he was about to get sick, so I had to get up again.

"Unlike Plato, my stories always have a moral, and for this one the moral is, 'Don't get married.'"

A boy named Donny spoke up. "Mr. Trimble," he said, "that doesn't sound moral to me."

Another attractive feature of this school is that you don't have to attend it if you don't want to, or if you're on the road the courses can be done by correspondence. It is the ideal school for children of traveling people.

On the balcony Barbara was now doing her homework. She did it faithfully every day, and in a silence she should have found disturbing. I was surprised that she was able to work, for in New York, in a cluttered, disorderly room, she has the radio going, and the television set. She talks on the phone while she watches Red Skelton on television and listens to any gags that might be interesting on the radio, switching her attention from one to the other and saying, "Listen, Frances, did you hear that?

Groucho just said—" In addition to all these goings-on she has a pencil poised on a piece of paper and is doing algebra. The miracle is that her report card is marked "very good" in all subjects, and "excellent" in deportment.

The cloud was up now, hiding the cone of Vesuvio—it was white and gray. I heard the clock towers of Naples bonging out six o'clock. It was time to go out, and I said, "Hurry up, Barbara."

Gathering up her books, she said, "Poppy, will you ever learn that it's not 'hairy ape' but 'hurry up'?"

I am at times astonished myself that I have been unable to shake off my Austrian accent. I, of course, cannot hear myself, but since I have lived in America from the age of seventeen, it is curious how strong the accent still is. Only a year ago I went to England, and I used some royalties that had accumulated there to buy myself a complete British outfit—Lobb boots, a Briggs umbrella, a Lock homburg, and a conservative suit and topcoat made by a recommended tailor. I also had my throat examined by a Harley Street specialist. In this British makeup I took a walk with Barbara on my return to New York. We were in Central Park, and a man approached us. He asked what time it was. I hung the Briggs umbrella on my left arm, opened my London topcoat, and reached into my waistcoat pocket for my watch. "Quarter to one," I said—and that is all I said.

The man smiled. "Oh, *Sie sprechen Deutsch.*"

"You see, Poppy, you don't believe it when I tell you," said Barbara after he had left. "Do you think in German?"

"That's another thing that puzzles me—no, I don't."

"In English?"

"No, I don't think in either. I think in pictures, because I see everything in pictures, and then translate them into English. I tried to write in German; I can't. I made an attempt to translate one of my books, and it was very difficult and sounded awful. Then the Swiss publishers Scherz engaged an old lady, the widow of a German general, to translate the book, and when I read it I said to myself, 'How odd! It's another book.' I liked it, but I could never have done it myself."

"What do you mean by pictures?"

"Well, when I write, a man comes in the door. I see it as a movie—I see the door, precisely a certain kind of a door, and I see the man."

"In color? Do you dream in color?"

"That depends on the subject. Happy dreams are usually in color, especially flying dreams."

"How do they go?"

"They are the best, and I have them after indigestion sometimes, when I eat late and heavily. I am like a bird, and I fly all over and see everything from high up, which is my favorite perspective."

"And you have no vertigo?"

"None whatever. I fly at will low over the ground and swing up and sit on the edges of high buildings, and visually it is the greatest pleasure."

"You love painting more than writing?"

"Yes, I would rather paint than write, for writing is labor."

"Do you think you could be a great painter?"

"Yes, the very best."

"But why aren't you?"

"Because I love living too much. If I were unhappy as Toulouse-Lautrec was, or otherwise burdened, so that I would turn completely inward, then I would be a good painter. As is, I'm not sufficiently devoted."

"Is it the same with writing?"

"Well, yes. My greatest inspiration is a low bank balance. I can perform then."

"To make money?"

"Yes, to make money."

"But that's awful!"

"Well, it has motivated better people than I."

"For example, whom?"

"For example, Shakespeare."

"And if you had all the money in the world would you just be a café society playboy and waste it?"

At such turns in the conversation I impose silence.

"Poppy—"

"Yes, what now?"

"About the people you write about."

195

"We've had that argument before, and I'll run through my little piece again for you. I was born in a hotel and brought up in three countries—when I was six years old I couldn't speak a word of German, because it was fashionable in Europe to bring up children who spoke nothing but French. And then I lived in other hotels, which was a very lonesome life for a child, and the only people you met were odd ones, below stairs and upstairs. In my youth the upstairs was a collection of Russian grand dukes and French countesses, English lords and American millionaires. Backstairs there were French cooks, Rumanian hairdressers, Chinese manicurists, Italian bootblacks, Swiss managers, English valets. All those people I got to know very well. When I was sent to America to learn the hotel business here, I ran into the same kind of people, and these I know very well and I can write about them, and one ought to write about what one knows. I can write about you, or Mimi, or a few other people, but I can't write about what you call 'ordinary people' because I don't know them well enough. Besides, there are so many people who do, and who write about them well."

"Could you write about German ordinary people?"

"I can write about Tyroleans, and Bavarians, whom I have known in my youth, woodchoppers, teamsters, boatmen, peasants, and the children of all these people."

"But how did you find out about them, and understand them, when you didn't speak their language?"

"Oh, I understood them, as a foreigner does."

"When you were older?"

"Oh no, in my childhood; or better, when I started living and occasionally ran away from the hotel."

"And did you like that more than the hotel?"

"Of course. The hotel was like an all-day theater performance and one played along, but the other was real and important and something you never forget. I ran away often and played with other children, but I was always brought back."

"Do you speak German with an accent too?"

"Yes, of course."

"Do you speak any language correctly?"

"Well, I have the least accent in French, or else the French are very polite, for they always say how very well I speak it for a foreigner."

"That's all rather sad, Poppy."

"Well, it has its advantages. It's like being a gypsy, belonging everywhere and nowhere. When you are in Paris you want to be in New York and vice versa. You are made up of fragments — and just now it occurs to me it's a good thing that you know what you want to be, an American, that you speak your own language well. Stay that way, and don't let anybody change it — and now we really must hurry up."

"Poppy, try saying 'Hurry up.'"

"Hurry up."

"That's better."

We went to a restaurant overlooking Naples and the bay, highly recommended for its view at night. It was a "swell place" in the meaning of the Neapolitan who was in Capri. The entertainment started with a Spanish team of accordionist and dancer. She did a bolero with castanets that were like two hamburger buns, and as authentic as the dancing. He looked like an English pansy, and she spoke German, between songs,

with a Swiss who sat in front of us. The proprietor of the place followed the Spanish number with his own rendition of "Funiculi." He weighed over two hundred and fifty pounds, and made much of it, bumping with his stomach into another fat man, in rhythm, and to much applause repeated the obscene routine.

Then the orchestra started. It was like a thousand orchestras all over the world, and it played one of the melodies that are played everywhere, in all the bars on earth — "You Gotta See Mama Every Night, or You Won't See Mama at All." Barbara knew every single word of the three stanzas. She swung her legs back and forth, ignored the food and the view, and, with faraway gaze and very little voice, formed the words with her lips as if she were saying a prayer. At the end of the song she folded her napkin and asked, "When are we leaving, Poppy? I mean, for home?"

12.

"Proletariat of the World, Unite"

THE FOLLOWING day was a Sunday, and there in the park close to the hotel was a father with seven children and his wife. He had an old-fashioned camera, and he wanted to photograph the family. The wife sat on the lawn with Vesuvio in the background, and the children were grouped behind her according to their ages. The baby was in the mother's lap. The father issued loud Sicilian commands to watch the camera and to smile. The baby pouted, and the mother raised her arms and screamed at the father to hurry up, but he was focusing his camera. The baby started crying.

"Oh, these European fathers with their happy family life!" was Barbara's comment.

"I beg your pardon, but the same scene could take place in Central Park. Only there would be one child, and a Kodak. Sunday and the father at home usually leads to tears in any country."

The baby leaned back and looked pitifully at its mother. The mother arranged herself in a Madonna pose, looked down at the baby, and yelled in voice hoarse from habitual screaming, "Hurry up!" The picture was taken.

We walked on.

"Look at all these men lying in the street! Isn't it a disgrace?" Barbara observed next. "What are they doing here?"

"Well, they are probably poor fishermen who have worked all night and now are resting in the sun. The idea that the Italians are lazy stems from the fact that tourists get up late and walk out into the heat when these people are taking their siesta. Italians work early and late in the day."

As we came near them several of the prostrate men got up and approached us, holding out torn hats and caps. I gave them some money, and suddenly the whole group came to life.

"They look more like bums than fishermen to me," said Barbara.

"Look, Barbara, one day I'll take you down to the Bowery in New York, and you'll see the same thing. They hang around the streets in the summertime, and in winter they're in the municipal lodging house or in some mission in Chinatown."

"They're foreigners."

"No, darling, they're not. But anyway, I'm a foreigner, and if I hadn't decided to go to America you wouldn't be an American.

America—and I love it every bit as much as you do—is a country of foreigners who got there sooner or later."

There was the usual silence that follows such arguments. This time Barbara broke it. "Poppy, do you have some change? Charlie told me there's a wonderful museum and aquarium that one must see. I can find it myself. I have a guidebook."

I don't know what the final result will be, but, as parents, we have let Barbara grow like a tree, with a minimum of pruning. So far it's been all right. One cannot guarantee anyone much in this life, and most of the children I've seen guided through its maze with strictness and all the available apparatus of protection have foundered and become unhappy people.

It seemed to us that the only thing one can do is to guarantee them a happy childhood, or at least create the climate for it. At times this entails worry, such as: Will they fall off horses and break their necks? Will they turn into freaks of one kind or another? Will they be impossible to get along with?

I suffered the doubts again in Naples, when a long while after her departure for the museum and the aquarium she did not return. I took a taxi and went to both places.

"Oh, yes, the *bambina* has been here," a man at the aquarium said, and at the museum I received the frightening information that a man in a long dark coat had driven away with her. Nobody knew the number of the car, for it was a Vespa, a motor scooter, and she sat at the back of it, holding on to the man. "No, she didn't scream," said the doorman of the museum. "She smiled."

"What did the man look like?"

"If anything, like an agent of the police."

Several people had collected. The doorman shrugged his

shoulders and looked around among the faces. Had anybody observed him? Dark hair, dark eyes.

"Italian?"

"Yes, of course, Italian."

For a moment I saw her body being fished from the Bay of Naples. At home I would have called the police or the FBI. I rushed back to the hotel, reproaching myself, and ran to the desk. No, they had not seen the child. I went up to the room, and there she was, writing a letter to her mother.

"Poppy," she said, "I met a wonderful man near the aquarium. When I came out I asked some people the way to the museum, but nobody could understand me, and then he came along and said he'd take me. He showed me all through it and bought me some photographs of the statues. He's the nicest man. I hope you like him. He wears a long black leather coat." She added, somewhat doubtfully, "Do you mind?"

"Why should I mind?"

Later we met the new friend in the lobby. He was elegant and polite. He suggested a small hotel for lunch, and there we ate on a balcony overlooking a busy street. The food was interesting. Italian food, when well cooked, has a curious effect. They bring a large plate of pasta, and you think you'll never be able to finish it, but suddenly the plate is empty and you look for more. Barbara had advanced to the stage where she enjoyed fried octopus.

As we left the hotel our guest asked the proprietor his name.

"Tomaso Fettucini," said the proprietor, handing out cards.

"Just Tomaso Fettucini? Not even *commandatore* or *dottore?*" asked our friend.

"No," said the other. "Just Tomaso Fettucini."

It seemed that the man in the black leather coat had received some democratic indoctrination from Barbara during the visit to the museum, for he now turned to her and said, "Allow me to introduce to you the only man in Italy who has no title."

We returned to our hotel, and Barbara went up to lie down.

"Your child has informed me that you are a writer," said the man. "Naturally, I love my country, and I should like to be of help to you. I am at your service. I can get a car for you at a reasonable price." Suddenly he turned. "Do you know that man passing through the lobby there?"

"Yes, that's Lucky Luciano," I answered.

Somewhat disappointed, he continued, "And the man walking with him?"

"I met him but I don't remember his name."

"That's one of the chiefs of police of Rome. He's assigned to Signor Luciano and is with him all the time. They're going to the races now. When it's cold they go to a warm place. When it's hot they go to Capri. The chief of police never had such a wonderful time. He takes his family along. It seems that crime pays—for the police at any rate."

I told him that the doorman of the museum and I had suspected him of being of the police himself.

"Not quite," he said. "Usually when I wear this coat I'm thought to be a labor leader, and I have therefore named it 'Proletariat of the World, Unite.'"

He said "Good-by," he would call the next morning, and if there was anything I needed he would be honored to be of assistance. He had many friends, he said. He went down the stairs, got on his motor scooter, and drove off.

I went over to the manager. "My child," I told him, "introduces me to everybody by his first name. Who was the man I just spoke with?"

"Oh, you don't know? That's his Grace, the Duke Mariano Imperiale di Francavilla."

I went upstairs. "You're doing all right with your friends, the ordinary people," I said to Barbara. "First Lucky Luciano, and now a duke."

205

The lighthouse blinked instantly. "Well, they're very nice people, and today I overheard Charlie say that without him Dewey wouldn't be governor of New York, and O'Dwyer wouldn't have been mayor of New York and also that he gets blamed for everything the police can't solve. When they have nothing else they can hang on people, they accuse them of being a friend of Lucky Luciano's."

Quite early the next morning the telephone announced, "*Il Duca* is on his way up."

When the duke took off the formidable "Proletariat of the World, Unite," he looked like an American businessman of Italian ancestry. His clothes and shoes were American style. He liked American cars, smoked American cigarettes, read American magazines, and went so far in his enthusiasm for the United States that he praised chewing gum, Coca-Cola, and catsup, and held the quality of American aspirin and gasoline to be above all others. He walked up and down, sat, got up again — as most Italians do when they are busy with talking. He seemed constantly to be sorry for being around and having an important name and title. "I like the American custom of first names," he said. "My friends call me Mariano. If you will allow me — come, Ludovico, let us go get a car to drive us to Positano. You must see Positano." He put the "Proletariat of the World, Unite" on again, lit an American cigarette, admired my American typewriter, bowed graciously to Barbara, who had decided to stay at the hotel while we went to get the car, and ran ahead to ring for the elevator.

We walked to the noisy quarter that is the "downtown" of Naples, a place as turbulent as the middle of a revolution, a web of streets so narrow that two bedsheets hanging together span them. You don't see the sky on account of the wash, and the smells in the air are as evident as shirts and stockings.

I stopped and took inventory of the scenes I could see without turning my head. Here they are: A cat sharpening her claws on a bag of charcoal. Two children sitting on the sidewalk, eating a kind of confection which a peddler manufactured in a decorated wagon standing nearby; he shaved ice off a block and then poured over it one of several kinds of syrup. Five more children were waiting. Argument between two men. Picture of the Madonna, candle-lit, in the hall of the house on the right. Argument in two windows above, and mother scolding boy in street from a window on the ground floor. Old man writing figures on the wall of the house. Straight ahead a donkey cart; next to it two nuns walking toward me. A shaft of light piercing the narrow canyon, illuminating the two bedsheets, the white of the nuns' headdresses, and the faded green canvas side of a Punch and Judy show which was stamped, as are so many objects in Italy, with the letters "U.S.A." in black.

"Come, come, Ludovico, don't be afraid," Mariano said. I looked about as we entered a house that had the air of a cave of bandits. We climbed six sets of stairs, and on every floor we heard a Neapolitan argument supported by shrill children's voices. The street sounds faded away. Mariano rang a bell, and a door opened, to my astonishment, into one of the most orderly homes I have ever seen. Observing a black grand piano in the living room, I thought of the late Captain Patterson of the *New York Daily News*, who once told me that there were more grand pianos on the lower East Side of New York than in all the rest of Manhattan.

This home was as quiet as the street was noisy. In the hall was a coat stand, and on the wall hung several oil paintings—not collectors' items, but originals sincerely executed. The living room and the dining room were spotless, and on a couch in back of the table sat the owner of the apartment, who excused himself for not rising, as he had just come out of the hospital, following an automobile accident. His right arm and hand were raised as in perpetual greeting, both being encased in plaster. Only two fingers were free, and in consequence, being an Italian, he had difficulty speaking; he was limited to the gesturing of those two fingers, which were like two caterpillars dancing on a tree trunk.

Mariano had made the climb to talk over some business with his *amministratore* and to obtain a car and driver to take us to Positano, and the owner of the car presently appeared. He looked like Ben Turpin. Everything was arranged over a cup of coffee served in thin china. We went out again into the street concert, and I was still astonished at what I had seen, for one never would think that the houses actually held warm, orderly, and quiet rooms.

Back at the hotel we found Barbara waiting for us in the lobby. Mariano steered us through the crowd to the restaurant of the untitled man, and after lunch we proceeded toward Sorrento in the car with the cross-eyed chauffeur. It's wise to get an Italian to drive for you here, as he will anticipate the donkey caravan, the children playing in the street, the parked car of the tourist around the next tight bend. Barbara sat next to the driver. She watched the scenery for a while, then fell asleep.

The beginning of this trip is not inspiring. We hasten first along a road that reminds you of the Pulaski Skyway or any such passage through the part of a large city which is given over

to factories, piers, warehouses, and freight yards. The scene improves at Portici and at Resina, the station of the Vesuvian funicular. Portici and Resina stand on the ruins of Herculaneum, which, together with its plebeian sister-town Pompeii, was destroyed by the eruption of 79 A.D. The ancient city of Herculaneum lies at present about twenty meters below the new towns.

We come to Torre del Greco, a souvenir and coral-jewelry town, after some driving amid scenery that is less pleasant than a ride through the Pennsylvania countryside. The road goes upward to Boscotrecase and Casabianca, and the enchantment is still to come. We also pass Torre Annunziata, distinguished as the center of the macaroni and canned-fruits industry.

At Valle di Pompei is the Santuario della Madonna del Rosario, a church with an uninspired modern façade, but containing a wonder-working picture of the Madonna, with the rosary. The picture was taken to Naples on the occasion of the last elections and the beneficial result is well known—the Communists were defeated.

Beyond the Valle di Pompei are fields of cauliflower, ar-

209

tichokes, and tomatoes. The world is still plain, and lined with the soft greens of chestnut trees and filbert bushes. Forests lie along the hills. Hereabouts countless springs—most of them benevolent and warm—run unused into the sea. By way of Vico, one turns past the Punta di Scutola and arrives at the point where magnificence begins. The plain of Sorrento is before you.

There are arguments about Sorrento, and people hold that other places farther along the road are more magnificent; it's like arguing whether the sunrise or the sunset is more beautiful. Sorrento lies in a magic garden, and most of its hotels perch at the edge of high cliffs. Along here stood the house in which the poet Torquato Tasso lived. The house fell into the sea together with the ground on which it stood.

Near that spot is Mariano's villa. Its garden is immense—in fact, it's a romantic park rather than a garden. In it grow grapefruit, oranges, lemons, and tangerines. The orange grove is lined with palms, beyond which is an ancient balustrade—and a sudden descent of several hundred feet down to the sea. From here you may see Vesuvio, Naples, and Capri, and it has been written about the place: "See Sorrento and die." There is always singing in the garden, and you will find in shady places under the trees young girls with garden shears, busy trimming the thin top branches of the orange trees. In one part of the property there stands a mill for pressing olive oil. Its mechanism is as ancient as the Bible.

The mansion had to be opened for our visit, and the electricity was not on. White sheets covered the statuary and most of the furniture. Our unexpected arrival upset the servants, who scurried around not knowing what to do first, but we asked that nothing be disturbed on our account, and said we would be grateful if only the beds were made.

After dining by candlelight Barbara and I were each given a candlestick and escorted to our rooms by personal guides. Barbara said good night to me from her doorway, and her words echoed down the vast corridors—it was as if one were speaking loudly in a cathedral. I judged from the sound of my own voice that my sleeping apartment must be a hundred feet long and as high.

In what seemed to be the middle of the night I was awakened by a flickering in my eyes. It was the light of Barbara's candle. She was wrapped in a gray silk coverlet, and it took me some time to decide where I was.

"Listen," she said, trembling. "Listen to it! It's been going on all night."

There was a sound similar to someone's being hit with a blunt instrument. "Plop, plop, plop," it went. I got up and put on my dressing gown and slippers and lit my candle. "Let's see where it's coming from," I said.

We walked out into the corridor and listened. There was the "plop" again, and also a creaking sound, and then laughter, which under the circumstances could be described as eerie.

"Now listen," said Barbara, going into her room. I followed. We heard voices, and the "plop, plop" continued. "I know there are no such things as ghosts," Barbara said in a tremolo, "but come here and see, Poppy." She had found some slats missing in a wooden shutter, and, looking out into the garden, we saw figures in a milky haze walking over the trees.

I opened the shutters. After a while the scene explained itself. Frost was expected, the fruit was ripe, and the people were working late to save the crop. The "plop, plop" sound came from overripe oranges falling to the ground. The people were running about on a framework of chestnut poles, tied in a vast system over and around the trees, like a glasshouse without panes. The device covered the entire garden, and at regular intervals in the network were small huts made of sticks and straw where reed mats were kept. The people had climbed up on ladders and were stretching the mats across the poles to shield the trees. The latticework swayed visibly sometimes, but it held together, and the younger workers amused themselves by doing acrobatics on it.

213

—

A LOT OF grapes grow along here as well, and Tiberius is said to have preferred Sorrentine wine above all others. If ever you have seen the apricots ripen along the foot of Vesuvio and observed the violence of the blossoming trees; if the warm, perfumed air that rises has made you groggy—then you will understand this wine. It is out of the volcanic earth; it is not a wine with a bouquet, it is too insistent; it's a strong wine, a good wine.

Voltaire has said that man is the only animal that drinks when it is not thirsty, that laughs, and that makes love the year round.

Everyone who comes here takes easily to wine. Look at someone and he smiles; you hear laughter in every street; and the babies seem to fall out of trees as the oranges do in Mariano's garden. Also, I have never seen a child cry in Capri, in Ischia, or anywhere along this road.

The next day I finally rebelled at eating any more spaghetti. We were standing in the center of a village where we had stopped to eat, when I saw the hope of a change in diet.

A man appeared with a hunting dog. The dog had no leash, and the man led him gently by an ear. He bent over the dog and seemed to guide him in the way a child might lead a small sailboat in a bathtub. Presently he took off his cap and placed it on a stone bench that was part of an ancient fountain. And from somewhere—perhaps from his sleeve—he seemed to pour quail into the cap. He got into a heated argument with some onlookers over the price of the birds.

I suggested to Mariano that I buy the quail.

"He will ask too much from you, and you will pay it,"

Mariano said. "Let me go and buy them." He was wearing the "Proletariat of the World, Unite" again, and, as I had feared, he was immediately suspected of police connections. As he approached the man the quail disappeared. The owner swiftly secreted them about his person and said with knowing eyes, "The hunting season, signore, does not begin until the fifteenth of the month." And so we ate spaghetti again.

IN VIETRI SUL MARE is a ceramic factory that turns out vases, tiles, and various souvenirs of excellent quality. We visited the plant.

In dank, dark rooms the artisans, dressed like beggars, sat on three-legged work stools. In one room a man turned his potter's wheel with bare feet, and an apprentice, a child, kneaded the clay. The little boy looked up as we entered, the potter grunted at him, and the boy bowed his head and doubled his efforts. His small hands rolled and pounded the gray mass. On wooden trays stood dozens of the ceramic donkeys that you see in the world's souvenir shops—the ones with oversized ears and large clay baskets on their sides. Another child stirred mixtures of clay in wooden troughs outside in the yard.

Mariano is of that class of Italians who have a feeling of responsibility for the people. He will talk to anyone in the street as if he were his brother. "Conditions such as we have seen just now," he said, "are the best propaganda for communism. These people work hard, and none of them earns enough even to feed himself decently. There are Italians that don't eat spaghetti— because they cannot afford it, except, perhaps, on Sunday. They eat polenta."

Back at the hotel that night I opened my old travel book on Italy and read Gregorovius, who visited Italy in 1853. It hasn't changed. I translate:

> Here let us sit at the edge of a chestnut forest between myrrh bushes and look at the land before us. . . . Here are gold-blond muscatel grapes that are made transparent by the sun; here the white, pure grapes from which the *vino buono* is made. All the grapes are heavy, and each is faultless. Beyond are fields of Turkish corn, and olive trees. In this terraced landscape framed by stone walls, each foot of land is cultivated.
>
> Can one believe that here in the center of such plenty the peasant is poor? Looking over this terrain, one would

217

assume it to be El Dorado, lived in by the happiest of people; yet, as you walk through this paradise, the people you meet all wear the look of hunger, of misery. All these fruits one gets for nothing do not supply a living for the native. He would starve to death were it not for corn meal, which is the staple of his existence. The cause for the misery is in the agrarian conditions. . . . The farmer owes a fourth of his income as rent to the landowner—in this case, Prince Colonna. It is the old curse of latifundia that impoverishes the people. Usury knows no bounds; even from the poorest, ten per cent is taken.

In the case of bad crops—and they often follow year after year—the farmer drowns in debt. If he borrows money or grain, the interest ruins him; the rich and the cloisterers wait for his ruin, until at their own price they acquire his property and he becomes their vassal and work-man. I have had much opportunity to observe these condi-tions, and as a rule the process is as follows:

First, the debtor sells the ground, but the trees (*gli alberi*—which means also the grapevines) remain his, for the time being, and, continuing to care for them, he also continues in his indebtedness. Soon he offers to sell the trees as well as the ground, and now he is completely the tenant-farmer—he and his family are in bondage.

He sells his wine—for himself he uses the second press-ing. He needs bread, but wheat is much too costly: he eats polenta, buying or planting Turkish corn. All the natives eat polenta, as a kind of meal or as cake—as such it is known as pizza. When you meet someone on a road and ask him what he ate for breakfast, he answers, "Pizza." "And what will you have tonight?" "Pizza." The yellow corn paste is cooked in the form of a pancake on a flat stone over coals and eaten very hot. The family sits in a circle at meals. With it they sometimes eat salad, and in high times there is oil to season the salad. Occasionally there is a watery soup made of vegetables, chicory, and other herbs. Wine stimulates nervous energy, but it doesn't nourish; one can imagine, then, with what excitement the people look toward the harvesting of the corn.

Toward the end of July the ears form, and then the plant needs rain. If none falls and the incessant sun scorches the fields, the people become afraid, and the daily processions start in the late afternoon to beg the saints for rain. Near madness, the women scream, *"Grazie, grazie, Maria,"* as St. Anthony is carried through the fields. The monks gesticulate. . . .

As we drove through this same landscape with Mariano, he explained that the pizza we know is a de-luxe creation compared to the pizza the peasants make of polenta. Barbara found her voice and said, "The best pizza I've ever had was at the San Marino in New York." Mariano nodded politely.

The first impression of Positano is peculiar. One arrives on top of it and sees it below, in a semicircle. Mariano said that wherever you went in this town you had to go up or down, and the first days in Positano you had acute pain in your legs. He called on a friend who was not at home, but a neighbor said, "Just use your shoulder and the door will open." It was a fixed-up peasant house. The interiors of these houses are delightful, but the beds are awful. They consist of a frame of chicken wire resting on four wooden blocks, and if you sit down carelessly the whole thing collapses beneath you. You sleep in it motionless, with hands folded, like a corpse.

In this part of the country, except in a few select places, the

219

baths and washbasins are also of the most primitive kind. The inhabitants of Positano number about two thousand. Most of them live off fishing; some receive money from relatives who have gone to America; and the tourist season affords an income to others. In this city of stairs there is no weight that the citizen cannot carry on his head. Pianos, heavy trunks, and even the departed in their coffins are carried balanced on a man's head.

The houses are primitive—one large room with an open fireplace. Several have a sort of Turkish bath in the basement, sunk into the rocks, and it is assumed that these trace back to the Saracens. There is one palace in the town, the entrance to which is a remarkable gate flanked by columns decorated with the heads of Moors. During the Napoleonic wars, when one could reach Positano only by vessel, this house was the residence of Prince Murat.

Some sixty artists and writers, most of them of the garret type and as yet undiscovered, live in Positano. About two years ago a group of Americans bought several houses which they decorated and modernized. In the whole of Positano there is only one cow, and since nothing grows on the rocks, grass is carried down to it from the mountains. High in the mountains are two small villages that supply the town with vegetables, milk, butter, eggs, and charcoal. The peasants are obliged to climb up and down hundreds of steps a day, heavily loaded.

One is again and again astonished at the cleanliness of the streets and the houses. The combination bedroom-kitchen-living room shines, the clothes of the people are spotless, and one would never hesitate to sit at table with any of them.

All are filled with a passionate love of children that is returned with an adoration of the parents. When I saw parent talking to child it was always with the attention and intimacy of close friends exchanging important views. Mariano explained that although the people are friendly, one must have lived in Italy awhile—so that you bear yourself without the tourist's inquisitiveness and are at ease with them—before they let you come close. Even so, it takes time. They show at the beginning a certain subconscious contempt for the foreigner, since most of the visitors do not go to church, nor bother to hide excesses and irregularities.

The town's leading restaurant is a café called the Bocca di Bacco—the Cave of Bacchus—owned by the local priest and his five nephews. The latter wait on table, and one of them is a remarkable photographer.

To reach the beach from the restaurant, one passes the church and the statue of the miraculous Madonna which gave Positano its name. The legend says that in the time of the Saracens devout fishermen brought her from the south, and as they came to the bay on which the present Positano lies, the statue said suddenly, *"Posi, posi!"*—"Put me down, put me down!" The feast day of this particular Madonna—a large statue weighted down with jewelry—is the high point of the year. It is surprising that she doesn't ask the fishermen of Positano to take her away during the eight days of uninterrupted celebration, with trumpets blaring, constant explosions, drumming, shouting, and shooting all night long.

Positano fishermen who have emigrated to Brazil and Argentina send large sums of money to insure the greatest possible glory for this feast. The last evening of the celebration all that

221

the church can contribute in glory and drama is displayed: prelates wrapped in clouds of incense; nuns leading children dressed as little monks and angels; also, half-naked little cupids, representing the god of love, marching along in the parade with six-year-old bishops in miters. The people are well-formed, and, in spite of the many stairs, the girls have slim legs. The young men pelt the procession with flowers. Rugs hang out of windows, and everything is decorated with the most elaborate artificial flowers.

Black-haired adoring men smile at their girls in recognition; even the prelates and nuns are gay. Everyone wanders happily about, laughing, talking—and then suddenly someone starts a prayer or a hymn. Although hands are folded and voices are raised in holy song, the eyes still rove, and there is always an answering smile through the rain of flowers as the throng wanders, singing, down the steps to the decorated fishing boats. Immediately after the church music a trumpeter starts an aria from *Aïda,* and the orchestra follows his cue. By now the celebration seems to have nothing whatever to do with religion, although there is a good deal of drinking at the Bocca di Bacco in honor of the Madonna, and hours later a torchlight procession is organized again to take her back up to her church. At the stands that sell pizza and wine every boy finds his girl.

It is most remarkable that in all this gaiety, day or night, you will never find grossness. If you see someone staggering, it is usually a foreigner; the Italians retain their grace. The most simple fishermen and peasants move with the ease of dancers. They never get rough or accost one another. They drink the cheapest raw wine, and it only makes them happy.

After the Madonna is put back into the church, with her gown covered with paper money the people have pinned to it, life continues in the Bocca di Bacco, where all Positano meets. Here is the mayor, son of an aristocratic Neapolitan family— able, friendly, and only twenty-eight years old. Here is the poorest fisherman, and here are tourists. The wealthy mingle with a ragged painter who lacks the money to buy paint but has enough to nurse a glass of Lachryma Christi.

The view from the restaurant includes three large rocks that lie in the water offshore and are called The Cocks. Here is the story of how they got there:

Once upon a time there was a ruler who wanted a castle in a hurry. He found a sorcerer who promised to do the job in three days. The sorcerer was a gourmet and fond of roosters, and as his price he asked the duke for all the roosters in Positano. Upon the order of the duke, all the roosters were requisitioned, slaughtered, and sent to the sorcerer—all, that is, except one. It belonged to the daughter of a fisherman and, since she loved it dearly, she hid it in her bed. In the dawn, the workingmen of the sorcerer came flying through the air, carrying large rocks for the foundation of the castle, and, with the first ray of the sun, the hidden rooster crowed. Whereupon the sorcerer declared the contract broken, and the workingmen dropped the rocks into the sea. And that is how Gli Galli were created.

The end of the celebration is again a scene from an opera. The last one to leave the Cave of Bacchus is a talented young painter, crippled from the waist down, who is carried home by the son of the local gravedigger.

—

THE MOST beautiful hours in this stretch of land are toward evening when the sun rolls down beyond the horizon. It sets the sky aglow and makes liquid fire of the sea. We started at such a time to climb the stairway-like road. Barbara was soon a hundred steps below, and Little Bit labored upward behind her. They rested every twenty steps. When we came to the restaurant at the top, sky and sea were purple and indigo, and out over the waters lay a thin red line. The restaurant seemed to hang in the sky.

The place was crowded. Mariano picked a large table on the cliffside at which a young couple sat. The man was a young American who had let his dark hair grow to the length of Italian fashion. He talked with his hands, moving them as if he were

examining an imaginary vessel of extreme delicacy. Mariano leaned over to me and whispered, "Diplomatic Corps, Rome."

The young man's companion was of the most beautiful and serious Italian type, too young for her getup, which was that of a Hollywood femme fatale. She was listening to him with rapt attention, her head inclined toward his. As I looked over the menu I heard them discussing the old question of whether American or European women were better off. I signaled to Barbara.

The young man said, "But our women have absolute equality in everything!"

The girl leaned back. With her eyes almost closed and with finality she said, "Who wants equality when you can have domination?"

"What will you have?" the waiter said.

Barbara, schooled by Charlie, ordered her own dinner, to the astonishment of the waiter and Mariano. The proprietor him-

self brought the wine. He must have heard that American tourists expect a certain protocol in the serving of wine, for with great ceremony he pulled from an oddly shaped bottle, that had no label, a naked cork — which I'm sure had been inserted in the kitchen especially for us. He went through the ritual of smelling the cork and pouring me the first glass of potent, "laugh of the stomach" vintage.

It was getting dark, the wind brushed over the sea, and it was like sitting on the prow of a ship silently sailing into the Mediterranean night. Sweet, heavily perfumed air floated the body as well as the mind. The wine was easy to drink. A robust woman carried in a large platter of rice with chicken, olives, mussels, and tomatoes; from below came the laughter of the people of Positano, and then the ringing of the church bell.

The couple we sat with had refused wine; instead, they

sipped the local mineral water and looked completely happy. The young man was again molding his invisible vessel as he talked about Italy and his love for the land and the people. Later he introduced himself as a Philadelphian. The girl called him Tom.

Several feet away from us a group of young Italians, all handsome and elegant, surrounded a round metal table. They were gay, and after a while there were as many bottles as people at the table.

The abstemious diplomat at my right asked Mariano something about population and matters political, and then the couple were served a fish so beautiful that it should have been in an aquarium rather than on a platter. The two ate silently, washing the fish down with bubbling water—a hard thing to watch. When the entrée was gone they ate artichokes and then had some tea, which, in this area, is abominable. The man sipped his tea from the end of a hollow-shafted spoon, his Adam's apple traveling up and down with each swallow. At last he put down the spoon. For a while he looked as if he were worried, but finally he seemed to find the words for what he wanted to say. I thought it would be about love, and it was.

"Teresa," he started hesitantly, and then began his molding again. With determination, as if he were composing an editorial, he continued, "The Italians are the most misunderstood people in the world. The Italians are not lazy, they are not liars, they are not cowards and thieves—and I'm going to say that over and over again until people will believe it."

"Thank you, thank you," said an Italian who had sat down with us. At the round table there seemed to be a commotion. All the young elegants looked our way and then stuck their hands together and talked excitedly.

The conversation at our table changed to other themes. The patrons of the round table left the terrace and the bottles were cleared away. We paid and, together with the American and the girl, started the descent, passing from housetop to housetop, until, suddenly, under a street lamp, we saw the group which had sat at the round table.

One of the young men, in a state of maniac elation, detached himself from the rest. With eyes glaring and face flushed, he ran over to the American, slapped his face, and challenged him to a duel. The American stood there frozen, looking the way one would when unexpectedly slapped in the face. By the time anyone realized what had happened, the young man had turned and disappeared with his group. It was like a scene in a play.

I heard later that the next morning the formalities were carried further, in Positano; the challenge was properly presented, with seconds going from one hotel to the other.

The explanation for the incident is simple. The soft, warm wind had miscarried the word *not*. All the Romans at the round table were sure they had heard the American say, "The Italians are lazy, they are liars, they are cowards and thieves—and I'm going to say that over and over again until people will believe it."

"This is very serious," the girl said the next day. "The young man is of the Roman aristocracy; he has challenged you. If you do not accept the challenge your situation in Rome will be impossible, for everyone will scorn you. Also, the Roman would be doubly insulted if we gave him the true explanation—he'd think you a coward. What is there to do?"

In the end the American composed a letter which may well serve as a model in such difficult cases. This is how it went:

My dear Prince_____:

Last night you slapped my face. You were somewhat under the influence of alcohol, and I was too astonished at the time to react. I presume that the slap was part of the procedure of challenging me to a duel.

I am an American, and since dueling has been out of fashion in my country for many years, my lack of proper training prevents my accepting your challenge. I suggest, however, two ways of settling this matter. First, I shall give a small dinner at the restaurant where we ate last night, and I herewith invite you to attend. When you reach the state of intoxication of last night, I shall return your slap and explain the matter to you, and after that I hope we shall shake hands.

If this suggestion is distasteful, then I offer an alternative. I shall go into the street and look for you, and when I find you, I will do my best to beat the hell out of you.

I hope you will accept for dinner, at about eight. Bring anyone you like.

Sincerely,

W_____ C_____

There was a great deal of speculation all day, but around seven the prince climbed the steep road upward. As he entered the restaurant, the American walked toward him and extended his hand. The prince grasped it.

Barbara and I, strolling in the garden of our hotel, came upon the young American. I said, "How clever of you to have solved the problem so well!"

"Oh, it wasn't my idea. I was completely paralyzed. I couldn't think of a thing to do but get shot. It was Teresa's. 'Write this,' she said, and dictated it. I translated it into English. I'm going to marry her next month," he said, smiling happily.

Barbara also smiled, the way the cat that walked over the Chianti bottles had smiled.

Later Mariano and I discussed the incident of the duel over another load of spaghetti.

"Ah, I am glad," he said. "It seldom ends so pleasantly. Usually it is hopeless." He shivered and drew around himself the "Proletariat of the World, Unite." "The Americans are changing everything in this world," he said with a little sadness in his voice. "It used to be that one had to get up early in the morning and go outside Rome and stand there in the fog in a top hat. Now it's all done with a punch in the nose."

He waved at an acquaintance, who came over and joined us.

"What are you talking about?" asked the man.

"We are discussing the impact of things American—morals, manners, food, and inventions—upon Europe. We were speaking about a duel by punch in the nose instead of saber or pistol."

The other man was a Roman, as was Mariano. He resembled the saints as painted by El Greco, and had that same wooden ecstasy and clay coloration. He said in a precise professorial diction that he also liked American things—that is, most of them, and that the duel reminded him of another American invention—one that had almost been adopted in Rome—the gossipist.

He looked at me. "We have here in Italy," he said, "the cult of the family, signore." He turned from me to Mariano, who confirmed this. "That does not mean that there exists no gossip, or that this gossip is without foundation." He stopped to underline his words and continued his lecture while moving his right arm like the pendulum of a metronome. "It means that gossip is one thing and the cult of the family is another."

Mariano nodded, and the other ticked on, "It never, never, never appears in the papers. Am I right?"

"Right."

"Now there was in Rome a Sicilian of questionable birth — and badly put together too, with a face like a rodent sniffing among ordure. Am I right, Mariano? Ah, he was not exactly the Apollo Belvedere. A little frightened man at first, and working hard and honestly, he was of so mediocre talent that the editor assigned him to go and take down the names of people who arrived and left Rome. He had no hat, his trousers were held up with string — no?"

"I did not know him then," said the kind Mariano.

"*Ecco*, this specimen of a journalist was also an admirer of things American, and since he had to go to hotels to get the names of people who had checked in and out, he had access to the reading rooms, and he found there American publications, among which were some that publish these gossipists. And he read in his own paper that one of them had just arrived in Rome and had been received like a king. This big gossipist was granted an audience by the Holy Father, he lunched with de Gasperi, he was even invited to the homes of some prominent Roman families. Our little ratscribbler, his eyes bulging in beady excitement, followed him everywhere. He became a disciple. He interviewed the great man — who occupied the royal suite of the Excelsior, free, in return for mentioning that the service there was superb — and after that his admiration for things American was without bounds.

"He wrote a profile of this *canaglia* from overseas, which won him the admiration of the American *canaglia,* and the American went with him to persuade the aging editor of the Roman paper to allow that *mascalzone* to write a gossip column. Out of the drab cocoon fluttered a full-fledged gossipist, and, I am sad to say, his column was an immediate and wild success. It was entertaining, at first, and nobody minded much.

"The little rat became a person to be reckoned with. He who had had to content himself with the affections of the dirty girls of Trastavere moved to the Via Veneto, to lodgings close to the Excelsior Hotel. He appeared in a new tie, and then in complete wardrobes designed by the best tailors. Paracini made his shoes. He changed his friends and acquired a mistress, for whom he bought a ring at Bulgari's. It went all the way up to an Alfa Romeo. True, no?"

"Yes, true."

"His bombastic ego knew no limit. He was so in the clouds that one thought he'd break his undercarriage as he descended the stairs to the Piazza di Spagna. He was seen everywhere. The rooftop restaurant of the Hotel Hassler, the wintergarden of the Excelsior, and the elite night clubs of Rome became his confessionals. He went to Capri, to the Riviera, to Paris. He had two secretaries and a dictating machine.

"He developed a complex which was a mixture of *folie de grandeur* and a feeling that people feared him. He entered a room or a restaurant with an ominous air, pausing in the doorway to decide whether or not to go in. Once seated, he examined the audience carefully, and, like a detective in an American movie, his eyes went from one face to the other, as if choosing whom to arrest. Here and there he would briefly honor a table with his presence, always sitting sidesaddle, and scribbling continuously in a little notebook which he shielded by placing his left forearm in front of it on the table.

"He wrote unashamedly of things most private and scandalous, and between these intimate revelations he sandwiched the *folie de grandeur* explosions of his mind—politicking as well as gossiping, suggesting to the government policy in matters most grave, casting doubt upon the integrity and ability of people in high official positions. When he ran out of provocative items and when gossip was slow, he put his wretched memory to work and served up old scandals. He attached phenomenal importance to his scribbling, and so, unfortunately, did a great many other people. Some were really afraid of him. No?"

"Yes."

"One day he published something that caused great unhappiness between two families. I do not say that what he wrote was untrue. But had it been left private, time, the intervention of relatives, the children—many circumstances might have come to the help of the unfortunate couple. As it was, when the affair became public through the meddling of this *canaglia* the scandal rang from all the bell towers of Rome. The complexion of the whole matter changed. Something had to be done. The result was a challenge to a duel, unhappiness in two families, a suicide, two ruined marriages, and misery for six children—four in the family of the guilty woman and two in that of her lover.

"This *vero mascalzone* walked about looking darkly, like the Three Fates, and he did all their work—he spun, he measured, he cut off the thread of destiny. People were really worried. It was decided that this could not go on.

"It was hard to get at him. He moved very carefully, as a little rat will, but he was too vain to refuse invitations from persons of prominence, and so, when he was asked to an important dinner, at a large house, he graciously accepted. He came in tails. After dinner the ladies went to the salon to gossip; the men retired to the library for coffee, and in a quiet little room adjoining it the gossipist was given a beating that he will remember all his life. He tried to escape; he fought and scratched and bit and kicked his way to a window, forgetting that it was high above a courtyard of stone, and he jumped and fell from the balcony and broke his legs, and some bones in his right hand. He spent six months in the hospital, and as a result we have no more gossipists.

"Now he's back with his old friends, there are no more free meals, and his clothes are wearing down to the texture of those he wore before he became famous. He walks on worn heels. He sees the ground again. One notices him talking to himself and making gestures in the street. In a little *trattoria*—you must go past the Pantheon to get to it—he eats fettucini and spaghetti with quiet devotion and gulps down tumblers of cheap wine. After that he is in a trance, sucking on a toothpick while he dreams of the glories of the past. He has to work hard, pecking a living off his typewriter with his one-finger talent. He reports without comment the arrival and departure of people that no one has ever heard of. *Sic transit gloria mundi.*"

"Alas," said Mariano, "I do not think it's right to send a poor fellow to the hospital. I suppose the best thing would be if people lived properly and truly observed the cult of the family and of honor. Then there would be no need or chance for anyone to write anything that would cause tears or suicide."

"Ah yes. I must go home now," said our friend, and he took off his hat and bowed and turned.

"You must excuse him," said Mariano. "It concerned a second cousin of his—that is why he is so vehement. But it is exactly as he told it."

"What was that word he used for 'rat'?" I asked.

"*Topo grande*—a big mouse. A mouse is a *topo*. Mickey Mouse is Topolino, and so is the smallest car made in Italy, the little Fiat. *Topolino* means a young mouse. As for the breed of professional gossipers, that is not an American invention. Remember what Suetonius wrote about Caesar? And in the sixteenth century we had the *Ragionamenti* of Pietro Aretino. He was a blackmailer who lived off the fat and the fear of the nobles. He tacked scurrilous notes on columns in the city. The only difference is that the slander of the ancient *canaglie* has become classic literature and is very readable today."

13.

Vesuviana

"DO YOU WANT to come and see Vesuvio?" I asked Barbara
the next morning.

"No," she said, "especially if you're going to wear those awful
yellow shoes."

I continued to lace my most comfortable pair of footwear.
Mariano came, and he said that sightseeing was much too
exhausting for children, and especially hard on a little dog. He
had brought with him a niece who was studying medicine at the
university of Naples. She was a modern American-type girl,
and there was an immediate understanding between her and

Barbara. In a few moments they were sitting together on the terrace, discussing subjects of social, economic, and world importance. Our departure was barely noticed.

On the way down the elevator got stuck. The operator, a short stocky boy, had the habit of turning around after it started and scrutinizing the occupants. With us in the stuck elevator was a robust Hungarian woman wearing a low-cut, clinging silk dress. The elevator boy leaned back in his corner and stared at the orchids and the décolletage.

Mariano suddenly exploded. Crumpling his gray fedora, looking hard at the boy, and in that anguished tone that distraught parents use with children, he said in Italian, "Will you take your eyes off this lady?"

The boy blushed. He looked up at the ceiling and, from there, always avoiding the woman, down to the floor. He had trouble making his eyes travel around the corsage, until Mariano said kindly, and like a father, "Why don't you turn around, little one?"

The boy did so, and remained in that position until ten minutes later, when the current was on and the elevator worked again.

While we were waiting for the car Mariano noticed my shoes, and he said with true Italian politeness, "What a sensible pair of shoes to visit a volcano!"

I had kept these shoes in the back of a closet in New York for years; they were old but never worn. They were made for me by a Swiss cobbler. They are as formless as a newborn pup and of a mean shade of egg yellow that has refused to change for the better, although they have been polished many times. Over the years, as I have smeared dark cream on them, the right one has

turned the shade of a ripe persimmon, the other a screaming red like a Chinese lacquer. Even exposing them to the elements did not improve them, but they were too expensive to throw away.

"In Italy you can wear them and nobody will pay any attention," a much-traveled friend had told me, so I packed them. And then I found to my regret that Italians are very particular about their boots, insisting that they fit like gloves and be of simple design. These multicolored clodhoppers were made especially for walking in the high mountains, with soles as thick as a club sandwich and iron caps at the heels and tips of the soles. All things work out eventually, and before the day was over I was glad that I had ordered them from Mr. Molnar, *Schuhmachermeister*, 22 See-Strasse, Zurich. Their day had come.

In the car on the *autostrade* that leads to Portici, Torre del Greco, and Resina, I shifted position and crossed my legs. The left shoe came up like a spotlight, and my polite companion asked with feigned interest where one could have such a pair of shoes made. After we had discussed the history of them, and of shoes in general, he ended his observations by saying that while they would be very good on Vesuvio, their great value would become apparent to me when climbing Etna or Stromboli. "Vesuvio," said Mariano, "is a promenade compared to the others.

"For the volcano ahead of us," he went on, "we do not have the absolute respect that the Japanese have for Fujiyama; nevertheless, we have an affection for Vesuvio in spite of all the troubles it has caused."

The funicular, built in the 1880s, goes to within about a thousand feet of the summit. The famous song "Funiculi! Funicula!" was written about it.

As you ascend Vesuvio, the window of the funicular frames the most carefully worked out designs for Paradise on earth. All the shades of green are here, beginning with the deepest bottle color of palms that stand in shaded spots, progressing to the lighter greens of the foliage of fig, lemon, orange, peach, and apricot trees, to olive orchards, chestnut forests, and finally to the pallor of the frail leaves and platinum-blond blossoms of the mimosa. The largest fields of light green are those terraced vineyards which produce some of the best wines of Italy. Representative of the region is a white wine called Soma, the Surrentine wine favored by Tiberius, and a strong wine called Lachryma Christi. This stretch of earth is so fertile that it reminds one of the tropics. The demon Vesuvio, between his outbursts, is a lavish giver. He has covered himself with rich soil and fertilized the land with his volcanic ashes. Here, heaven is below and hell above.

No matter how often you see it, the color of the sea far below delights you; the white hulls of the Capri ships lie on it like billiard balls on green cloth. The houses, painted in pastel

colors, would disturb the picture in other latitudes, but here they are proper.

The funicular wobbled over a hump, the clattering of the cog wheels slowed down, and in a pleasant station the trip came to an end.

In contrast to the pink and fat conductor of the funicular was the guide we encountered there. My companion, who loves comfort and came on this trip reluctantly, said, "Look at him! He is at his ease in his role as the devil in the Inferno." The observation was apt, for the man could have played a role in Hades. He was sharp of face, his skin mottled and umber-colored; he wore an American battle jacket and had emerald-green eyes. There were about five other guides in sight, and a sign saying it was unlawful to ascend without a guide. The fellow who approached us, however, acted as if he were the sole custodian of the volcano and attached himself to Mariano and me. In back of him was the observatory, and it was the precise color of my right shoe.

The guide started out with us, carrying the overcoats and camera, and we walked for about fifteen minutes in silence. There was some vegetation—a small pine here, there a yellow broomflower called *ginestre*, a tough kind of grass; a goat was tethered wherever patches of it appeared.

The volcano itself loses its shape as you get closer to it. It is a melancholy scene, and in a little while the muscles at the back of your leg let you know that you are climbing.

"Don't ever speak badly of the Swiss again," said Mariano, and he looked for a rock to sit on, because his feet had begun to hurt. There were now rocks all about, of approximately the same size—huge cannon balls with soft surfaces—the ammunition of the volcano.

The guide noticed my shoes and expressed admiration for them. Silently I apologized to their maker, for they felt like slippers now. It is a curious thing that in the mountains heavy shoes are lighter to walk in than light ones; these held the foot firmly and gave me a solid stance, which was very important, for not having to worry much about what I stepped on, I could pay attention to the landscape. There were frequent stops now, to catch the breath, and the panorama extended itself more and more. As you turn from the road you find the scene swimming in a violet haze. The vegetation below has moved together into one all-over velvety green mantle. There is no sound, no rumbling, no hissing—there is only a soft swish of wind; and this carries to you alternately the scent of lemon and orange blossoms and of roses, and, at a shift of the wind, the smell of hell: sulphur oozes up out of cracks and you enter a lunar landscape. You are truly in the domain of Faust. It is worth all the trouble to come here and let this scene surround you. It is grim. On your left is a river as wide as the Hudson at Albany, but it is frozen; its color is indigo, and it drapes itself in astonishing serpentines from high above you down to the right of the observatory. From a distance, the stuff of which it is made looks like burned fat, and you think that when you touch it, it will crumble like old piecrust. But you find it to be as hard as glass.

This is where the real climb began, and here stood a man, all alone in this wilderness, who had the concession of renting sticks to visitors. The sticks were long, of peeled wood, and extremely good to walk with. Now came the trouble of climbing. The guide went ahead, carrying our coats, and soon our sweaters too. Often we asked him, "How much longer?" And on we went, following him, staggering along, placing one foot ahead of the other, for the path was narrow and consisted entirely of slag. I was in reasonable comfort, but Mariano was in misery.

I am used to skiing on dangerous terrain and never experience any vertigo, but the cone of Vesuvio is a frightening place to be, and gives you the sensation of walking on the edge of the Empire State Building. There is nothing to keep you from falling in; stone and ashes roll down the outside and the inside of the crater as you walk—or rather, crawl—along it.

You can look down into the crater, but there is no fire or boiling mass of lava visible. Nothing moves except the vapors that rise from both the inside and the outside of the crater. The crater itself, like all immense surfaces that are of one kind of material, changes suddenly with the light that plays on it. One moment it is as static and stony as a moist dungeon; the next, it shimmers, as the sunlight passes through a thin cloud, like the milky glass snowballs that are hung on Christmas trees. Direct afternoon sunlight molds it, and then it looks like a herd of elephants imprisoned in mud. It is indigo where the shadows stay, and at the edges of crevasses are strips of yellow light. While we were watching this a cold wind came, and I had the sensation of flying. As fast as clouds tear past the windows of an airliner, shreds of vapor rose and were twisted into spirals and torn away; at times the crater disappeared from view altogether. As the fog closed in, the guide warned us not to go out of his sight.

He lit matches, held them close to the ground, and they produced a large yellow flame that fed on natural gas in the atmosphere. Then, for a moment, he left us sitting at the edge of the crater and leaped agilely away through the fog. He returned with a stone, carrying it in a thickly folded newspaper. It was burning through the paper when he reached us.

The guide, probably in an effort to scare us, said that about a dozen Americans who refused guides had fallen into the crater. They had been trying to take pictures and lost their footing. He also told a remarkable story of an Italian who had tried to save the cost of a guide and almost perished. The fellow was a shoemaker's apprentice of Sorrento. He climbed to the crater alone. Emptied by the last eruption, it looked reasonably peaceful, and the shoemaker, finding it dull, amused himself by tossing rocks into the mouth of the crater. Heaving a particularly large one, he lost his balance, began to slide, and miraculously caught himself on a small ledge formed by hardened lava. There, hanging over the inner rim, he remained for two days until a guide who came up with a tourist heard his cries. The guide went for help, and with the aid of ropes the cobbler was rescued. He was stupefied by the fumes and also in a state of shock, but after a week's hospitalization he returned to Sorrento and was famous from then on. "The moral," said the guide, "is never to go anywhere in Italy without a guide." When he had finished the story I was very glad he was there to lead us away from the crater, perhaps to a good restaurant. We stumbled downward in the sulphuric, soupy mist.

As long as volcanoes cook their stone, growling with a bad-tempered rattling of pots and pans — but controlled — they are a safety valve for the fiery core of the planet. And, it has been said, some of them are connected with one another beneath the earth's surface.

There are some useful products of volcanoes too: The mudstreams that flow from them harden to form a precious building material. The ashes, which are fired into the air for miles and, like the atomic cloud, assume the shape of a mushroom, return to earth as one of the best fertilizers known. Volcanic bombs, called *lapilli*, are the slag of brimstone. The product of the highest volcanic activity is lava. A glowing stream of molten stone, it spills over the crater, and only twenty years after it hardens it covers itself with a thin layer of greenery, which in time becomes the most luxuriant vegetation.

The explosions of a volcano are of a periodic nature, like the tempers of a madman. After it has let off steam, it rests and seems in accord with the world. It is exhausted, the fires are low, and sometimes they go out altogether. In time the crater fills with water, forming a lake that may be of exceptional beauty. The richness of the land attracts people, and whole villages such as we see at the foot of Vesuvio are built from its lava. Suddenly the fire mountain shakes again. In the diary of Vesuvio—since man has kept track of it—there have been about seventy eruptions. At one time, from 1500 on for a hundred and thirty-one years, the mountain was so still that trees and bushes covered it and cattle grazed in the crater. In 1631 it exploded again, killing over three thousand people and destroying the surrounding villages with ashes, fire, falling *lapilli*, and seven streams of lava.

In the early part of the twentieth century Vesuvio again produced a tremendous spectacle—a flow of lava that lasted eleven months. It shook the ground and blasted a cloud of ashes thirty-three thousand feet high. By the end of April 1906 the show stopped as suddenly as it had begun.

If the ascent to the crater is tiring, coming down is more so; your knees get weak, and at every step you sink ankle-deep into the slag. Soon we reached the place where we had rented the walking sticks, and, turning them in, we walked easier now, back to the broomflowers, the goats, and the pines.

"Where do we eat?" asked Mariano with some enthusiasm.

Close to one station of the funicular is the Hotel Eremo, belonging to Thomas Cook and Son. It is at a height of 1995 feet, and the prospectus says that it has hot and cold water, fourteen rooms, and a magnificent view. Unfortunately it was closed. But the observatory was open, and the general hellish air that hangs about Vesuvio is present in compact form inside the building.

It is the counting house of disaster. The walls are decorated with pictures of eruptions and photographs of exceptional fire bombs and the various directors of the observatory. On the desk of the present director, Professor Imbo, stands an ashtray made of lava. In the vast recesses are various seismographs in glass cases, recording the mood of the volcano. I asked the young man who showed us through this building if the mountain showed any signs of agitation, and he took us to one of the seismographs and showed us the record of the last week.

The needle occasionally had marked periodic tremblings. "Nothing serious. This is the professor coming downstairs, in the morning," said the young man, pointing at a small disturbance. And then, pointing at others, he said, "This is the funicular arriving and departing; this was a motorcar; and this is you and your friend." At the right side of the band, which is about the size of a sling in which one might cradle a broken arm, was a more violent writing, swinging from left to right. "That," said the young man, "is something far away. Might be an earthquake in Japan or California, but something minor; we won't read about it in the newspapers." The rolls of paper used to trace the activity of the volcano are covered with a film of carbon, and this is done in very simple fashion. Petroleum is poured into a tiny gutter attached to a handle, and then lit. The roll of paper slowly passes over it, picking up soot.

In the basement of the observatory is a room unique in the world: it's like a dungeon in an ancient castle. In the center of it, surrounded by a heavy banister of stone, is a circular platform that stands free and is so constructed that it is level at all times. In time of great activity, when the whole mountain shakes, a consecrated scientist can stand here and, with his instruments about him in the banister, measure the disturbance going on, the shaking of the very building in which he works. It's about as happy a place as the room which contains the electric chair.

The observatory stands on a spot that so far has been safe. Masses of lava have moved past its door, down into the fields, the gardens and the villages, setting fire to everything on the way. The lava flows on until, inexplicably, as if some authority out of pure caprice suddenly gave the order to stop, it halts. "It is," said a native, "as if the chief of a gang of bandits suddenly gave the command to stop plundering, burning, and killing, and to fall back into order and form ranks—that's how suddenly the flow of lava stops."

Most of the natives, however, don't mention bandits in connection with Vesuvio. They see in it destruction—the evidence of the wrath of God—and ascribe the sudden stopping of the lava flow to the powerful intercession of the saints to whom they have prayed. The saints, however, are sometimes angered by the avarice of certain individuals. The story is told of a Neapolitan lawyer named Cavallero, who had built himself an estate on the slope of Vesuvio and spent a good bit of money making it a show place. He entrusted the property to the care of St. Januarius and over a period of time spent a good deal of money on celestial insurance. He built a beautiful chapel for the saint, placing it in the most probable path that a lava stream might take. He bought scented candles and, with his family and servants, frequently prayed there.

During the last (1944) eruption of Vesuvio, the lava stream headed toward the property of the lawyer. There was time to save the furniture and many other treasured possessions. Signor Cavallero's employees and neighbors begged him to act and offered to help, but he refused, explaining that it was the duty of the saint to look after the place. The lava did not stop; it ate up the chapel and rolled on toward the house. Signor Cavallero took the keys to his estate and, with a bitter curse, threw them into the hot liquid, as all his property was ruined.

In the middle of the month of August of the year 79 A.D., about six weeks after the coronation of the Emperor Titus, movements of the earth at Vesuvio were observed, but no one thought them dangerous. On the twentieth of August of that year sounds as of distant thunder were heard, and then these signs of upheaval were repeated—still no one thought of danger. It is recorded that the birds ceased to sing, cattle became uneasy and bellowed, and all the dogs tore at their chains and barked. The sea was in motion, but only the farmers began to look toward the sky, fearing hail. On the morning of August

twenty-fourth the sky was pale blue and cloudless, the sun shone, and it was unusually hot, even for August. Suddenly the earth heaved, and from Vesuvio came a deafening explosion. Day turned to night. Lightning struck, and frightened birds that had taken to the air began to fall in a cross fire of burning *lapilli*. Thus began the destruction of Pompeii.

It is told that when Sam Goldwyn gazed upon the ruins of Pompeii he turned to a companion and said, "See what happens when people start something and haven't got the money to finish!"

All the sayings attributed to Mr. Goldwyn are zestful and apt; so is this one. Pompeii has the air of a classical subdivision gone bankrupt and abandoned. When one sees it, the image of grandeur one has had of it is dissolved completely. A homey spirit still lives there. It is very small and sympathetic; it is as if

250

High Tor had spewed lava on a friendly little town like Nyack, N.Y., or as if Newcastle, Delaware, had suffered an earthquake. Even the most elegant houses in Pompeii are comparatively small, the size of modern American homes. The arangements of rooms are intelligent, the streets are narrow, and the only place of real space is the arena. On almost every street corner stand the remains of a bar.

On entering Pompeii, the tourist is assaulted by a battalion of guides—not compulsory here. They speak almost every language badly, and the easiest way out is to engage one. The

visitor understands Pompeii immediately: it is logical and simple down to its leaden plumbing, gardens, glassware, and cooking utensils. Large blocks of stones were placed at street intersections, so that people could cross without getting their sandaled feet wet, either in rainwater or the refuse usually there. I always regret, when visiting Roman ruins, that we have nothing to match their beautiful baths.

The most interesting part of the ruins were, to me, a set of plastercastlike figures of extreme simplicity of line. They are people who were caught in the disaster and calcified. The suddenness of their dying froze the expressions on their faces. They gasp and reach, twist in agony with mouths open; a mother holds a baby; a couple embrace each other. The forms are fluid, as articulate as the best in modern sculpture. In one group is a little dog about the size of a fox terrier. He appears so lifelike that you wait for him to shift his position, scratch himself, or get up and run away. Since Pompeii is small, the visit is not tiresome; it is a promenade among the ruins.

Every Italian immediately informs you that the citizens of Pompeii were vulgarians, drunks, and libertines, and that the nobler people were buried in Herculaneum, a city that lies buried under the houses of Resina.

In Ecuador once, in the jungle, I ate in a restaurant with only one table. The tablecloth apparently had served for many other meals, and on it were red stains of the specialty of the house, a soup, and also egg stains. After I had chased the flies away the soup was served, and with it a greasy pewter spoon. As I wiped the spoon clean another customer, who sat opposite me, and who was on his first trip in these regions, asked the owner of the establishment if the soup was clean. The restaurateur was offended and said brusquely, "Certainly. A man has cooked it." In a restaurant outside the ruins of Pompeii that same kind of soup was served us on that same kind of tablecloth.

After the soup we had spaghetti, and I have never eaten better—although I had had wonderful spaghetti the day before. This happened to me again and again. Just as the music fits the landscape here, so does the spaghetti fit the stomach. *Spaghetti Inside* would be a good title for a travel book on Italy. You find the hard dry wine of Soma good also, and you don't particularly mind the spots on the tablecloth; you are becoming Italian.

A boy came and offered to shine our shoes. A car filled with American tourists arrived. A man in the garden started to sing "Funiculi, Funicula." And the whole scene—from the ruins of Pompeii to the table of this restaurant—was dominated by the cone of Vesuvio, which, on a sunny afternoon like this one, is the most delicate shade of lilac.

Mariano drowsily observed my shoes as the boy polished them. Presently he said, "Please write down for me the address of that Swiss bootmaker. My feet are on fire."

BARBARA WAS in bed, but awake, when I got back to the hotel in Naples.

"How did you and the Italian girl get on?" I asked.

"Fine. We studied for a while and then listened to the radio."

I went over to the window to have another look at Vesuvio. It seemed smooth and peaceful from below. Then I unlaced the comfortable shoes and went to bed.

"Poppy," Barbara called, "that cat with the mice in Ischia— you remember—what can anybody do about a thing like that?"

"I'm afraid you can't do anything."

"Did you ever save an animal?"

"Yes, I saved a donkey once."

"How?"

"I bought him."

"Then why didn't you buy the cat and the mice?"

"Because it wouldn't accomplish anything. The man would just go out and get another cat and other mice. You'd have to shoot the man to stop it."

"What about the donkey?"

"That didn't accomplish anything either. I was riding up a steep hill in San Pedro del Tingo, in Ecuador, and came upon a donkey, not much bigger than a dog, loaded down with two sacks of wheat between which sat the owner. My horse was strong, and I offered to carry the sacks. The halfbreed told me to mind my own business and proceeded to beat his animal with a heavy stick, to make it go faster. The poor donkey was covered with mange, there was barely any hair on its tail, and its ankles were swollen. I kept yelling at the man, and finally he got off and kicked the donkey with his boot and ran off into the fields. I jumped my horse over the fence and chased after him. When I caught up with him, he fell on his knees and swore with folded, upraised hands that never, never would the donkey be abused again. I rode away, feeling awful.

"As I took my usual walk around Tingo after the evening meal I passed some huts and heard a strange sound, like the oranges falling in Mariano's garden. I traced it to a kind of shed. Inside was that same halfbreed. He had tied the donkey to a cross beam and was hitting it systematically with a club. When he saw me he stopped. I bargained with him for the donkey,

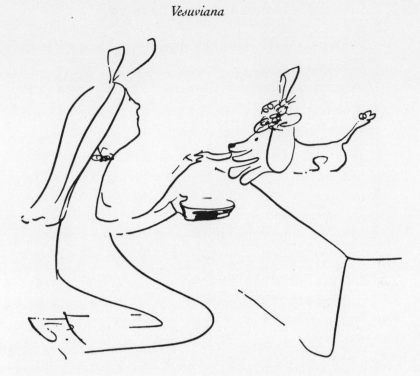

handed over the money, and took the animal away. I forgot to tell you—the man who had lent me the horse had also sent a sergeant as escort, and I asked this sergeant to shoot the donkey. Afterward he said, 'It accomplished nothing. He will get another donkey and beat it to death. To put a stop to it you should shoot the man.'"

"Is that all one can do, Poppy—shoot the donkey or the man?"

"No, I have to go back to my little piece—that in the sphere where I have responsibility—"

"I know. But outside of that, isn't there anything that can be done?"

"Well, one can attack the problem on an economic level."

"Buy all the animals?"

"No, buy good will, or touch the pocketbook where it hurts."

"You mean fines?"

"No, on the contrary. For example, a traveler or a society could insert small ads in the newspapers, or give coachmen a card on which is printed something like:

> Use the whip
> And the tourists won't tip.

That would make sense to him. And instead of arresting people, or threatening them, you could organize an annual beauty contest for the best-fed and best-cared-for animals. Say a Sicilian coachman won the first prize. His horse would get a golden ribbon to wear in its mane, or a disk with an inscription. Then the others would also try to win a prize. It would become fashionable to have a fine-looking horse. Fashion is next in importance to money in things like this."

"How about traps?"

"There too you would have to appeal to the pocket rather than to morality if you wanted to accomplish something."

"Give a prize to the trapper who didn't catch anything?"

"No. But build a better and much cheaper trap—one that might release a charge of painless, instant-killing vapor, harmless to the pelt. The awful tooth-edged traps that maim animals and lessen the value of the catch might go out of fashion."

"You don't think that appeal to man's better nature would help?"

"Here and there, yes. But people are what they are, and one cannot be the policeman of the whole world."

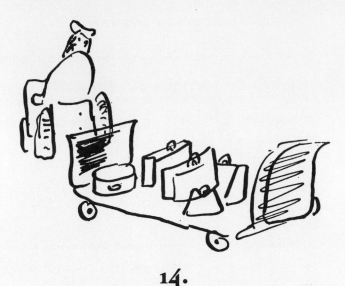

14.

I Always Travel
on Holidays —
A Christmas Story

OUR LAST night in Naples was disturbed by the shooting off of
fireworks and cannon, in honor of one of the most revered
saints in Italy. By early morning the citizenry was all out in
costume, celebrating. Bands played. Statues of saints wobbled
down the flower-strewn street, borne on the shoulders of the
faithful. Barbara and I and Little Bit went out to watch the fun.

The street was jammed. The section of the procession crawling toward us was made up of the Sons of San Rocco, led by a
man in a top hat and a pale blue satin shoulder sash. Behind him
marched the *carabinieri*. Then came the band, the clergy, and the

statue of San Rocco. The man in the lead carried a silver stick, like a drum major's, and just after he passed us he knocked on the ground with it. The procession came to a halt. He left his post, walked over to us, and doffed his top hat. "I know you're leaving today," he whispered, "and I got something important to tell you. It won't take a minute." We moved away from the line of spectators, and while the band played "There Is No Stain in Thee" he said in New York jargon, "Mister, if at any time you need anything in Italy, or if you're in any kind of trouble, or if Miss Barbara needs anything, or if there's a revolution or anything—you never can tell—well, Charlie wants you to know, you got a friend. All you got to do is get in touch with him."

"That's very nice," I said, "but I haven't done anything for Charlie."

"Well," he said, looking tenderly at Barbara, then at me, "your little girl introduced you to Charlie—and that means an awful lot to him. And you shook hands with him and had dinner at his table." The man had tears in his eyes and his voice was choked. "Things like that mean an awful lot to him. Charlie's a very lonesome and sentimental guy. Don't forget—anytime you need something, just call out. Good-by now." He moved quietly off through the crowd and rejoined the procession, which started up again at his signal. He looked back twice, waved his white-gloved hand, and smiled.

The lighthouse was dark for once, with sadness. She said, "Poppy, is it wrong to feel sorry for people like that?"

"If you need authority to feel sorry for anyone, you can go to religion, which commands forgiveness and love."

"Well, don't you?"

"I find it easier to feel sorry for those who don't live at the Excelsior, bathe in Capri, and drive in chauffeured Cadillacs to the races."

"Oh, but it's all right for your characters to sail on yachts with two chimneys to attend a ball in Venice! And what have they ever done to deserve it?"

"It's funnels, Barbara, on a yacht, not chimneys."

"Oh well. Poppy, what kind of saint is San Rocco?"

"He's the patron saint of dogs. Didn't you notice the statue of a dog next to his statue?"

"How come?"

"He lived in the woods, all alone, and a dog brought him food."

"Oh, incidentally, Poppy, Thoreau didn't live in Concord, New Hampshire, but in Concord, Massachusetts."

We continued our walk to the Excelsior in silence.

In the lobby sat a somber man — American — most probably the president of a vast corporation. He was dressed with immaculate severity, in an uncomfortable, too tight, double-breasted gray suit. He wore a tight collar. The very small knot of his tie was stuck halfway between the collar button and the upper rim of the collar. He had high black shoes, the laces tied, the shoes tightly closed, and the ends of the laces stuck inside the shoes. His scared secretary approached him as if he were a bomb about to go off. Several people with briefcases were seated around him. The hotel porter came and handed some tickets to the secretary.

The important man glanced up impatiently, for he had been disturbed. He asked for the tickets, and the secretary handed them to him. He nodded and then with a curious smile said to the men who sat around him, "Gentlemen, I make it a habit always to travel on holidays."

Someone translated this for the benefit of those who did not speak English, and they all nodded in agreement, as they would have to anything he said. "There's always room," he said. "Trains and planes are empty."

"Ah, yes, I never thought of that," said the others, looking at one another.

The porter came and handed us our plane tickets. We drove out and found the gentleman of the golden pince-nez and the tight collar already sitting in the almost empty Naples-Rome-Paris plane.

The plane took off. After we had stopped at Rome lunch was served. The stewardess handed out the trays and served the wine, and then she stopped at the seat of the important passenger. He seemed to be ill. She walked forward and returned with the captain, and such is the discipline of flying personnel that it was only the next day that we found out, reading the papers, that the man who was a very important executive had died on the plane.

We arrived at the Hôtel St. Julien le Pauvre in time for the flag-waving and the tinkling of the bell. This time our rooms were on the same floor as the old lady's, but across the court.

The valet said, "We'll get the mattress for you, monsieur, in just a moment. Don't lie down yet."

The lighthouse flashed immediately. "You're not going to let him take it away from her, Poppy, I hope?"

I asked the valet, and he said that the mattress was below, in the room of a young man, and the maid said, "Don't be upset about it. He's a Czech—one of the useless at the Parrot Cage."

The Parrot Cage is what the United Nations building in Paris is called by the French.

In a short while valet and maid returned with the good mattress from below. I wanted to send it in to the old lady, but it was no longer a gift. It looked as if a dozen people had been beaten to death on it. The condition of French hotel mattresses in all but the very best hotels should be referred to the ministries both of health and of tourism.

We had to go and get a health certificate for Little Bit, so that she could get back into the United States.

I can recommend to all who travel with dogs the services of Doctor Grobon, Lauréat de l'Académie Vétérinaire de France (three medals). He has an office off an inner courtyard. The waiting room is lined with photographs, most of them of dogs, and some of cats. The photographs are signed, "To the good Doctor Grobon, who has saved my life," and other such appreciative sentiments. They are signed "Azore," "Toto," "Tintin," "Minou," and other names. The charges are very reasonable, and Doctor Grobon gives free consultation to animals of people unable to pay. He examined Little Bit and wrote out a certificate of health, stating that the animal showed no symptoms of *le rage*.

I was very busy. I told Barbara to buy a few gifts to bring back to her mother and to friends. She returned from her shopping expedition with the following: a magenta suede leash, a dog collar adorned with golden fleur-de-lis, a corduroy and velvet coat of the latest canine fashion, with a pocket and handkerchief, a portable doghouse of wicker in the shape of a castle with four little towers, with windows on both sides and a

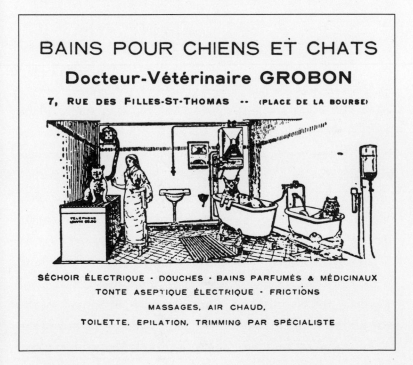

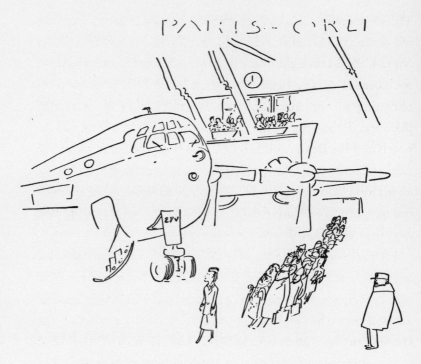

foam-rubber mattress with a satin cover—all this bought on the Rue St. Honoré, where no one gives anything away.

Just before we boarded the plane at Orly a telegram was handed to me, asking me to write a Christmas story for *Holiday* magazine. I put the wire in my pocket and gave Little Bit a sleeping pill. It worked so quickly that she missed the dinner aboard.

The dog slept soundly, but I was wide awake. I was thinking of the Christmas story, of Tyrol and the snow-laden trees, of Wendelin and the cows and horses that live in the inn, of the manger there, and the snow and the Christmas scenery and the Christmas mood, and the story of the deer with the binoculars.

Then I started to think of other things. I thought of Armand in the garden in Versailles, who told his little boy that there was no Santa Claus. I thought of the emptiness of the life of Patrizzi — the absence of any happiness when he had all the means of obtaining it, and his flight from place to place in search of pleasure. I thought of the disembodied people of the palace hotels and the Beau Monde ball, of the Italian columnist, and of Lucky Luciano in Capri and the remark the duke had made about him: "Crime pays — for the police at any rate." And then I thought of the executive dying on the plane, and how he had said that he traveled only on holidays.

I fell asleep after the stop in Iceland. By the time we arrived in New York, I thought I had the material for a Christmas story, and I sat down and wrote the first draft. I let Barbara read it, and she gave it her highest approval, which is not an outburst of enthusiasm but rather an absence of criticism.

When something seems what she calls "sharp," she retires to her room, where the work is read over the phone to the intimate circle of her friends. This was "really sharp" — she picked up *my* phone.

"Frances, listen to this," she said. "'I Always Travel on Holidays, A Christmas Story by Ludwig Bemelmans . . .'"

I quietly left.

IF ONE WERE to cast this story for pictures, the first actor that would come to mind would be Mr. Sullivan as he appeared on the screen in *Great Expectations*. Mr. Reallybig has that much weight, but then you'd worry about his accent, for Mr. Sullivan is definitely English, as they would say in Hollywood. And the mind and projection of Mr. Reallybig would be like that of some of the roles the late Dudley Digges played, or perhaps we'd better look at some pictures with Claude Rains, who has had experience in scenes played in the hereafter. But let us put the casting off and look at Mr. Reallybig as he himself is.

His face is the graph of a lifetime of fighting, of success. He never laughs, he never smiles, his mind is a weighty business machine that computes constantly and never errs. He brushed illusion aside when he was in his tough beginnings. His compensations are accomplishment, good food, good wine, and the company of his equals.

In his immense head the pale eyes are like tunnels; through them one cannot see into his mind or his heart. His voice is high

and issues from a wide mouth that is almost always open—not
to make talk, for his words are few. When one listens carefully
there is a faint trace of a foreign accent. He has the painful
breathing of the overweight and nervous; he walks slightly
stooped, and the doctors expect him to die of a heart attack.
Dieting might put it off, easing down might, but Mr. Reallybig
has his own therapy, his own views. He feasts, and then goes for
the cure to Montecatini or Vichy.

His interests are vast. They stretch from lead mines in Africa
to timber in the Canadian North. He is international and holds
two passports (it is better not to be a citizen of the country in
which you have your business; it makes things easier just to be a
resident).

Mr. Reallybig loves the feeling of owning things; as well as
does his mind, his hands know things: the feel and weight of
properties, of soil, and of the products of labor. The ticker
machine in his head is never at a standstill (think, think, think).
He visits his many plants and terrains regularly, and this is no
longer a matter of long voyages, for this story takes place about
ten years from now and the distances to all places on earth are
short—it is, in fact, more trouble to go from New York to
Philadelphia than to Africa or Paris; once you are aboard the
Superjet, these are as close as Brooklyn is by subway.

Mr. Reallybig lives in one of the last private houses on Fifth Avenue. (He is protected, in a real-estate sense, by owning the two adjoining houses.) His comfort is assured by a French cook, a Swiss butler, an English valet, and seven other domestics. At the time this story begins there is also a governess to watch over little Billy, his grandson.

Mostly Mr. Reallybig lives alone. He is disappointed in his children. His daughter married for love, his son became an artist, and the child of this son, a child of divorce, is sometimes left with the grandfather, the way one leaves a pup in a good kennel. Little Billy is a sad-eyed, quiet child; he seemed to be old when he was born, and the grandfather has much hope for him.

The house is furnished in the manner of a modern Medici — the most important antique dealers were given carte blanche. It is therefore carpeted, wainscoted, frescoed and gilded. Double doors keep noises out of a bedroom done in blue and gold. Mr. Reallybig sleeps in a bed that stood in one of the first châteaux of Navarre. Its four massive carved columns support a canopy heavy with a million stitches of tapestry. The headboard is crowded with a relief showing cavalry in combat; against this rest three large pillows (for Mr. Reallybig has asthma and sleeps most comfortably in an almost sitting-up position). At both sides of the bed are bellcords, again of most rare needlework, and further distinguished for having felt the pull of the hand of Napoleon I.

Mr. Reallybig does a great deal of work in bed during the night. He makes use of a dictating machine that is built into his night table and of a special reading light and a desk that hang like a bridge over his bed. On this table are always a bottle of water and a very fine glass, into which, lest he forget his identity, are cut his initials. Bottle and glass stand on a tray; then come papers, books, pads, pen and pencil, and so on. Here we see Mr. Reallybig for the first time. He is dictating something of importance. He has just returned from Europe aboard a plane of the line of which he is chairman. He reports his observations—he is at the part where he complains about the hostess. He had noticed that there was a degree of familiarity between this employee and the passengers, of which he did not approve. He wants the girl in question brought up short; he gives her name and number (detail, detail). Also he wants a general order on proper deportment issued immediately. After finishing this, Mr. Reallybig stops the machine and pours some water into his glass and drinks it. Then, with his mouth open, he leans back into his pillows and thinks of the day ahead.

It was one of the occasions on which little Billy had been left with him. It was Christmas time. In an hour or so his valet would run his bath, and then he would have breakfast, and after that he would take Billy to the park.

In the lobby of the well-managed house Mr. Reallybig lifted his arms and the butler maneuvered the fur-lined coat so that he could comfortably get into the sleeves of the garment. The butler handed him his hat and cane, the clock in the hall struck ten, and a door opened. Billy, washed, combed, dressed, and buttoned up properly, appeared. Miss Talmey gave him a clean handkerchief. Another door was opened (it was snowing outside), Billy took his grandfather's hand, they left the house and walked a few blocks, where they came to Mr. Flannelly, the policeman who directed traffic at Fifth and 65th. (Mr. Flannelly once subdued a crank who, with loaded revolver and long premeditated intent to kill, had gained access to the house of Mr. Reallybig. When Mr. Reallybig asked the cop what he wanted, he asked for two tickets to *La Tosca*. Mr. Reallybig, thinking his life worth something more than that, had sent him a season subscription for Wednesday nights, and renewed it every year. He had also given the cop's son a position in one of his enterprises.)

Mr. Flannelly's ears were lit up like red electric-light bulbs. He brushed the snow off his sleeve and sang out, "Merry Christmas!"

"A Merry Christmas to you," said the heavy man, and with careful sliding step crossed the avenue while Mr. Flannelly held up the traffic.

"Merry Christmas!" said Billy and gave his hand to the cop. "I like Mr. Flannelly very, very much," said little Billy.

"I have great confidence in Officer Flannelly," said the grandfather.

"The other day I had a rather long conversation with him," Billy continued. "It was in front of the zebra's enclosure, and I asked Mr. Flannelly if the zebra was a white horse with black stripes, or a black horse with white stripes."

"And what did he say?"

"He said it depended on how you looked at it."

"That's very clever," said Mr. Reallybig.

"Grandpa, why is Mr. Flannelly only a policeman and has to stand in the cold for hours?"

"Because we need a man we can trust near our house, and because many very important people live around here."

"I'm very glad he's there," said little Billy. "And I believe anything he says."

270

"Yes," said Mr. Reallybig, "you may safely do that. I would believe anything Mr. Flannelly says myself."

Billy looked back through the falling snow and watched the officer as he moved his arm in short, choppy motions to make the traffic come faster out of the park, and then he heard the shrill blast from his whistle, and everything stopped. It was the time in Billy's life when he wanted to be a policeman, but he wanted to be one in the park and on a horse.

Mr. Reallybig and his grandson walked down Fifth Avenue, and they came to a department store.

"Grandpa, is there a Santa Claus?"

"I'm glad you asked me that," said Mr. Reallybig.

They were almost in front of a Santa Claus, who stood there ringing his bell.

"Look at him," said Mr. Reallybig. "Take a good look at him. He must be about sixty, and in all this time of life he has not been

271

able to make a go of things. You'll find him sitting on a park bench in spring, maybe down on the Bowery in a flophouse in summer; he collects unemployment insurance the year round — he's a liability. He's what we used to call a plain bum, but now they have fancy words for it. And all along the avenue you'll see them, and all over town, and in other towns there must be thousands of them. There, look, there's another one! Look at his shoes."

This Santa Claus hopped from one foot to the other. He wore low brown shoes, worn at the heels, worn at the soles, and over them he had a kind of black cloth puttee to give them the air of the kind of boots that Santa Claus would wear.

Mr. Reallybig continued his lecture. "Now, mind you, boy, if you own a department store, or if you manufacture paper that goes into Christmas cards and boxes and newspapers and magazines and books that people give away on Christmas, then it's a very good thing. All holidays are good for that — Father's Day for the necktie trade, Mother's Day for candies, and Easter for new hats and clothes which people put on for the Easter Parade. What I mean to say is, I haven't anything against it. For example, we own forests. So why is it good for us, Billy?"

"Because paper is made from wood."

"Very good, sonny. You know what I mean then."

"Yes, Grandpa."

Mr. Reallybig continued his walk with Billy, and they slowed down at every Santa Claus. Some were tall, and some were elegantly dressed, and all of them were old, and all were cold.

They walked over to Madison Avenue, and then across to Park Avenue.

"Merry Christmas!" said the doorman of a fashionable restaurant.

Mr. Reallybig and Billy went down a few steps, very slowly. With his mouth open and breathing heavily, Mr. Reallybig was freed of his fur coat and shown to the best table in the place.

"You sit here, Billy, beside me."

After Billy had finished his ice cream, and as the owner of the place himself lit Mr. Reallybig's cigar and poured his brandy, Mr. Reallybig again talked of Christmas.

"There's one thing I want to tell you, Billy, that's good about Christmas—and all other holidays. Remember this—they are the very best days on which to travel."

"Why, Grandpa?"

"Well, what do people do on Christmas, for example?"

"They get presents and light up the tree."

"And what else?"

"They go to church."

"Yes, and what else?"

Billy's Christmases had been confined to getting presents and going to church with Miss Talmey.

"What else?"

"I don't know."

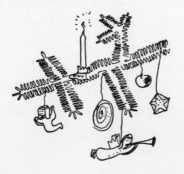

"Well, I'll tell you. They congregate. They sit together all over the land and stuff themselves on turkey—very good if you own a turkey farm. Now while they do that is the best time to travel for people like us. Planes and trains are empty and comfortable on holidays. I always travel on holidays. Remember that, Billy."

"Yes, Grandpa."

The year after, Mr. Reallybig sent Billy abroad. He thought that the boy should learn languages and see the admirable and efficient country that is Switzerland. On Christmas morning he decided to visit his grandson. The valet held the greatcoat, and the master left the house. He got into his limousine, and Officer Flannelly waved it forward. The car was on its way to the airport.

Mr. Reallybig was never wrong. The plane for Paris was ready, and he was the only passenger aboard it. The machine left the ground, sailed upward, and, looking from its window, Mr. Reallybig saw that in a matter of minutes it was far out over the sea. Some planes that once had been considered fast hung like petroleum lamps in the air below.

The chef of the plane himself came forward and suggested the various courses for dinner. A real table, magnetically attached, and solid, was placed before the lone passenger. On featherweight china the steward brought some stone crab claws and dished out a little mayonnaise and uncorked a bottle of wine. When Mr. Reallybig had finished, the first course was cleared away.

The steward came back with a plate of turtle soup and some sherry. He tipped the bottle and waited for Mr. Reallybig to give him the sign on how much of it he wanted poured into the soup. The steward held the bottle close to the plate and looked at Mr. Reallybig, and Mr. Reallybig stared ahead at the back of the seat in front of him. His mouth was open as usual. The steward said, "May I?" and then cleared his throat and said respectfully, "Beg pardon, Mr. Reallybig."

When there was no answer he called the hostess, who called the captain, and it was noted that Mr. Reallybig was dead.

BETWEEN THE controlled pressure inside the plane and the thin night air outside, there was no longer any difference for Mr. Reallybig. He found the door opened for him by what must be an angel (for aren't they blond and beautiful?), and this one had an intelligent face besides, and was precisely the kind of a girl he would have engaged as a secretary. She bent her arm in a sharp motion, looked at a golden chronometer, and floated off, leaving a train of light, a path of silver sequins, on which he followed.

The great plane had swooshed on silently, for it was so fast that its roar was audible only long after it had passed. As in a flying dream, in great comfort and ease, Mr. Reallybig progressed, not knowing how far or fast or indeed by what means he traveled. He encountered mist and banks of vapor, and then he approached a luminous place, the size of what might be

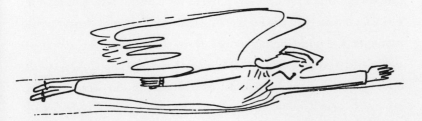

contained in the arc of a rainbow. The vapors solidified, and there appeared an immense shell of white marble, perhaps the length of Long Island, and on this stood a structure of many towers and countless floors, its front the color of cold salmon, its roofs green-gold. (Have you seen the Casino in Monte Carlo? It reminded one of that, except that it was vastly more beautiful and its door alone was higher, wider, and more ornate than the whole Casino.)

On the carpet that ran down the stairs stood a doorman, who came forward with both hands outstretched. He pulled himself together at the last moment and, coming to attention and saluting, he said, putting as much welcome into his voice as possible, "Mr. Reallybig!"

"John," said Mr. Reallybig. "John, you used to be at the old Plaza. How did you get here?"

"Yes, sir," said John. "It was my ambition always to be the doorman of the greatest hotel—and *this* is really out of the world, the utmost in G.L."

"What is G.L.?" asked Mr. Reallybig.

"Gracious living," said John.

Mr. Reallybig, blinded by light, left the doorman and walked up into the hotel.

Oh, how great was the welcome here! The assistant manager ran for the manager. The manager, a peppery little man with a pince-nez and bright eyes, presented himself and smiled his official pleasure. In the midst of all this bowing and scraping the manager suddenly looked worriedly at the clock over the reception desk, and he said with his hands held together in a pose of apology, "A thousand pardons, Mr. Reallybig, but your suite is not ready yet. You see, you are too early. We are not conditioned

to the new speeds—you are not really here yet. All this progress down below—it interferes with the order on this side. You are not due here until four hours from now. In the meantime, make yourself comfortable in the lobby."

He took the esteemed client to a comfortable sofa near the door to the dining room, and standing at the door of the dining room was none other than Pierre, Mr. Reallybig's favorite maître d'hotel. Pierre jerked his head back in surprise and then waved with his menu and smiled his most expensive smile, that which was reserved for only the best and the most generous of gracious livers.

Mr. Reallybig sat back on the sofa. This, then, was what he had been so afraid of for so many years! How foolish that he hadn't come sooner! How sad that he couldn't tell little Billy that it was marvelous, and that all of it was to the contrary of what was thought below! It wasn't tiresome at all.

And poor Officer Flannelly—he wished he could tell him too. The policeman could be standing outside swapping jokes with John the doorman, where it was warm and comfortable. (There is always a great friendship between cops and doormen.) These reflections made Mr. Reallybig glow. He could no longer sit still. He walked over to the glass door of the dining room.

277

He had always called them the *right people* — oh, and they were there, those that had gone before him, the great society of enjoyers, the people who really knew how to live, the pushers of the revolving doors of Palace Hotels, and the ones he had seen in Biarritz, Paris, and St. Moritz, and crossed with and flown with, and the champion canasta players. And of this vast group there were also those who had snubbed him below, the ones he could not call his friends. Well, here they were. In four hours — no, now it was only in three and three-quarters — he would be in there, with them, an equal, a life member — no, a forever member — of the most exclusive set on earth — no, in heaven.

He walked to another seat from where he could watch the dining room. Was it lunch, was it dinner, was it Christmas dinner or New Year's Eve up here? The white-gloved lackeys carried silver trays, immense but seemingly featherweight, and on them were arrangements of Lucullan taste, pieces that would have won prizes at the most severely judged culinary contests. Surely the man that directed all this was the great Brillat-Savarin himself. The meal must have gone on a long time, for the diners — the men in tails, the women in evening gowns and weighted with fortunes in jewels — turned slowly and graciously waved the lackeys away, and so pheasant followed woodcock, and wild duck, and chukar partridge, and all other birds, and succulence went back into the kitchen, from which it again came forward in new arrangements and with ever-increasing gastronomic perfection.

Oh, things were so wonderful Mr. Reallybig could hardly sit still.

The wine waiter was bringing a bottle in a basket. Mr. Reallybig wondered what it contained. The bare wish to know sufficed; as if a movable crane bore a television camera, the bottle came into focus, the wine waiter tilted the basket carefully so Mr. Reallybig could read the label (he did not even have to put on his glasses), and the man, the wine waiter, smiled in recognition. Wasn't he the one who had been at the Golden Snail in Paris? Yes, yes, that was the man. Well, then, there was not only the guarantee that the vintage was the best, but also that the bottle had had the best possible care and would be served with respect and in the best tradition and in the right glass. Oh, how nice! Mr. Reallybig had the pleasure of seeing it opened, and he watched the wine waiter take it to the table. Ah, they had had enough of that too, for again they turned as they had before and nodded their thanks.

Mr. Reallybig sat and watched a silent orchestra play.

The assistant manager approached. He smiled and, looking

at the alabaster clock whose emerald hands were moving slowly toward the hour mark, said, "Not much longer, Mr. Reallybig." Suddenly he jerked himself forward and, excusing himself for his neglectfulness, offered food and drink.

"You didn't even have time to finish dinner!"

"Yes, I was suddenly called away," said Mr. Reallybig.

"Well, then, allow me."

He clapped his hands, and a wagon loaded with delicatessen of the most costly and rare kinds appeared. In a mosaic-like arrangement were not only the good Bluepoints and the delicate Little Neck clams from the eastern seaboard of America, but the oysters and shell things of all the world, the small Olympias from the State of Washington, the little *praires* of the Norman coast, the Italian and Greek and Portuguese *crustae*, the *scampi* and *langoustines*, the *oursins*, the sea snails and conches, the whole register of delights of the sea, and in between the wings of a swan carved out of a block of ice sat a huge pale blue can marked Product of the Soviet Union, which contained the most select, the largest gray fish eggs, covered with the greenish ooze whose potent fishy smell was drawn into the widened nostrils of Mr. Reallybig. He had gotten up, and his face was almost in the caviar; he wore the expression of a baby crying for its nurse. The servant took a soup spoon and heaped

caviar on the thinnest of buckwheat cakes. *"Encore, encore,"* said Mr. Reallybig as he devoured it, and with it he drank cold, cold champagne from one of the bottles that once were reserved for the British House of Lords, the most brut vintage.

"Encore," said Mr. Reallybig, ignoring all the other goodies.

When finally he had had enough, the golden wagon was withdrawn. Leaning comfortably back and folding his hands over his stomach, Mr. Reallybig was about to close his eyes. He was happy, he was relaxed, even his mouth was closed. Looking up, he saw a huge mirror framed in trellised orchids that were made of jewels, the leaves cut in transparent jade. The glass was at such an angle that it reflected the gaming rooms of the hotel. He saw people sitting around a roulette table, and attendants in golden slippers supplying the players with winnings. They sat among columns of chips, their faces wore the masks of real players — the expression Mr. Reallybig wore even when not gaming. All was as it should be, as he had hoped it would be; nobody lost. He relaxed and closed his eyes.

Mr. Reallybig was a wary man. Suddenly he felt a person nearby, and he opened his eyes. Someone cleared his throat and came forward from behind a column. "Nice to see you here," said the man. "I'm the press agent for this joint."

He sat down near Mr. Reallybig as he had done in his haunts below — at attention, his gaze alert, his rodent nose sniffing. His left arm was on the table — he had always sat so, jotting things down in a minuscule notebook. It was just a habit — he had nothing to ask.

"Oh," said Mr. Reallybig and sat up. "Well, hello, Larry. Happy to see you."

The small man left as he had appeared. He scurried away,

saying, "Well, I'll be seeing a lot of you." He turned back before going into the dining room and waved with a small, cold, bloodless hand.

Mr. Reallybig waved back at him, and he waved with enthusiasm and smiled, and the other—now in the dining room—pulled the corners of his mouth down and bared his teeth in the tired rodent smile with which he had met and parted with people on his nightly rounds below. Mr. Reallybig remembered that the man had been a columnist.

Mr. Reallybig asked for the manager, and he said, "How does a rat like that get in here?"

The manager's eyebrows tilted. "Rat?" he said, and then, pointing in the direction Mr. Reallybig had indicated, he said, "Oh, you mean Larry Ophul?"

"Yes," said Mr. Reallybig.

"Well, a friendly little rat," said the manager.

"Why, that man has done an awful lot of mischief! You know the Morocco in New York? Well, just take this one instance. I was there one night—and you know how it is with columnists, they are important people, so important that they eat and live freely—and he sat there at a good table, eating and drinking on the house, and everybody who passed stopped to talk to him— the women smiled and the men bowed. I sat on the other side of the room, opposite him, and you know I don't like to wear glasses—well, I didn't see him, and it seems he waved at me, and

I didn't wave back, and the next day he printed in his column that I looked sick and was about to undergo major surgery, and the stocks of all my corporations dropped several points."

"But you knew you were all right?"

"Certainly."

"And you gave orders to buy up everything, and you profited handsomely by it. You owe him thanks."

"I never looked at it that way. Still I ask, How does a rat like that get in here?"

"Do you mind if I sit down?" said the manager. He looked at the clock: it had gone forward half an hour. "It won't be much longer, Mr. Reallybig," he said. "Now about Larry Ophul—"

Mr. Reallybig put his hand on the manager's arm to stop him. "You know, he wrote a profile of me for that awful magazine."

"I know," said the manager. "As far as what you call awful things go, he has done much worse than that."

"Well, then, explain to me how he gets up here."

"If you'll let me, I'll try. You say he looks like a rat. That's right. He was almost lost at birth, but there are doctors who will labor over a creature—they take an oath to that effect. It would have been better to wash him down the plumbing, but here he was, blue and premature, and his life was like his birth. Now he is important, but he's always near a wall or door, and when he

284

spots you he runs and jumps at you and digs into you with his little dead eyes, his bad teeth, his naked skull. He looks, and he is, awful. Don't you feel sorry for him? You know, you still have ordinary human emotions—that is, for two more hours."

"You are very understanding," said Mr. Reallybig.

"We must be most understanding, we must be," said the manager. He looked at Mr. Reallybig. "It is easy to be kind to beautiful women; one can love the morning, horses, flowers, ships and dogs, books and paintings, music, a devoted servant, even a factory or money—all that is easy to love, but a mean creature with sparrow bones, who picks free food off plates and is disliked and without an alibi—in life that's difficult even to have around."

"You are most tolerant," said Mr. Reallybig. "But tell me what he has done to justify his membership here."

"If we weren't tolerant, who would be? As for Larry Ophul, I might say that he has done a lot—oh, in the domain of politics, in the department of humanity. He was a shining patriot on every day, he waved the flag of his country and did so many good things that to list them would be tiresome—for the kiddies, for the blind, for the cardiacs, for the soldiers."

"But all for a purpose," said Mr. Reallybig.

"That I grant you," said the manager, "and that is why we

ignore it. That stuff hasn't done him any good whatever. But you remember the murder case in California, about ten years ago, in December, where a jealous husband shot a man he thought was his wife's lover? Big names, famous trial?"

"I remember," said Mr. Reallybig.

"I cite that only as an example — there were many such cases. To come to the point, Larry Ophul had gotten this information from one of his informants and published it. The husband read it; he killed the man, was found guilty, and is still in jail."

"But that's terrible," said Mr. Reallybig.

"Upon first examination, perhaps," said the manager. "By the way, would you like a little more champagne while we're waiting?"

"Thank you, no," said Mr. Reallybig, who had moved forward to the edge of his chair. His mouth was open again, his eyes were tunnels in the painful, hard mask he had worn in life.

"You'll see what I mean — I'll try to explain." The manager folded his hands. "It never occurs to the ordinary person — you will be shocked when I tell you this — follow me carefully. It is never clear to the people, and is hidden from them by the machinations of so-called do-gooders — no, that's not the way to begin either . . .

"Let's go with the man who shot the lover, to jail. Take anyone, take the worst criminal — do you know that the world would end without evil? Let me explain. The Supreme Court judges and all other judges — the district attorneys, prosecutors, and magistrates — every day of their lives they should humbly bow with gratitude in the direction of the penal institutions to which they send offenders. Without the criminal, where would they be? And in that same category are the vast numbers of policemen, jail attendants, professors who teach law, makers of iron bars. Oh, if the world were to be an honest place, where would the locksmiths be? And if everyone was good and true you could dismiss all lawyers, their clerks, the printers of legal books and stationery.

"This can go on endlessly, Mr. Reallybig. I don't have to tell you how far—to the writers of detective stories and the servants they employ, the cigarettes consumed by private eyes, the salaries of the columnists and crime reporters, fingerprinters, and the vast equipment of the G-men and their junior G-men clubs, the manufacturers of burglar alarms—what would they do without the burglars? Mr. Cagney, where would he be? And Mr. Bogart? You can go on and on."

In the fashion of a businessman getting his point across, the manager beat his right fist into his outstretched left hand and said with passion and conviction, "Mr. Reallybig, I say to you, here and now, and I've said it over and over again—half the world would be without a livelihood. It would be necessary to invent crime. One would have to create murderers, burglars, and gangsters. Life would be hopeless without crime. And would you believe me that nobody, but nobody, recognizes that the poor, misunderstood, and forgotten crook is the walled-up and forgotten martyr of the piece?"

"The hero," said Mr. Reallybig with a trace of sarcasm.

The manager had exhausted himself. Mr. Reallybig sat rigid, staring ahead. "Come, come, Mr. Reallybig," said the manager, "you've done quite a few things that weren't exactly according to the book, and I don't mind telling you that you were extremely clever at it."

Mr. Reallybig said, "I gave a planetarium to the city of—"

"Don't tell me—I know. We know everything here. My hat's off to you. You're on the preferred list up here. Mr. Reallybig, we're proud to have you with us."

Mr. Reallybig pocketed the compliment, and the manager looked at the clock. There was an hour and a half to go.

"I'll see you in a little while," said the manager and left.

Mr. Reallybig was restless. He got up and walked over to the dining-room door and pressed his nose against it to see better.

A woman was seated there, someone in the highest circles, really one of the right people, who had never acknowledged his existence on earth. She looked at him, and he thought he saw the trace of a smile of recognition, and she came close to the door, her immense jewels swaying. There was a large chandelier overhead, but she cast no shadow, and suddenly horror bathed his eyes, and despair took his legs from him, and he swayed, for as she came near he saw that she was hollow, that she was a glass woman with a thin covering of cobwebby stuff which had given the illusion of life at a distance. Mr. Reallybig clung to the back of a chair as she moved away, and he sank into it, and he looked as he had when they had found him dead. He managed to lift his hand, and someone called the manager.

"I have a grandson," he said. "Little Billy. I must see Billy—I have to tell him something. I have to tell him—I must let him

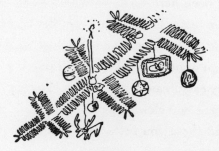

know that everything I told him is wrong. Please, please, is there a way I can get to him? I will do anything," he pleaded humbly. He dragged his feet; he was for the first time in his existence a beggar.

"I don't know," said the assistant. "It's never been possible before, and I don't think an exception is made to the rule. Anyway, we have no precedent; up to now, no one has—that is, as long as I've been here—no one has asked for a return."

The manager came, listened to the pleading, and looked at the clock. To Mr. Reallybig's surprise he said, "Why not?"

"How do I go about it?" asked Mr. Reallybig.

"Oh, it's very easy," said the manager. "You simply lean back in that chair there and close your eyes and think of where you want to be, and there you shall be."

The important man, who had always moved with ponderous precision, ran to the chair and threw himself into it, leaned back hard and closed his eyes—and then he was gone.

As if dictating an important letter to his private secretary, Mr. Reallybig had said, "The Palace Hotel, St. Moritz, Switzerland. Quickly, please, it's most urgent."

Suddenly there was crisp, crackling snow underneath his feet, sleigh bells rang, a porter saluted, and the owner smiled. "We didn't expect you, Mr. Reallybig. We're filled up, but we'll make room somehow!"

Mr. Reallybig ran into the high, heated lobby, and around the Christmas tree, and to the hotel owner who trotted along he said, "Don't worry about me. I'm not staying. I'm looking for little Billy."

The owner said, "I'm sorry, but he left with his governess some time ago. They planned to sail on the *Queen Elizabeth*."

"Excuse me," said Mr. Reallybig. He sat down in the nearest chair and leaned back and pronounced the name of the ship. The columns in the hall of the Palace Hotel and the chandelier began to rock, and the peaceful, ice-covered lake outside turned green and turbulent, and the stamping of the machinery came through the floor and chair. The saloon was decorated with holly and frosted pine boughs.

"Mr. Reallybig," said the purser of the *Elizabeth*, "what a pleasant surprise! I didn't know you were aboard."

"Forget about me," said Mr. Reallybig. "But tell me, where is little Billy?"

"They were aboard on the last crossing," said the purser. "They are in New York now, I suppose."

Mr. Reallybig looked at the clock. "Dear Lord," he said, for the first time in his life humble, and his eyes filled with tears. He ran to a leather-upholstered chair, and closed his eyes again, and gave his own address. The columns stood still, the swish of the water stopped, and suddenly he was outside his house and one of his men was scraping ice from the sidewalk.

"A Merry Christmas to you, Mr. Reallybig," said the janitor. "You just missed them. They went down the avenue."

Without waiting for lights, Mr. Reallybig began to run. He was ashen, and cold sweat was under his hat. *Oh God, good God, grant me this one favor! I have never before prayed! I have never asked for anything!* He clenched his hands in prayer and ran on—and he envied the Santa Clauses who were ringing their bells, and he would have thanked his fate if he could have been the poorest and coldest and the most hopeless of them, and he ran on, searching, and at last, down near the library on Forty-second Street, he saw them. Miss Talmey had Billy by the hand, and he was talking to her.

Mr. Reallybig ran after them, and he cried, "Billy! Billy!" He was almost at the boy's side when a cop took hold of his sleeve and said, "Somebody wants you, Mister."

Mr. Reallybig found himself in front of a travel agency. Unlike all other shop windows along the avenue, this one was without Christmas festoonery, tree, or candles. It offered a smart display of the signs of the zodiac in pale blue and chromium, and the supercharged jet liner hung in the center. From the door of the place, in the neat uniform of an air hostess, came the graceful and intelligent blond girl who had escorted him from the plane, and with her correct smile she again smartly bent her arm and looked at her chronometer and said in her absolute and polite fashion, "If you please, Mr. Reallybig."

"Oh, there you are," said the manager, smiling his official greeting.

Mr. Reallybig was back in the palace of gracious living. Two lackeys, immaculately attired, held open the corridor doors.

"Your suite is ready, Mr. Reallybig," said the assistant manager, pointing to the door.

"No," said Mr. Reallybig, and then he screamed, "Nooooooo!" like a madman.

The glassy rigor was in his feet. He fell to his knees and held up his folded hands. "I must, I must—you must let me speak to little Billy! It's the only important thing in my whole life! He mustn't be like me! He mustn't believe any of the things I told him! Please, I beg of you!"

The manager looked at him and said, "It's too late. Besides, everyone has to find out for himself."

Suddenly there was a crowd in the place, arriving from some mass exit from life below. The manager said, "I'm terribly busy—excuse me."

Mr. Reallybig had always gotten his way by insistence. He now shouldered his way through the newly arrived people who stood about him. He pushed Larry Ophul out of his way and took hold of the manager by both lapels of his coat and screamed, "You take care of me! It's little enough I ask. You know who I am—"

The manager interrupted, "Sorry, but I must really go now."

Mr. Reallybig relaxed his grip, and he turned toward the lackeys. He came to the corridor and he walked into eternity. He was to be forever afflicted with uncertainty and doubt; nothing in time, matter, or motion would be as he thought it was. At least that was the way Larry Ophul, who walked for a

292

while beside him, explained it. It was like the stuff Ophul had written below—of swindle, insincere friendship, the hope that others' luck and happiness would go smash.

"Well, I'll be seeing you," said Larry Ophul, and he smiled his rat grin and went off.

The glass feeling reached to Mr. Reallybig's hips. He dragged himself down the corridor—it was like the scraping of a dried leaf, windblown, over cement.

He came to his room and had a very pleasant surprise, for here was all his furniture. The magnificent bed he had had below, the carved pillars of Circassian walnut that supported the canopy, his own carpet and the Napoleonic bellcord. He felt at home until he looked in the mirror. Then he had to lie down. He lay down very carefully, and as he waited there and strained his mind for a weapon with which to combat his terror, sentence was again pronounced on him, as it would be over and over again, forever. He got panicky and screamed, and his glass hand reached for the bellcord, ever so carefully, for he was terrified of falling out of bed and breaking into a thousand pieces.

In the mirror he had seen himself as empty as the woman in the dining room.

The door opened and a lackey entered. Mr. Reallybig begged that two mattresses be placed on the floor, to the right and the left of the bed, so that if he fell out he would not break. Then he screamed again, for the servant had come close, and Mr. Reallybig saw that it was the man, the would-be murderer, whom Officer Flannelly had caught.

Mr. Reallybig did the wrong thing—he tried to flee. Suddenly, with a crashing sound, he broke into pieces, as he would over and over again in all eternity.

15.

The Bowery

I'M SLOW-WITTED in some things. I asked Barbara the next day, "Did you read that story to *Frances?*"

"Yes," said Barbara. "She thinks it's the greatest story she ever heard. She's scared to death."

"Frances is Doctor Lincoln's child—no?"

"Yes."

"I thought they were in Saudi Arabia?"

"Well, you've heard of Mossadegh."

"Yes, but that's in Iran or Iraq or whatever Persia is called now."

"Well, Poppy, you know the whole Middle East is in flames, so naturally at the last moment they decided not to go."

"Oh. And what about Little Bit—don't they want her back?"

The symptoms, well known and always the same, began to appear. The chin started to tremble.

"All right, you can keep her. Bring her along now—we're going for a ride down to the Bowery."

"What for?"

"To look at some bums."

"What do you want to look at bums for, Poppy?"

"To illustrate the Christmas story, I need models for Santa Claus."

In the car she asked, "What kind of bums are you looking for?"

"Nice ones."

"You're going to make them nice?"

"Well, Santa Claus has to be nice."

"But you're not changing the awful grandfather?"

"Well, I was thinking about it. I'll change him a little."

We were driving down Fifth Avenue, and near the Plaza a distinguished old man in a greatcoat with a fur collar walked across the street toward Bergdorf Goodman's windows.

"That's the grandfather type right there," said Barbara.

I agreed that he seemed to be a very hard man.

"What do you want to change him for, Poppy? You're not going to make him go to heaven in the end, I hope?"

"No, not that, but, after all, it's a Christmas story, and Christmas is a time of cheer and gladness. And at Christmas time you don't want to bring any more misery into the world than there is already, so that when people have read it they feel

like jumping out of the window. And as for the theme that evil is necessary—it really isn't. Anyway, if you follow that proposition you arrive at the point where it's all right to make soap out of people.

"If you believe that evil is the axis of the world you join the company of Faust, of the Marquis de Sade and Machiavelli. You walk backward over eroded landscapes, and the tumbleweed of lost hope rolls with you. The only hand you can take is that of a philosopher like Nietzsche, and by way of the madhouse or suicide end up in hell."

"But then it's just going to be—" Barbara started.

"A Christmas story," I said.

"I knew that would happen."

It was windy, and there were few bums on the Bowery. I drove across the bridge and up to Brooklyn Heights, to a place from which I like to watch the sun set on New York harbor.

Brooklyn has assets other than Murder, Inc. It has a cemetery in which Lola Montez is buried. It has a lovely park. And it has a feeling of being home to people. Its citizens around the Heights section might live in a small town, far removed from New York. They find time to stand and talk in the streets; they wave at each other. Unlike New Yorkers, they smile and go home with quiet, slow steps.

While the most fashionable section of Manhattan looks out on a panorama of insane hospital, prison, railroad bridge, and the various municipal and public service structures across the river, the view from Brooklyn Heights is truly beautiful.

The sky was the color of a sheet of copper reflecting fire. Around where the sun sets it was the red heat of metal. The orange fire of the sunset was reflected in the thousands of Manhattan windows that face south. The east-lying fronts of the buildings were in the deep violet, gray, brown, and purple that play over lava.

A curtain of sleet moved against Manhattan. It looked like rose-colored ashes, and it sailed across the bay in even tempo, and then bashed itself against the skyscrapers. It fled along the streets and out of them up into the sky. It was yellow there, and another gust carried masses of it up the East River against the darkening houses. It was lit up as it passed through the immense bridges, whose wiring is like that of giant harps.

The foghorns doubled their volume. I took my binoculars from the glove compartment and looked at a small tramp steamer coming up the bay. It flew the Greek flag. It was one of the boats that come by way of the Bay of Naples. Perhaps part of its cargo was the opium crop of Istanbul and Iran. By the law of perspective it was now four inches long. It was in a line between the Statue of Liberty and Staten Island. The circular military reservation on Governor's Island, and the old fortress, looked as if a pastrycook had shaken powdered sugar on a chocolate cake. The lights of moving cars blinked on the bridges, and overhead the running lights of planes flashed on and off.

A curtain of snow and of night sank down on the panorama. I drove back over Brooklyn Bridge. On such nights as these I like to wind through the old streets at the end of Manhattan Island, especially the one in which the smell of coffee roasters hangs. We saw some bums pressing their noses against coffeepots, delicatessens, and restaurants with thirty-five-cent dinners. It was all a melancholy Christmas card.

"Are you going to leave the columnist in?"

"I think so."

"But you'll change him—you'll make a great guy out of him, a literary character like your friend Mr. Leonard Lyons, or a Gigi Cassini, or a dynamo like Winchell."

"No, I think I'll leave him as he is. On the other hand, columnists are such easy targets."

"Oh, you're afraid they won't let you into your favorite spots after it comes out."

I said nothing for several blocks.

"Poppy, did I hurt your feelings?"

Rapprochement like this is never made without ulterior motive. "No, no—what is it you want?"

"I'm hungry. Where are we going to eat?"

"We can go down to the fishmarket and eat at Sweets, or Sloppy Louis' on the waterfront. There's a good Italian restaurant—Bentivengas, where gangsters hang out, and also the mayor and usually the police commissioner."

To all this she reacted with indifference.

"How about Twenty-One?" I said.

"We're not dressed properly."

There was a red light, and to the right, at the windy corner, an emaciated, hatless man, tall and with a beard, held the lapels of his coat closed. Snowflakes stuck to his eyelids. He stood outlined in the light of a cheap eating place. He looked like John Carradine.

"Poppy," Barbara said earnestly after staring at him a long time, "I wonder, if Christ came to earth, could he get a table at Twenty-One?"

I said, "Don't tell that to anybody, or they'll make a Christmas story out of it before I can."

We finally decided on Bentivengas. I was reading the menu when Barbara said, "Look, Poppy, over to the left"—and there was our friend from Naples, the one who had left the procession to deliver a message from Charlie. He came over to us, his napkin stuck in his collar. "Remember what I told you," he said. The gravel voice was again soft and low, as in Naples. He sounded like Pinza with a strep throat. "And that goes any-where," he added, nodding vigorously. Then he returned to his own table.

After dinner we drove back uptown, and I locked myself up to rewrite the Christmas story. When it was done I mailed it off.

Shortly afterward I received a galley proof of the story. Barbara picked it up and read it. She made no comment then, but later she called her friend Frances.

"Hello, Frances. Honestly, you remember that last bitter social satire of Poppy's—that wonderful Christmas story? Well, you ought to see it now. It's—it's like Dickens. He's changed the bad columnist and made him a plain embezzler. All the crooks are toned down. Mr. Reallybig doesn't go to hell any more or break into pieces. He just disappears in the end, after trading his clothes with an old bum and appearing as Santa Claus. As usual, Poppy has to love everybody."

Books Forming a Series
By and About Ludwig Bemelmans

Other Titles in Preparation

Ludwig Bemelmans [signature]

Bemelmans tales overflow with whimsical eccentrics, somber head waiters, and a long string of charmingly irresponsible and wholly unlikely people and situations. The plots of his stories lead to improbable solutions. We journey with him through western Europe and Latin America, and we learn first hand from this master writer and illustrator of exisiting warmth in people and places. His exuberance for life and humanity creates nostalgia, a fresh glow and a yearning for more of the same. His writings and book illustrations brim over with light-hearted satire and joyful humor. In short, Bemelmans makes us feel good.

This book was composed in
Cochin and Nicholas Cochin Black
by The Sarabande Press, New York.

It was printed and bound by
Arcata Graphics Company, New York
on 60# Sebago cream white antique paper.

The typography and binding were designed by
Beth Tondreau Design, New York.